John Mole was educated at Oxford University and at the renowned international business school INSEAD. In 1971 he joined a leading American Bank in Pittsburgh. In 1980, after several years in Athens and the Middle East, he returned to the London Branch, becoming its General Manager in 1983.

Since leaving Oxford, John Mole has kept up his literary interests, writing reviews for *The Times Literary Supplement* and several uncompleted and unpublished novels. This hobby culminated in the comic novel *Sail or Return*, published in 1985. He resigned from the bank in that year to write full time. A second novel, *The Monogamist*, came out in 1986 and was followed in 1988 by the humorous business book *Management Mole*.

John Mole is married, with four children, and lives in London.

*Also by John Mole*

MANAGEMENT MOLE

and published by Corgi Books

# Thanks, Eddie

## John Mole

**CORGI BOOKS**

THANKS, EDDIE

A CORGI BOOK  0 552 13450 3

Originally published in Great Britain by Bantam Press,
a division of Transworld Publishers Ltd.

PRINTING HISTORY
Bantam Press edition published 1989
Corgi edition published 1990

This book is set in Bem Medium
by Colset Private Limited, Singapore.

Corgi Books are published by Transworld Publishers Ltd.,
61–63 Uxbridge Road, Ealing, London W5 5SA, in Australia
by Transworld Publishers (Australia) Pty. Ltd., 15–23 Helles
Avenue, Moorebank, NSW 2170, and in New Zealand by
Transworld Publishers (N.Z.) Ltd., Cnr. Moselle and
Waipareira Avenues, Henderson, Auckland.

Made and printed in Great Britain by
Cox & Wyman Ltd., Reading, Berks.

*FOR DAMIAN,*
*A BETTER KIND OF CLIMBER*

# Contents

# PROLOGUE

• • •

## After the Easter Banquet

'The riff-raff we let in these days,' said the little man in lace cravat and knee-breeches. 'I dread the loving-cup. I swear it gave me mouth ulcers last year.'

'It's all right for you,' said the new Governor of the Bank of England, stretching his long legs out towards the flickering fire, 'the Lord Mayor gets first go.'

The tradition of passing round a chalice of wine at the end of banquets for each guest to sip was a symbol of the brotherhood of the City.

'I'm glad that's all you have to worry about,' sighed the new Chairman of the Stock Exchange, scratching the side of his thin nose. 'The reptiles are baying again.'

'Reptiles don't bay,' said the Governor, author of a dozen financial thrillers under another name and a stickler for words.

'I bet Tyrannosaurus Rex bayed,' said the Chairman gloomily. 'I bet he howled and gnashed his teeth.'

They lapsed into silence, watching the flames flicker in the fireplace and dipping their faces into brandy goblets big as nosebags.

'The City's the only decent industry the country's got left and the press want to ruin that as well,' said the Chairman.

9

'Not their fault,' said the Mayor, who was on the board of a newspaper company.

'Whose fault is it then?' grumbled the Chairman. 'Just because there are a couple of rotten apples they condemn the whole barrel.'

'They're fishing,' said the Governor. 'When you ask for proof they say they have to protect their sources. Which means they made the whole thing up.'

They lapsed into gloomy silence again. The only sound in the Mansion House parlour was the ticking of a grandfather clock.

'So what do we do?' asked the Governor. 'Tell them to stop rocking the boat?'

'They'll think we've got something to hide,' said the Mayor.

'Who hasn't?' snapped the Governor. 'What do they think we're playing here? Monopoly?'

The burden of responsibility hung heavy on the protectors of the City, the griffins at the gate with sword and shield and red pointed tongue.

'Throw them a bone,' said the Mayor.

'What's that supposed to mean?' asked the Chairman.

'Give them something to chew on. When the wolf's outside the door you don't stick your fingers down his throat. You throw him a bone. Ancient proverb.'

'We can't shop our own chaps,' said the Chairman.

'We don't have to,' said the Mayor. 'We just nudge the papers in the right direction. They invent the rest. I know an editor I can whisper a quiet word to.'

'Anyone in mind?' asked the Governor.

'Not yet. We'll find some Johnny-come-lately too big for his boots,' said the Chairman.

They chuckled and passed the brandy and poured it into their individual goblets.

# •••
# *MAY DAY*

It was a crisp May morning, the first of the merry month, May Day. A youngish man, slim and dapper in a dark three-piece suit, plucked a red carnation from the façade of the Moscow Narodny Bank. He hooked his neatly furled umbrella in the crook of an elbow while he fixed it and considered for a moment whether he should wear a buttonhole with a black tie. Life must go on. Despite the tragic events of the night he felt light-hearted, optimistic, glad to be alive, whatever the uncertain future might bring. He hummed to himself as he strode jauntily down Threadneedle Street. 'Ti-tum-ti-tum ti-tum-ti-tum . . .'

The offices of Dividend Investments were in a new development of tarted-up warehouses at the eastern edge of the City. They took up one floor of Capital House, an old opium warehouse from the heyday of the China trade, gutted and scrubbed clean. It formed one side of a square around a cobbled courtyard. He walked briskly over the cobbles and up the steps, pausing for a beat to let the automatic doors sigh open. A fleshless man, scoured pink, in blue and red military uniform with thick gold stripes on his sleeve, snapped to attention behind a desk.

'Morning, sir.'

13

'Morning, Sergeant. Carry on.'

He made straight for a waiting lift and pressed the button for the fifth floor. By the time the door opened he had his keys ready to unlock the reinforced glass door. With a sharp pang he realized that he was now the only living keyholder.

The reception area was panelled in dark oak. Step back in time, said the panelling, step back to the old-fashioned values of thrift and tradition and respectability. Our long-established firm was founded way back in 1979, you can trust us, and here are some old engravings of the Bank of England and Saint Paul's and the Guildhall to prove it.

A door on the right boasted 'General Manager' in gold letters. A door on the left muttered 'Staff Only' in silver. A door in the middle, behind the receptionist's mahogany desk, said nothing. He went to the unmarked door, reached a practised hand inside and flicked a dozen switches. Concealed lights flickered on and a red light on the alarm system stopped flashing.

'Ti-tum-ti-tum ti-tum-ti-tum . . .' With the decisiveness of habit he went through the door marked 'General Manager' into another lobby panelled in the same dark oak as reception. He stood for a moment while he reconstructed in his mind George Livery's last moments. Livery had been working late. He had staggered into the lobby clutching his chest and collapsed on the floor. Mentally he drew the outline of Livery's body on the carpet and respectfully stepped round it to go through an unmarked door into a kitchen where he switched on the coffee-machine cook had prepared the night before.

While he waited for the coffee to brew he went through the connecting door into the dining-room. It had windows along one side and a door that led into an ante-room where guests gathered for drinks before being ushered to the table. Both rooms were decorated in Barbican Nouveau, teak and chrome and white leather, with prints of exotic birds on the wall in aluminium frames. He walked round the long table, inspected the cocktail cabinet and the sideboard, glanced at the floor, to make sure nothing was out of place. He was particularly attentive to the ante-room, straightening the sofas and putting his hand down the back of the white cushions, as if he had lost something. All clear. Nothing to worry about. Fingers crossed.

'Ti-tum-ti-tum ti-tum-ti-tum . . .' He went back to the kitchen, poured coffee into a Doulton cup and carried it back through the lobby into the general manager's office. He looked round the empty sanctum, breathing in the smell of coffee and wax polish and cigars and thick pile carpet. He opened the venetian blinds and sat down in the high-backed leather chair and put his cup carefully on the leather-bound green blotter. The red *Economist* diary was closed, the in-trays empty, the Reuter screen blank. It was innocent, ready for a fresh start, swept clean like sand for the next ephemeral footprint.

'Eddie!'

The grating, reproachful voice made him jump. He saw who it was, framed in the doorway to the secretary's office, and let himself sink slowly back on the farting leather cushion, trying to pretend he had not been leaping to his feet. Tall, pale, veiled in black, she looked like Death herself.

'Eddie, how could you?'

'How could I what?'

'Sit in his chair.'

'Easy. I aimed my bum and bent my knees. I do it several times a day.'

'It's Mr Livery's chair,' she hissed.

'He doesn't need it any more. He doesn't need anything any more.'

Death sobbed, turned on her heel, and disappeared. Eddie got up and followed her. She stood in front of an open filing cupboard dabbing her eyes and looking at herself in the mirror fixed to the back of the door. She took off a voluminous moiré patterned coat but kept on a black pillbox hat with a spotty veil designed for easy eye dabbing. She wore a black silk suit and black gloves.

'It's a bit soon for the funeral.'

'Where's your respect?'

'More to the point, Nora, how did you know he was dead?'

Nora looked at herself in the mirror and pursed her lips. She was made up to look as though she had not been made up and her lips were much brighter inside than outside. She took off her hat and shook her hair, mourning hair, straight brushed. Black tears, made of jet, dangled from her ears.

15

'You phoned me.'

'Just as long as I know. What time?'

'How should I know? Eight o'clock.'

'I was still at the hospital. Make it ten.'

'Wasn't there anything they could do?'

'Nothing. He was gone before he left here.'

She threw her head back and slapped her forehead with a clenched fist as if she was rubber stamping it. Like all Nora's movements it was slightly awkward, uncoordinated, as if she were aiming somewhere else.

'What are we going to do, Eddie?'

'You can take off the funeral gear for a start. Your relationship with Mr Livery was purely secretarial. Then you could check the ante-room again. You wouldn't want anything left lying around.'

'That's why I came in early.'

'Go and do it, there's a good girl.'

'This isn't true, is it, Eddie? Tell me it's not happening, tell me someone's making all this up.'

'It's not true and someone's making it all up and it's all in your imagination.'

'He's got a luncheon at National Midland today.'

'He'll have to skip that one.'

'I never picked up his bifocals.'

'He won't be needing them for a bit.'

'He was ever so cheerful and suddenly he said, Oh dear.'

'Oh dear.'

'Oh dear, he said.'

'That was a bit of an understatement. In the circumstances.'

She glared at him, her fist still fixed to her forehead.

'You don't know what I've been through. How can you know? How can anybody know?' She closed her eyes and moaned again, removed the fist from her forehead and put it in her mouth.

'They could put two and two together. Mrs Livery noticed his shirt was tucked inside his underpants. She said he never wore them like that. She accused the doctor.'

'Oh no. I could have sworn . . .'

'She said it was common.'

Colour burst through the white mask on Nora's face.

16

'What will she do?'

'She might forget all about it. On the other hand it could prey on her mind. She might start asking questions.'

'If she finds out . . .'

'They'll be after us. We have to cover our tracks.'

She looked at him blankly, blinking through tears black with mascara.

'What do you mean, after us? Who's "they"?'

'General Manager Dead of Shock in Office Love Nest. Heart Massage Messenger was Go-between. After-hours Orgy Kills Bank Supremo.'

'What are we going to do, Eddie?' She took a deep breath and pulled her broad shoulders back, reminding Eddie of an over-sized figurehead on a sailing ship.

'Do what we always do. Yes-sir-no-sir-three-bags-full-sir.'

'But they'll find out.'

'There's always a way out, Nora. We just have to think of it. Leave it to me.'

A bell rang.

'There's the post.'

'Eddie?' she said, halting his escape at the door, 'You won't tell anyone, will you?'

'No, Nora.' The bell rang again.

'It's not for me. I don't care. It's for his sake.'

Underneath the flummery and posing Nora must have been genuinely upset. Eddie's feelings took him by surprise. He felt sorry for her. For Nora! He must be slipping. More important was that he had something over her. It might come in handy in the future.

'Don't worry. Of blessed memory, Nora.'

'Thanks, Eddie.'

He sauntered out into the general manager's lobby. It was furnished with a haven of sofas around a low coffee table, illuminated by a crystal chandelier and dominated by a portrait under a spotlight. It was a colour photograph of a middle-aged man fudged to look like an oil painting. He posed at his desk, one hand on a telephone and the other on a diary, a man of authority, a captain of industry, a chairman of the board. The scarcity of hair on his smooth, receding crown was compensated by black and bushy eyebrows brooding over eyes that were hooded yet protruding, like a crocodile's. His other features were lost among the wattles and swelling cheek pouches of the rest of his face. The identity of the great man was not entrusted to the competence of the artist. A brass label on the bottom of the frame announced 'Percival Wheeler, Chairman and Chief Executive of the Dividend Group of Companies'. Eddie stood in front of the picture. His impertinent good looks, sharp but cheerful with a crooked smile and straight nose, were superimposed on the captain of industry. He straightened his tie and smoothed down his dark curly hair and gave himself a cheeky grin. He switched on the spotlight and his reflection disappeared.

'Ti-tum-ti-tum ti-tum-ti-tum . . .' He went into the entrance lobby and brought the mail-bag in from outside the front door where it had been dumped and went through the door marked 'Staff Only'. It opened into a large open-plan office. Coming from the management suite across the no-man's-land of reception was like entering another world. There was no panelling or subdued lighting here, no coffee-machines and soft cushions. The people who work here are different, it said, they do different things, they are not as important as the people on the other side. It was brightly lit with neon tubes, furnished with grey and silver metal. Freestanding partitions about five feet high divided it into a warren of cubicles and passages. The partitions, the floor, the walls were covered in fuzzy grey carpet, bristling with static. Stepping lightly and trying not to touch any of the surfaces Eddie went straight to a row of four telex machines against the wall and tore off the messages that had come in overnight. He read them carefully as he threaded his way back through the maze to the lobby. He picked up the mail from the reception desk and took it through the unmarked door into his post-room. He liked to get it all read before the staff arrived.

'Ti-tum-ti-tum ti-tum-ti-tum . . . We'll keep the red flag fly-ing . . .'

At five to nine he sat at the reception desk to tick off the names of the staff in the attendance register as they arrived. He could have done the job just as well in front of his television screen in the post-room. But he liked them to know they had him to thank when they were marked down as arriving on time even when they had not. As usual Norman, the Chief Dealer, was the first to arrive. He was in his early fifties but could have passed for sixty-odd. His ancient gaberdine mac and shuffling walk, eyes downcast as if prospecting for cigarette butts, would have gone unnoticed at a refuge for down-and-outs.

'Bad news this morning, Norman.'

'Hong Kong dollar down?'

'Mr Livery. He closed out his options. Squared his position.'

'What did you say?'

'Mr Livery passed away.' Eddie forced his cheerful face into an expression of mourning.

'Swifter than a weaver's shuttle his days have passed leaving no hope behind,' intoned Norman.

'Sorry?'

'Does Mr Wheeler know?'

'He'll be here later. He had a heart attack.'

'Who? Mr Wheeler? God bless us.'

'Mr Livery.'

'Ah.'

'Just thought I'd let you know.'

'Thanks, Eddie,' he sighed and shambled off into the main office, shaking his head, body language he employed to ward off whatever news threatened his conviction that he had seen it all.

'Fleas? Have you caught the fleas?' said Freda Grafton, slamming open the glass door. She was a busy, bustling woman with a frizz of greying hair and a permanent frown. She was Head of Administration, nominally Eddie's boss, a pretence they kept up once a year when she gave him the envelope with the notification of his pay-rise. Nothing else connected them except a line on the standard work of corporate fiction entitled Organization Chart.

Eddie shook his head, unsurprised, as if an enquiry about personal infestation was the usual greeting among the staff of Dividend Investments.

'I knew it. That Louise telling stories again. She says they're in the walls. And in the partitions. She's a troublemaker that one. If I have to look at the bites on the back of her legs again I'll slap

19

them, so help me. I'm seeing them now. Out of the corner of my eye. All of accounts is scratching themselves. We'll have to fumigate this place . . .'

Rumours normally lasted about ten days. They covered the spectrum of plausibility – impending closure, redundancy programmes, Legionnaire's Disease from the water cooler, cockroaches in the coffee-machine, impotence from the neon lights, radiation from the computer screens, death rays from the satellite dish on the roof. They gave shape to the general feeling of impending doom associated with boring work. This week it was fleas in the fuzzy wall carpet. It was eclipsed by Eddie's news of a doom that no longer impended but had fallen fair and square on their boss's head.

'Mr Livery,' he said, the mention of management silencing her instantly, 'passed away. Last night.'

She clapped her hand to her mouth and turned round to glum Larry Chivers, Chief Accountant, sidling past behind her. He was thin and pale and insubstantial. Livery called him – used to call him – the ghost in the machine. He averted his gaze, as he did whenever he was looked at.

'We've lost Mr Livery,' she said. Startled, Larry looked round to see where his boss could be hiding.

'He died last night,' added Eddie, putting him out of his confusion. They observed a few seconds silence, each waiting for the other to express the first condolence.

'I've got a salary review with him this morning,' murmured Larry. Or bellowed. With Larry it was hard to tell the difference.

'Better get out the ouija board then,' said Eddie.

By half past nine there was a sense of industry in the main office that the employees of Dividend Investments rarely experienced, a buzz of excitement more usually associated with stock footage of dealing rooms on the television news or commercials for building societies than with real life. Nora typed out an announcement for Eddie to stick on the staff notice-board outside the toilets but like all information on staff notice-boards it was an empty formality. The real news grew like barley sugar on a string.

'. . . heart attack . . .'

'. . . stabbed in the heart . . .'

20

'. . . collapsed in the office . . .'
'. . . the scaffolding collapsed . . .'
'. . . buried alive . . .'
'. . . buried by the market . . .'
'. . . in Leadenhall Market . . .'
'. . . knocked down by a delivery van . . .'
'. . . couldn't deliver . . .'

Between the caucuses of speculation and rumour went Eddie, listening, gathering, gleaning, enticing with a crumb of fact the conjecture away from its more fanciful flights and with crusts of disinformation steering it away from the truth. The colder the trail to his own small part in Livery's demise the better.

● ● ●

Nora stood behind Livery's desk and closed the venetian blinds. He had never liked to look out on the council flats and seedy buildings of Spitalfields and the squalor of Bishopsgate where it abandoned the shiny glass and marble of the City of London and degenerated into the stained concrete and crumbling brick of the borough of Tower Hamlets. She bit her bottom lip and let the tears run down her face. She would look a sight and the staff would gossip but someone had to weep for Georgie. The rest of the staff only talked about what was going to happen and who was going to take over and what was in it for them. Didn't they care? Don't they have any feelings? Anyone would think that death was just another excuse for not turning up for work.

She opened the top drawer of the desk and began to sort out his personal belongings. She put them into a cardboard box to be sent to his wife, no, his widow, Mrs Edwina Livery, Mrs George Livery no longer.

'What about me? Does my name change? Is there any sign of what I suffer? Do I have to keep my grief a secret, like my love?' That sounded quite nice. She'd put that on her wreath, sealed inside a folded piece of paper, like a confidential luggage tag. She jotted it down in her shorthand pad before she forgot. The smart alecs who said shorthand was a thing of the past, a relic of the days before dictating machines and word-processors, forgot that it was a very convenient way of keeping things secret from men.

Spare bifocals. Gold-plated cigar-cutter. Silver hip-flask. A black and white photograph of a young woman with a fifties perm in a small silver frame. Three Cross pens engraved with various corporate logos. A disposable lighter. A silver golf tee. An indoor putting set. Five ball-bearings on a cradle, tick tick tick. An oblong leather case with a gold lock containing masonic regalia. A little silver model of an old Bentley. A leather case of business cards. A pewter tankard. Membership cards for the Bankers' Club, the Lombard Association, the Threadneedle Society. Tags and badges and lapel pins for Henley and Ascot and Epsom. A Rotary badge. She caressed these and other men's things with gentle fingers before wrapping them in tissues and putting them in the box.

'Oh Georgie.'

There were other objects which she did not put in the box, things which a wife should not see. These she put in the empty in-tray to be transferred to the bottom drawer of her own desk. The key to a hotel room in Harrogate on a long wooden tag. A shrunken head with a tiny shrunken penis dangling round its neck. A colour photograph of a young woman in an eighties bikini langorously draped on a beach lounger. Books of matches advertising discreet little restaurants. A pink coral heart on a key-ring. A front-door key strung on a black lace garter. Mementos of her own life as well as his, lives now over and done with. Oh Georgie. Who could replace him?

'Wheeler's on his way up,' said Eddie. He came in without knocking and she bristled. Their enforced complicity had made him too familiar.

'*Mister* Wheeler, you mean?' With heavy heart she put the cardboard box on the in-tray and carried it into her office.

Percy went straight to the alleged scene of the tragedy with Eddie without taking off his velvet-collared coat. He stood under the crystal chandelier with his back to his portrait. Although there was a definite resemblance, skilful use of the airbrush concealed from the public a number of details that rounded out the whole person: the scurf in his vigorous eyebrows for example, or the matching hairs that sprouted from his ears and nostrils. He was a stocky, pear-shaped man. On his sloping shoulders even his well-tailored clothes looked as though they still had the hangers in. He stooped over the carpet and surveyed it through hooded eyes. 'Did he say anything?' he asked.

'About what, sir?' asked Eddie. Bosses feel more at ease with subordinates who are obtuse.

'Last words, that sort of thing.' The speech therapist employed by the media consultant he patronized had not succeeded in wholly eradicating the Brummy consonants that lurked among his class-less vowels.

'He was undergoing a mystical experience when he expired.'

'Mystical?'

' "Jesus, I'm coming," he said. He was a religious man under-neath. I told Mrs Livery. I thought it would comfort her.'

'Livery religious?' Wheeler's eyebrows shot up his forehead like a pair of crows taking flight.

'Deathbed repentance. You can't deny him that, can you sir?'

Wheeler quizzed him with his hooded eyes, trusted the inno-cent look on his face and passed on.

'You gave him artificial respiration before you called an ambulance?'

'Yes Mr Wheeler.'

'Mouth to mouth?' he asked, incredulous.

'Yes,' said Eddie, trying to stop himself visibly retching at the thought of George Livery's moist, purple lips and bristly mous-tache and furry tongue. It had been bad enough thumping his chest on the floor of the ante-room and watching half-naked Nora fish his dentures out and labour over his flaccid chops with her smudged red mouth. A tremor of nausea seemed to pass across the corner of Percy's mouth too.

'What was he doing here at six o'clock?'

'Working late sir.'

'Working late? That doesn't sound like Livery.'

'He said he had something important to do. He wanted to give something to Nora, his secretary. Miss Truelove.'

'Was she here?'

'Oh no. She'd gone home.'

'Why were you here?'

'I always wait until the end of the computer run. Then I lock up.'

Wheeler's eyebrows came back to roost and he looked hard at Eddie. For the first time he began to have misgivings about his story. Livery's sudden appetite for work had made Wheeler suspicious.

'Then what happened?'

'I'm sitting at my desk in reception when I hear a shout – no, a sort of strangled cry. I come in here and see him on the floor, sort of writhing around and pulling at his collar.' Eddie gave audio-visual reinforcement to his story by clutching his collar and rolling his eyes. In his experience it gained nothing to be economical with the truth. The more lavish with it you were, the less people noticed the bits you missed out. He refrained, however, from going the whole hog and lying on the carpet to kick his heels.

'Tragic.'

'It gave me a fright, I can tell you.'

'Terrible.'

'It was the way he would have wanted to go, Mr Wheeler. On the job.'

Together they gazed down at the spot on the carpet where George Livery was purported to have rendered up his spirit.

'I wonder what brought it on.'

'Over-work?'

'Livery?' asked Wheeler, rhetorically, but nevertheless obtaining a reply.

'Oh yes, sir. He'd started to go through the files.'

The crows were startled again.

'Files? How do you know?'

'He had one in his hand when he came out of his office. I had to prize it out of his fingers when the ambulance came. Company property. I couldn't let it out of the office, could I?'

'What file was it?'

'What file?'

'What file!'

'I don't know. I didn't look. I mean in the circumstances . . .'

'Show me.'

'Show you?'

'Show me!'

'Show you what, sir?'

'The file.'

'The file.'

The crows were performing an aerial samba by now. Eddie was not prepared for the summoning of evidence. One of the many misconceptions about important people in high places is that they are only concerned with applying broad brushes to big pictures. They have got where they are as much through attention to detail as to the strategic generalities. Percy Wheeler was no exception. A lifetime of looking after the pennies, gathering mickles, buttering the edges of the slices before the middle, had taught him the value of thoroughness.

'The file!'

'It's in the main office.'

He left Wheeler pondering mortality in the velvet pile and went into reception and through the door marked 'Staff Only'. He threaded his way through the fuzzy grey maze to the automated filing cabinet that held the customer files. It was untended. Louise, the filing clerk, was gossiping about Livery to the girls in accounts. He picked a file out at random. The Panama Investment Company. When he came back Wheeler snatched it out of his hand.

'PANIC,' he muttered. His face turned bright red and his jaw muscles rippled and his teeth ground above the hum of the air-conditioning. Eddie hoped he would not be thumping his chest too before the morning was out. He wished Nora luck with Percy's mouth; his lips were so thin she could cut herself.

'Panic, sir?'

'Panama Investment Company. Have you shown this to anyone else?'

'No, Mister Wheeler.'

'Good. Keep it that way. I'm relying on you. I want the utmost confidence. If this gets out in the wrong way . . .'

'You can trust me, Mister Wheeler.'

Percy tucked the file under his arm and marched to the general manager's office.

'Thanks, Eddie.'

● ● ●

'Mr Simple for Mr Wheeler,' announced Eddie.

Any female of any age and of any disposition who met Harry Simple experienced the same sensation when she first saw him: a sudden intake of breath, a tremor somewhere behind the breast-bone, as if she had been given a mild electric shock. Despite the tide of grief on which she was tossed Nora was no exception. He was tall, slim, elegant, black hair swept back, blue eyes, tanned face, firm jaw, straight nose, shy smile, deep and beautifully modulated voice, scent of musk and tweed. He wore a perfectly tailored dark blue suit with double vents and a soft pyjama-striped shirt and pink and maroon silk tie. Like Eddie he wore a button-hole for May Day, a pale yellow rose, but not in honour of the workers' day. His May Day was the maypole on the village green, choirboys warbling over Oxford from Magdalen Tower, relics of a golden age, not promises. He stooped slightly in front of her desk, a courtier's bow, and for an instant George Livery was submerged. She pulled herself together and gave him the tradi-tional secretarial greeting.

'Do you have an appointment?'

'Gosh. He just phoned me. Pole right round he said. I say, sorry about the bad news and all that.'

Behind his back Eddie performed one of the silent impersona-tions he was famous for in the lower bar of the Samuel Pepys, this time his chinless Sloane. Nora glared at him as she opened the door into the general manager's office.

Percy stood masterfully with his hands on his hips looking out of the window. Nora had taken away his coat. His light grey double-breasted Chester Barrie suit, unbuttoned, floated round him like a new blazer on the first day of term. He looked through his scowling reflection at the smoke-grimed churches and red-brick tenements and warehouses and markets, the narrow streets already filled with scuttling office workers 'going down the lane', poking and ferreting among the barrows, Nigerian market mammas, round and gaudy as hot-air balloons, wizened Bangladeshis in astrakhan caps and long white beards, turbanned Sikhs with shiny briefcases, muscly men with loud suits and Rolls Royces parked on the pavement, down-and-outs and drunks

26

looking to earn a few shillings by clearing up the rubbish. He could see into sweat shops where Asian men and women and children made leather clothes and jeans and frocks and saris for the shops below, into storerooms piled high with Japanese cassette players and Indian brassware and Chinese toys, into little offices unchanged for a hundred years except for a telephone. Bathed in the warm breeze of the air-conditioning, peering through the slats of the Venetian blinds, it was like being in the posh stateroom of a luxury cruise-liner moored in an exotic port.

Unlike the late lamented Livery he liked the view. He preferred it to the regimented, sanitized, automated bustle of City streets and office blocks. He knew what it was like to roll up his sleeves, work long hours, haggle and bargain, take all his capital out of his back pocket and put it on a single deal, cash on the nail, no questions asked, no tax returns. That was real business. He had never been comfortable with Dividend Investments. In theory its business was straightforward. DI collected the surplus cash of all the other subsidiaries of the Dividend Group and invested it in bank deposits and securities. But Percy preferred real things. He liked to count notes and kick tyres and see the bricks and mortar.

'Mr Wheeler, Mr Simple to see you,' Nora announced in a simpering contralto before spinning like a model on a catwalk and making her exit downstage left. Wheeler continued to look out of the window while he counted to ten, listening to Harry pad across the carpet. He let him stand for another couple of beats before turning round.

'George Livery dropped dead last night,' he said by way of greeting.

'I know. Poor old Livers.' They observed a five-second silence. The formalities concluded, Percy resumed.

'That's why I'm over here for the morning. Get things sorted out. We'll have to make an announcement.'

'I'll get right on to it,' said Harry like a keen school prefect. He was Director of Public Affairs, Director of Investor Relations and Official Spokesman of the Dividend Group. Wheeler himself took on these roles when there was good news to announce: profit rises, dividend increases, acquisitions, pay rises, bonuses. Harry looked after the bad news: dips in profits, redundancies, closures, complaints to the Press Council, briefings of libel lawyers, appearances at public inquiries.

'We'll need a new General Manager.'

'I'll get old Kingers on to it.'

'Who's he?'

'Kingmaker. The executive search chappie.'

'Headhunters? Cannibals. Bloodsucking cannibals. Why should I pay a year's salary in fees just to get some empty suit?'

'That's how you recruited me.'

Percy had a reputation for many things and tact was not one of them. Yet he managed to suppress the obvious reply as the crows over his eyes fluttered on their perch.

'Internal promotion. That's the answer. No recruitment expenses and you can pay them less. Get Personnel to find somebody in-house.'

'That's an idea,' said Harry. He did not say what sort of an idea he thought it was. It was best not to contradict Percy directly.

'There's just one thing, Percy.'

'Yes?'

'Off the top of my head I can't think of anybody in-house who knows about investing money.'

'You're right there. They only know how to spend it. How about the old-boy network? That's what I hired you for, Harry, your connections.'

'Nice to know my abilities are appreciated, sir. I'll ask around.'

'Get on to it. There shouldn't be a problem. The City's having another shake out. The banks are letting people go.'

'Gosh, come to think of it I bumped into a chap at the Contango the other day. Bright chap. Harvard Business School, lending experience, dealing room, high-flier, fast track, just got passed over for the top job. We'd have to pay him but he'd fit the bill.'

'I don't want a yuppie. I want someone lazy and stupid and middle-aged and thick as two planks and unsuccessful and anything for the quiet life who I can pay peanuts.'

'Pay peanuts and you get monkeys,' said Harry, embarrassed at using an Americanism.

'Exactly. I want a sleepy baboon who spends all day scratching his balls and wondering where the next banana's coming from. There are plenty around the City. Try the clearing banks.'

'I see why you don't want to use a headhunter. This isn't the job specification they usually get.'

Percy's hooded eyes narrowed, sizing up Harry, making it plain that he was considering whether to share a confidence.

'I've got plans for Dividend Investments, Harry.'

'What sort of plans?'

'Not very long-term plans.'

'Gosh.'

'It doesn't make enough profit. It's cheaper for the subs to handle their own banking business.'

'You're closing it down?'

'I didn't say that, did I? Did I say that?'

'No sir,' conceded Harry. Percy liked to keep his subordinates guessing.

'Whatever I decide to do there won't be a job for a general manager by the end of the year.'

'Why not close it down now?'

'I would. But there's some unfinished business I have to get to the bottom of first.' His voice dropped and he leaned over the desk. 'Livery was working late.'

'I say,' said Harry, sharing his master's concern. Then he was struck by a second thought. 'What's so odd about that?'

'Maybe nothing,' said Percy. 'Maybe everything. When did the idle bugger ever open a file during working hours? Livery was the old school. The working day ended with lunch. The afternoon was for sobering up. So what was he up to? What was he doing that gave him a heart attack?'

'Gosh. You mean . . .'

'I don't know what I mean. Maybe he was up to something. Maybe he discovered something that someone else was up to.'

'Maybe there was nothing. Maybe he just had a heart attack.'

'There are rumours. There've been snoopers. Newspaper men. Sniffing round the company. I want you to keep your ears open. If you hear anything, let me know. If anybody on my payroll is up to something so help me I'll have their guts for, for . . .' He balled his fists and stared malevolently down at the PANIC file on his desk.

'Garters, sir.'

'What?'

'Garters.'

'What's garters got to do with anything?'

'I mean, er guts garters. Guts for. You said . . .'

'What are you blathering about?'

'Nothing. I mean apart from Livers working late there's not a lot to go on, is there? I mean is there anything else that looks fishy?'

Percy put both hands flat on the PANIC file and leaned over until his chin was nearly on the blotter, as if he were going to do press-ups, and opened his mouth to share a confidence when the door from the ante-room burst open to reveal Nora triumphant with a silver salver, as if it bore the head of George Livery instead of coffee things. She processed to the desk and unloaded the tray with meticulous ceremony, watched by the two men in irritated silence which she interpreted as gratitude.

'White or black, Mr Wheeler?' she asked, looking sideways at Harry.

'We'll look after it,' snapped Wheeler. He saw her recoil, noticed her puffy red eyes and added more ingratiatingly, 'Thank you Nora, that's wonderful. What would we do without you?' In silence they observed her retreat down the catwalk to her own office, the exaggerated care with which she closed the door, the final glance in search of approbation.

'Crème de la crème, sir?' asked Harry. He picked up the silver milk jug in two delicate fingers like an altar cruet and poured the contents in both cups. 'You were saying about old Livers . . .'

Percy leaned back in his chair, his hands still on the PANIC file, and eyed Harry.

'No, there's nothing else. But you know what it's like. One whiff of scandal and there'll be DTI inspectors and the Securities and Investments Board and the Fraud Squad round here before you can say, say . . .' He picked up his coffee cup and a chocolate biscuit and dunked one into the other.

'Insider dealing,' volunteered Harry.

'What's that?' hissed Percy. 'What are they saying? Out with it.'

'Gosh, nothing. Just a turn of phrase. Before you can say insider dealing. Manner of speaking.' He had come across another taboo phrase, like worker participation or industrial democracy, never to be uttered in Percy's presence.

'I want complete, complete discretion about this. This comes at a ticklish time. I happen to know they're working on the honours list right now.'

'I say. Sir Percy Wheeler. Very nice.'

'I've spent a lot of money, Harry. Boys' clubs, East End settlements, homes for alcoholics. Fiddlers and layabouts. Look what I've given to the Tories. I don't want it all chucked out of the window. If there's a whiff of scandal in any of my companies it won't do me any good at all.'

'Absolutely.'

'I've got to find out if there are any skeletons in the cupboard.'

Wheeler fed chocolate fingers into his mouth, munching briskly like a hamster with a carrot, frowning. Harry stirred his coffee with a puzzled frown as well as a spoon, as if something in the story was missing.

'What's the matter?' asked Percy.

'I'm not a hundred per cent sure of what you want me to do.'

'Just find me a general manager. A caretaker. I need someone to count the paper-clips and not poke his nose into what doesn't concern him while I tie up the loose ends and take care of Dividend Investments in my own time.'

'A bright future for somebody.'

'I'll give him a good reference.'

● ● ●

'Morning comrades,' chirped Eddie, putting the crate of food on the table in the middle of the kitchen. Lucy snatched an envelope from a clutch of kiwi fruit laid in straw and tore it open to pluck out the invoice. She checked there was everything she had ordered from the High Class Suppliers in Leadenhall Market, flicking the paper with a sharp fingernail as she went down the list.

'The creeps forgot the mangoes again.' She shook her head in anger. Lucy did most things in anger. She was about thirty, with a long face and long hands and long body, everything about her long including her Titian hair which she wore combed and crimped in Pre-Raphaelite tresses if she was in a good mood and a tumbling mass of rat's tails if she was not. Whatever her mood she clothed her angular body in the same Laura Ashley fabrics, their innocent little flowers turned to blooms of deadly nightshade and foxglove and laburnum under the toxic influence of her resentment. Today it was the rat's tails and a frown on her wide, freckled forehead.

'How much did you spend today, Lucy?' asked Eddie, as usual.

'Never you mind,' she said, as usual, spiking the paper on her cork notice-board with a skewer for everyone to see that the ingredients for lunch for Mr Wheeler and his guest – quail's eggs, truffles, salmon, strawberries and other delicacies, the more out of season the better – approximated to an average weekly supermarket bill for a family of four.

'What are they drinking with this lot?' he asked. 'I would have thought the '84 Sancerre all the way through. Unless you're doing your *Béarnaise brulée* with the salmon in which case it has to be the Graves.'

'Sounds all right to me,' said Rhoda, fumbling ineptly with her apron strings, but not as ineptly as when she came to untie them again after sherry, wine, port and brandy and whatever else she could lay her hands on before she went home. Rhoda helped out in the kitchen and served drinks and waited at table. She was short and round, like a cottage loaf, with a bun of dyed black hair that took ten years off her age, leaving her with about sixty.

'So what's going on, Eddie?' asked Lucy, chopping leeks with a cleaver and a fury that threatened to split the beech block into matchwood.

'How should I know?' said Eddie innocently, pouring coffee from the cona into a mug entitled 'I'm the Boss'. 'I suppose it's what Mr Wheeler's discussing in there with Mr Simple.'

'Who is he? The new manager? And Mr Livery not cold yet,' said Rhoda, dusting her nose from a powder compact she kept in the pocket of her apron. She was sensitive about her nose, with good reason, a handsome ruby conk accentuated by the pale Welsh face in which it was mounted. She plastered over it every few minutes but today tears for Mr Livery were playing havoc with the rendering.

'Hooray Harry Simple. He's Wheeler's Director of Public Affairs. His chief-of-staff. His step-and-fetch-it. You'd better watch it Lucy. He's a professional knife and fork man.'

'Nobody liked his food better than Mr Livery,' sniffed Rhoda, 'and his port afterwards. Poor man, God rest him, what a way to go.'

'He brought it on himself, second helpings of this, second helpings of that,' said Lucy, circumcising a courgette before submitting it to the chopper. Watching her at work on courgettes and leeks and egg-plants and cucumbers was unmanning.

'Come on Lucy, Livery was all right,' said Eddie, 'he let us get on with it.'

'There'll be changes,' said Lucy, 'You mark my words. I bet that's what those two are cooking up in there.'

'They're a funny pair all right,' said Rhoda, 'Put them in the blender and you might get two normal men.'

'What's a normal man?' challenged Lucy, tipping the chopped vegetables into a pan, stirring with a wooden spoon and tossing her unkempt hair out of her eyes. Ferocious and intense while she worked, Lucy gave the impression she was doing more than just cookery; alchemy perhaps, creating her own homunculus from the vegetable and animal matter she concocted. Rhoda and Eddie exchanged knowing glances. A proper conversation with Lucy in this mood was going to be difficult. Perhaps she was more moved than she cared to admit by Livery's death. She had cooked for him for the past four years – ever since she gave up her job as a social worker to do directors' lunches – feeding him up with the choicest meats and gravies and sauces and puddings. Some kind of bond must have formed, like that between a farmer and his prize pig.

'It's uncertain times,' said Rhoda with resignation. 'When I lost my first husband I thought the end of the world had come. The same with the second and the third. But you never know what's round the corner.'

'Will they be promoting from inside?' asked Lucy.

'Shouldn't think so,' said Eddie. 'There's no-one in the group who knows anything about investing money. They'll have to go outside. They'll be going to the headhunters. The Investment Manager at Premium Insurance is looking for a job. They ought to go for him.'

'How do you know?'

'Mate of mine's the head messenger.'

'Whatever it is it'll be the same old thing,' said Lucy, 'do this do that with never a word of gratitude. You work your fingers to the bone and then, suddenly, you're down the waste disposal. There's only one thing to do in life and that's look after number one. Rhoda, where's the cream?'

'So who's looking after things until they get a new manager?' asked Rhoda, opening the fridge.

'Wheeler himself is coming in every morning. He'll be having lunch here every day. I'll fetch you the Sancerre then, you can put it in the fridge.'

'Thanks Eddie,' said Rhoda, getting out her powder compact.

● ● ●

Liz pushed the snooze button and sank again into a tropical lagoon, her naked body warmed by the sun, an enormous sun, like an eye. The sound of a bacon slicer starting up in the next room dragged her back, set her teeth on edge, and she rolled out of bed. Half-past seven. Sunlight was streaming through the curtains and she hated them for it as much as she hated the chintzy little pink roses and the tassles at the sides and the bunched up material at the top, like baggy knickers. Fiona's choice of decor. Sitting on the side of the bed she scratched her thigh and reached for the packet of Camel filters and the black disposable lighter on the bedside table. No. Round her right wrist was a rubber band. With her left hand she pulled it up half an inch and let it go. David's idea. Punish yourself. Drive away temptation. David was full of ideas for self-improvement. It did not sting very much so she flicked it again, harder. Her wrist smarting she jerked a cigarette out of the packet and lit it and took a deep drag. 'May Day,' she said, noticing the date on the clock. 'May Day. Mayday. Sinking fast.' She stood up and went to the door, stepping over her clothes and

34

trying to avoid her reflection in the full-length mirror on the door of the fitted wardrobe. Common courtesy changed her mind. 'Morning Lizzie,' she said, blowing smoke in her face. She ran her fingers through her tousled blonde hair and peered at the bags under her eyes. She rubbed off the eyeshadow and the little black specks of mascara with the heel of her hand. May Day. She would have to snitch some of Fiona's cream again.

She stood at the door of Fiona's bedroom and watched her flatmate pedal her exercise bicycle, the source of the bacon slicer sound. She was wearing bright red warm-ups and had scraped her blonde hair into a pigtail. Her face glistened with moisturiser and perspiration. Walkman headphones straddled her head, the yellow box clipped to the handlebars. Liz remembered a black and white film about a secret agent using a bicycle generator to power a transmitter. Come in, London. Mayday. Mayday. This was the finale. Fiona had already gone through her exercise routine on the immaculately vacuumed pink pile carpet. The rest of the room looked like a show flat. Her clothes for the day, a grey pleated skirt, a blue blazer, a horsey Hermés scarf, hung pressed over the mirror on the wardrobe door, polished shoes underneath, underwear laid out on the bed. When Liz wore clothes like that she felt like an air hostess.

A clock on the bicycle pinged like an oven timer but Fiona did not hear it. Liz slouched over and lifted an earphone. 'You're done,' she shouted. Fiona stopped pedalling, wrinkled her nose and flapped her hands at the cigarette smoke. Liz put her hands behind her back while Fiona took deep breaths and touched her toes.

'Why do I always dream about the sun like an enormous eye in the morning?'

'Money. It's the eye on the back of a dollar bill.'

'David thinks it's my father. I need to bask in the approval of older men.'

'Uh uh. Money.'

'I only have it between snoozes.'

'Get up as soon as the alarm goes off.'

'I'd rather die. I'll put the coffee on.'

'Just juice for me.'

She was still hunched over the *Independent* on a third cup of coffee and a second Camel, twisting the rubber band round her fingers, when Fiona came in to the kitchen showered and dressed and made up and glowing and vibrant and alive and repellent. She opened the fridge, filled a tumbler from a Five Alive carton and sat down opposite her.

'Elizabeth. I need to have a chat with you.' Elizabeth. That meant trouble. What had she done? Transgressions fast forwarded before her – tossing the unsinkable lemon from a bath-time gin and tonic down the loo, leaving pants in the wash-basin overnight, growing penicillin on the Lymeswold rind in the sink while she was away for the weekend, surely not smoking again?

'At this hour of the morning? It's not even eight o'clock.'

'Listen Elizabeth, it's been wonderful having you here. It's not only your financial contribution. You're great to share with. You're a tremendous person, easy-going and relaxed and tolerant and attractive and good company. I'd envy anyone else who lived with you. You're a wonderful person.'

'Do you want to borrow money?'

'No.'

'Sleep with me?'

'No!'

'Why are you telling me this?'

'It's true.'

'Why are you boosting my confidence. Is my self-esteem showing?'

'Liz, please.'

'All right, out with it.'

'I'm going to have to ask you to leave.' She looked Liz in the eye and they stared each other out as they had learned on their assertiveness training courses.

'Oh. Can I ask why?'

'I'm selling this place and moving to Docklands.'

'Congratulations. That's wonderful news. When do you move in?'

'Next year probably. It's not built yet.'

'So we've got plenty of time.'

'Not exactly. I'm buying with someone else. The person I'm

36

buying with is moving in here. See how we get on first before we commit ourselves. So it's the end of the month, really.' She drained her glass and stood up. 'Look, I'm sure you'll find something else before you know it.'

Liz lit another cigarette. Fiona stood up, looked as though she was about to say something, and thought better of it.

'It's your flat,' said Liz.

'Let's talk about it tonight. I've got a meeting at eight fifteen.' She picked up her shiny black handbag and hurried out of the kitchen.

'Do I know her?' Liz called, but the only answer was the door slamming.

Half an hour later Liz closed the front door and turned down the east walkway towards Aldersgate. She walked quickly, breathing deep the fresh spring air, partly for the exercise and partly because she was late as usual. She swung an old leather music case with a metal rod on two leather thongs for a handle. In her office she had a reputation for her street style, her informal eclectic outfits, her disregard for the conventions of what went with what. Young typists would sometimes imitate her with disastrous results, contriving to look like down-and-outs. Liz always carried it off, just. The secret was not to contrive it at all. Her outfits were the result of putting on whatever she could find that was clean or at least spongeable ten minutes before she left home. If she wore a T-shirt the wrong way round it was because there was bolognaise sauce down the front. If she wore men's shirts and jackets it was because David's happened to be cleaner than hers when she got up. If she went bra-less, it was because they were all in the wash. If her hair was tousled and fluffed it was because she had left her hairbrush in the bathroom.

'You're a tremendous person, easy-going and relaxed and tolerant and attractive and good company. You're a wonderful person. But get out.'

Where was she going to live? Even if Fiona was selling up right now she couldn't afford to buy the flat for herself. She had fought off the shackles of a mortgage for so long that she was on the bottom of the ladder. Other than a dank bedsit in south London the best she could hope for would be a little two-bed something in

37

Chelmsford or Luton. Move in with David? He was a securities dealer and had to be at work by half past five. He had dinner at six and went to bed before ten. It would be like living with someone with permanent jet lag. He was only civilized at weekends.

'Spare the money for a cup of tea?' asked a little man in a corduroy cap and a shabby brown overcoat. He had a stiff neck and the left side of his face sagged as if he had been sleeping on it too long. She took a pound coin out of her jacket pocket and gave it to him. Always somebody worse off.

'It'll turn out all right in the end, miss,' he said, touching his temple.

'Thanks for the tip,' she said.

Besides, she liked living in the Barbican. She could walk to work instead of sweating it out on public transport. It gave her an extra hour in bed in the morning. Monumental slabs of brick and concrete put her in the right mood for earning a living. It made you feel that all that effort and struggle and ambition was not so important after all. It was comforting to have all those straight lines, right angles and earnest chunks of masonry, not to have grass and flowers and trees and real houses to remind you what life could be like. It was comforting to feel small and insignificant among the massive tower blocks and grandiose walkways, one of the little people sprinkled on architects' models, afterthoughts in a developer's mind.

Her boss, Warwick J. Kingmaker III, was waiting in the rear lobby for the coffee-machine to digest his instructions when she walked out of the service elevator, sneaking in the back way so the receptionist would not see she was late. Bluff it out.

'Jolly bracing,' she said jovially. Warwick sniffed. He was a tall, hollow-chested Chicagoan who wore horn-rimmed spectacles too big for his face and yellow ties and short-sleeved shirts with button-down collars and a pack of Marlboro showing through the top pocket.

'What?'

'Jolly bracing. The weather. Outside.'

'Right. You been to lunch already?' The intestines of the coffee machine burbled and fizzed on cue.

'Just got in.'

'Right,' said Warwick, looking at his watch.

'Breakfast meeting,' she lied.

Warwick, pronounced War-wick, was the London Vice-president of The Kingmaker Group, the executive search and outplacement company founded by his father, Warwick J. Kingmaker Jr. They specialized in financial institutions and had followed their American clients to London in the wake of the Big Bang, like grouper fish after sharks, hyenas after lions. One of the first heads Warwick had hunted was Liz's from the International Department of National Midland Bank where she had been an assistant manager. He had been impressed by her degree and the best suit she kept for loan signings and job interviews. The coffee-machine gurgled and burped.

'Listen Elizabeth, can we have a talk?' Elizabeth again. Her heart sank. His order was finally egested with a hiccup and splurt. He lifted up the flap and took the polystyrene cup out of the bottom of the machine and carried it away like a boy in an egg and spoon race. Liz selected a black coffee, extra strong. A pep talk from War-wick was all she needed. She followed him into his office.

'Elizabeth, you've done a great job for us over the past couple of years. You've got lots to offer. You've got lots of talent. You've packed a lot of useful experience into a short career.'

The good thing about talking to War-wick was that you did not have to use tricks like imagining him naked except for his tie or pretending he was a chimpanzee or had a parrot on his shoulder. He was unthreateningly absurd enough already. Liz attributed it to the interpersonal relationship courses he was addicted to. He was a consultant's dream. He signed up compulsively for every new gimmick whose brochure plopped through the letter-box. His natural shyness was overlaid with layer upon layer of acquired mannerisms. He leaned over the desk and looked frankly into her eyes and stretched out his arms. That was a new one.

'I want you to believe me Elizabeth when I tell you that you are a wonderful person. You have a great career ahead of you. You're going to go far.'

God, it was a partnership. He was offering her a partnership. How much? Quickly, how much? Her father would lend her something for a deposit and then with a decent mortgage . . . He looked up to the ceiling on the right. She recognized that one. Deep thought and sincerity.

'There's only one thing that worries me a tad, Elizabeth, and I think it's probably our fault and not yours.' His head cocked on one side he scrutinized her like a sparrow eying a crumb.

'Additood.'

'Additood?'

'Right. Additood.'

'I'm not sure what you mean.'

'I don't feel that you are totally committed to the organization and its aims. I've been picking up some clues in the way you've been behaving and I think it's a cry for help.'

'Have you been reading my personal body language again, War-wick?' she said accusingly.

'Why, Elizabeth . . .'

'Okay, out with it.'

He blushed and breathed out rapidly as he spoke, a trick to avoid stammering.

'Your non-adherence to the dress code, your time-keeping, your non-compliance with the internal reporting schedule . . .'

'What's that got to do with anything?'

'I know it's probably our fault and that makes me feel real bad but I sense you're not happy here, Elizabeth. I sense you want out and I don't think it's right that we should prevent that.'

'Are you firing me?'

'We're letting you go, Elizabeth.'

'Because of my additood?'

'And because you haven't made a placement in four months.'

She had rehearsed this moment. Deep down inside she knew it was coming. She had never met anyone made redundant who in their heart of hearts did not know it was on the cards, who almost welcomed it when it came. She ought to know: this was the third time it had happened to her. She knew how she was going to behave: cool, calm, mature, what's all the fuss, I'm too good for this lousy outfit anyway. She was therefore surprised at herself when resentment and anger and humiliation swamped her self-control. She felt herself blushing and hated herself for it.

'That's preposterous. After all I've done. Not even a warning? The market's down. Firms are unloading staff. I can't work miracles. Why didn't you tell me before what you wanted . . .'

'I'm sorry Elizabeth. Listen, you have all the resources of the Kingmaker Group behind you, an office for four weeks, a telephone, stationery, secretarial services, the works.'

She stood up and he jerked backwards in his chair. 'Watch this for body language,' she hissed, and stuck a finger in front of his face.

• • •

*NEW MOON*

'You're late,' snapped Wheeler.

He was standing in front of his desk holding the *Evening Standard* at arm's length. He only wore his half-moon glasses when he was alone. His head was sunk in his puny shoulders and his belly slumped beneath the top of his trousers. Harry closed the padded door behind him and advanced across the carpet like a rabbit across the snow, wary, ears cocked for danger. He assumed an attentive pose on the visitor's chair and subjected himself to Percy's stare.

'Sorry. I was tied up with the Equal Opportunities Commission.'

'What did they want?' barked Percy. Harry flinched.

'To see if we kept figures on women and blacks.'

'What business is it of their's?' snapped Wheeler, swatting the newspaper down on his desk.

'The Equal Opportunities Comm . . .'

'The buggers. I run a business. Not a social service. What did you say?' He pointed a stubby finger at Simple's tie.

'I said we had a positive, caring and responsible attitude towards the community.'

45

'In other words you flannelled. I suppose that's what I pay you for. Still it was a nancy thing to say. Why don't we hit back? Tell them the majority of my staff are minorities. There are women all over the place.'

'Women are not a minority. They're more than fifty per cent of the population.'

'Exactly. We reflect the population.'

'They're all typists and cleaners.'

'Listen, Harry, I don't need smart remarks. This isn't a debating society. I need some positive action. I'm sick and tired of being pilloried by the gutter press.' He picked up the *Standard* and held it under Harry's nose. His thin lips were moist and flecked with saliva. Harry turned his head away to avoid being sprayed. 'Look at this. "Dividend Share Price in the Dustcart." We've got property, insurance, funeral services, hospital laundries, road maintenance, a bus company, we've got a chunk of everything that's been privatized. Out of all that look at the photograph they use. A Dividend Garbage Gorger.'

'At least the dustman's black. I'll send it to the Equal Opportunities Commission.'

'Do something, Harry. Do it now.' He threw the paper across the room. He sat down behind the desk with his hands gripping the arms of the chair, as if he were in danger of being swept away by the wave of his indignation.

'By "do something" do you mean to our image or our share price?'

'Both. I need both of them considerably enhanced by the end of this month.'

'How about announcing a profit rise?'

'Another stick to clobber me with? When I make profits I'm exploiting the community. When I don't make profits it shows I'm no more efficient than the local authorities.' His face brightened with inspiration. 'I want a positive, caring, responsible image, Harry. That's what I want.'

'That's an idea,' agreed Harry. 'I'm seeing the Prince's Trust tomorrow.'

'I don't need you to give away my money. I can do that myself. They only think it's conscience money anyway. I want something innovative, something unusual. Do you understand, Harry? Are those words in your public school vocabulary?'

'Would a woman general manager for Dividend Investments be innovative and unusual enough?' He fidgeted under Wheeler's wide-eyed stare, planning a retreat across the beige carpet while it was still unstained with his blood. Approbation from his boss was so rare that he did not recognize it.

'Who is she? What's she like?'

Harry pushed a paper across the desk. It outlined the erratic career of Miss Elizabeth Goodman. Wheeler pondered it and flipped it back across the desk.

'Where did you get this?'

'I gave Warwick Kingmaker a call. Just to see what the market was like,' he added hastily. 'We won't have to pay a fee.'

'Why has she had so many jobs? Four jobs in four years.'

'She says it was to broaden her experience.'

'A job-hopper and a woman as well. Couldn't be better. Let's have her in.'

'That's an idea,' said Harry.

● ● ●

As they were representing the office at George Livery's funeral, Nora and Eddie took the car. They left at lunchtime in the venerable Humber limousine, motoring sedately out of the City in the direction of the suburban crematorium.

'I never thought it would end like this,' mused Eddie, 'he looked all set for his retirement party.'

Nora sighed in reply, looking out of the side window through the dots in her veil, drawing consolation from the curious and admiring glances of passers-by. She wished she were sitting in the back and Eddie was wearing the cap he used when he drove Mister Livery to official functions. Used to drive. Oh Georgie.

They were early. Nora declined Eddie's offer of a coffee in the Starburger opposite the cemetery gates and they strolled round the graves, browsing among the epitaphs.

'Funny how they don't seem such a load of rubbish when you're actually burying someone,' mused Eddie.

47

'I don't ever think they're rubbish,' said Nora, crisply.

'Do you believe in it all, Nora, eternal rest and being with Jesus and going to heaven?'

'What difference does it make if you or I believe in it?' she said. 'If it's true, it's true.'

'Opium of the people,' muttered Eddie.

They took their places in the crematorium chapel. Although they were business, and therefore entitled to sit somewhere in the middle, behind family and close friends, they went to the back pew, the traditional place for lovers, ex-husbands and wives, natural children, estranged relatives, enemies, victims, necrophiliacs, writers looking for material and people coming in out of the rain. It was where she had sat for her first ever funeral, a grander affair than this, packed with captains of industry and members of boards and directors of banks and masons and rotarians and freemen and their fur-coated wives. She was seven years old and her mother had not told her who was being buried or why they had come or why she was weeping behind her spotty black veil or why they had left while the coffin was being lowered into the hole lined with grass like they had in the windows of fish shops. Later, when she was nineteen and engaged to be married, her mother told her who her father was and why they had to sit at the back of his funeral. When Nora saw the widow Livery come in behind the coffin, leaning on a solemn young man, and go into the front pew, she closed her eyes and took a deep breath and put her hand on her bottom lip to stop it trembling.

When she opened her eyes again she examined for the first time the other occupants of her pew, besides Eddie. They were three women, about the same age as her, mid-forties, similarly dressed in black coats and little hats with veils. They were not together, and, like Nora, shot sideways glances at each other. Their mordant curiosity was at odds with their otherwise melancholy demeanour. They eyed each other surreptitiously until the homily was over and the clergyman switched on the cassette of the Lord Is My Shepherd and the curtains parted and the rollers revolved and they turned their gaze inward to the awful mysteries.

Their curiosity was soon satisfied at the ceremony of sizing up the floral tributes, lined up outside against the crematorium wall.

The widow led the procession, bending down over the tickets, holding them so she could read them properly, like a lost-property attendant. Then she stood and greeted the mourners after they had checked the wreaths to make sure the one they had ordered had been sent. Nora fingered the tag on hers with its secret message sealed inside. Mrs Livery came up to them, her face swollen with emotion. She was small and trim, with silvery blue hair.

'Nora. How lovely of you to come. And Joyce, you shouldn't have. And there's Wanda over there. I saw Betty just now. You're such good girls. He would have been ever so touched. The office meant so much to him. You'll all come back after, won't you? George would have liked that.'

She wandered off leaving Joyce with Nora. Joyce had long black hair down to her waist which Nora thought she was too old for.

'Were you his . . . you know.'

'Secretary,' said Nora.

'That's what I meant.'

'His last.'

'Right after me then. Before he moved to Dividend. He wanted to take me with him, you know.'

'Oh yes, he did mention you, once,' said Nora sweetly. 'Did you get something done about the varicose veins?'

'He talked a lot about you. Only last month in fact. Did he ever give you that diet plan?'

So that was where he had got it from. Nora forced a laugh. Better an alliance with an unknown enemy.

'I think we've got a lot in common. Did you ever have to massage his toes when he got cramp?'

'The poor sweetie. He got it whenever he walked back from lunch. Here comes Betty. She was the one before me, while he was running Commercial Loans.'

'She needs the diet plan more than me.'

Since the days when she massaged George's toes Betty had gone to seed. It wasn't so much her weight – Georgie liked big girls – but the way she waddled under it, splay-footed, as if she were pregnant.

'Hello girls,' she said, in a Welsh accent. 'The old bugger finally did it.'

'Did what?' said Joyce.

'Snuffed it, bless him. He always sweared he was going to when he got breathless. He knew it was coming all right. Mind you, that was twenty years ago, so he hung on a bit didn't he?' She giggled and looked round as if it were naughty to laugh at a funeral.

'You were his secretary too,' stated Nora.

'Five years. He was a one, wasn't he? Remember the little brass monkey that looked like a pencil sharpener? When you put the pencil in its willy popped out. He used to love springing that on the new girls. Oh he liked a bit of fun, Georgie did.'

'You can say that again,' said Joyce, flicking her long hair back over her shoulders.

'And did he still have that shrunken head he brought back from Australia?'

'And the shrunken thingie to go with it?' said Nora. 'Yes he had that. It's in my desk. I didn't think Edwina would appreciate it.'

'Nothing shrunken about George's . . . Hello Wanda,' said Betty. Nora looked enviously at Wanda. Her erect carriage, her simple well-cut clothes, her alligator bag, her perfectly cut grey hair, belonged to an elegance and stylishness that she coveted. Pity about the gravelly voice. She lit a long cigarette from a Dunhill lighter.

'George's old slags, eh? We should have jumped on the funeral pyre.' She coughed a fruity, brassy cough and smoke puffed through her nose.

'We were talking about his little ways,' said Joyce.

'The things I did for that man,' rasped Wanda.

'Not too loud, ladies, the widow's behind us, bless her,' giggled Betty.

'She'd learn a thing or two,' said Nora.

'Like who remembered her birthday . . .'

'Their anniversary . . .'

'Bought her presents . . .'

'Remembered her sizes . . .'

'Sent her flowers . . .'

'Booked their holidays . . .'

'Sewed his buttons . . .'

'Mended his zips . . .'

'Watched his diet . . .'

'Calmed him down . . .'

'Sobered him up . . .'

'Held his head . . .'

(And what they did not discuss, the kisses and hugs and cuddles in swivel chairs and visitors' sofas and empty offices and conference centres and airport hotels and company flats that always ended in him going back home to her, the widow.)

'I gave him the kiss of life,' said Nora, capping them all.

'Pity it didn't work,' said Wanda, bring them back to present reality.

They went back to the house in the Humber, Betty in the front with Eddie as she took up most room and Nora in the middle behind. The Liverys lived in the hinterland of the M25, nestled in the leafy suburbia that stretches from Watford to the sea, the padded rump that Britain sits on, soft and comfortable, larded with subcutaneous wealth, the country's fat store, the swollen arse of affluence.

'I love these leather seats,' said Joyce.

'Your bottom doesn't go numb like on nylon,' said Betty.

The house was in a cul-de-sac, sixties neo-Georgian, a brick box with a white triangle over the front door. The curtains were all drawn. Plates of little sandwiches with the crusts cut off, shrouded in white linen napkins, were laid out on the dining table in the through lounge. Eddie made himself useful by circulating with the sherry bottle while the four ex-secretaries stood at one end of the room with little plates and thimble glasses, aloof from the other thirty or so mourners. They looked round avidly, sucking in every detail. They had been to the loo, upstairs, so they could peek in the bedrooms, and offered to help carry plates around so they could examine the kitchen. None of them had been to the house before, seen where he spent his other life.

'That's the picture he brought her back from Eastbourne,' said Wanda. 'I remember choosing it.'

'See that photograph? Him at the golf tournament? He was wearing my tights it was so cold,' said Nora.

'I bet you didn't need them,' giggled Betty.

They did not stay long, uncomfortable, tacitly agreeing they had no place there. They received the widow's tearful hugs and thanks in the hall.

'I know you all did so much for him,' she said disconcertingly to Nora, the last to say goodbye.

'We'll miss him, Mrs Livery.'

'He was so hard-working, you know. Home late most nights, all those business trips, he was dedicated to his job, you know, dedicated to everyone who worked for him. He was dedicated to me too, you know, he did everything for me. We were married thirty years, you know.'

'How did you meet him, Mrs Livery?'

'I was his secretary.'

● ● ●

For a joke Eddie put on the chauffeur's hat he kept in the front glove compartment. He dropped the other three off at stations on the way back to London and then took Nora home to Streatham. She stayed in the back, sitting in the middle, looking neither to right nor left. Turning on to the Purley Way he saw in the driving mirror that for the first time that day tears were streaming down her face. When he parked he got out to open the door for her.

'You saw more of him than she did, Nora, or anyone else come to that.'

She drew herself up, smiled a brave smile and sniffed. 'Thanks, Eddie,' she said.

● ● ●

Eddie sat at the reception desk outside his office and ticked off the names of the staff in the attendance register as they arrived. He had the unusual experience for a Monday morning, indeed for any morning, of recording that no-one was late and no-one was absent. He could remember this extraordinary event occurring only once, the day Mr Livery started as General Manager. The circumstances were similar, in fact parallel, as this was the first day of his replacement by his successor. There was a circularity, a tying up of loose ends that confirmed Eddie's sense of history, its rhythm, its inevitability. He only wished he had more information on their new leader since the phone call from Mr Simple in head office late on Friday afternoon saying that the Chairman would be bringing in the new General Manager for lunch.

'Morning, Eddie. New bloody broom, eh?' said Norman, despondently.

'Who knows, Norman, perhaps the old broom on a different handle.'

Shaking his head, Norman padded off to find his antique woolly cardigan and broken suede slip-ons, the closest to slippers he could wear in the office.

Instead of arriving hangdog and taciturn, as they usually did, everyone walked in expectant and nervous. As soon as they arrived they gathered in clusters to gossip and speculate. Nora held court in her office in the management suite for Lucy the cook and Rhoda the waitress and Freda Grafton, Head of Administration. Freda's staff huddled in the main office around Trevor, her deputy. The finance staff congregated around Larry Chivers, the Chief Accountant, more in deference to his position than expectation that he could contribute anything, since, even if he did know something, he would be too tongue-tied to say it.

'. . . Nora says he's from another bank . . .'

'. . . Lucy says he's from the Bank of England . . .'

'. . . Annie says he's a troubleshooter . . .'

'. . . Bill says we're in trouble . . .'

'. . . Norman says we're going to the dogs . . .'

'. . . Bill says he's allergic to dogs . . .'

'. . . Maureen says he's got a dog . . .'

Carrying his shield of invisibility, an armful of envelopes and papers, Eddie flitted from one little group to the other, listening, gathering, gleaning and occasionally contributing to the only piece of solid fact he knew, that their new boss's name was Goodman.

Shortly after twelve o'clock the Sergeant phoned up from the ground floor lobby. They were here. Eddie stood by the front door and listened for the ping of the lift. The entourage was led by

Mr Wheeler himself, hands thrust deep into the pockets of the velvet-collared coat that flapped around his wiry body. Behind him was a young blonde woman, average height, dressed in a floppy linen version of a blue business suit, carrying a battered music case. Bringing up the rear was the elegant and charming Harry Simple, relaxed yet formal in medium grey flannel and a covert coat that looked as though it had seen real coverts and smelled real game, unlike the specimens that never leave the ambit of the Circle Line.

They went straight to the management suite. As Percy reached for the door it was sprung open by an unseen hand. Rhoda stood spruce in waitress black with a lace-trimmed apron and little cap, the monochrome crispness of her appearance alleviated only by her shiny red nose. She bobbed a curtsey to the visitors and stood aside to reveal the majestic figure of Nora, also dressed in black but certainly not a waitress, as magnificent in mourning as on the day after Livery's death. She advanced on the visitors from her office and had begun the speech of welcome she had been practising to herself in a solemn contralto. 'Good morning . . .'

'Morning, dear,' said Percy, and they all swept past her into the general manager's office.

'Where's Mr Goodman then?' asked Rhoda.

'He must have been held up,' said Nora.

Lucy came out of the kitchen, knife in hand. 'Where is he?'

'He hasn't arrived yet. There are only two of them in there. Mr Wheeler and Mr Simple.'

'Late again. Typical. The beef Wellington will be tough as old boots. They can choke on it for all I care,' and she dodged back into the kitchen in search of something to dismember.

While she waited for her new boss Nora went into the dining-room for a last-minute check. She closed the door behind her and admired the table that Rhoda had laid. The silver gleamed, the glasses sparkled, the mahogany glowed, the greens and reds of the hunting scenes leaped out of the placemats. She put the centrepiece carefully down on its silver tray in the middle and stood back to admire it, a tasteful arrangement of carnations and fern from the florist in Leadenhall market. She put the menu-cards in the silver lyre holders and the place-cards behind the dessert spoons, folding

54

them carefully so they stood up. She folded the starched linen napkins so they stood in a cone on the plates. She would have liked to make them into fans and stand them in the water glasses but Lucy always objected, saying it looked like a Berni Inn. She stood back and admired again, made a few minor adjustments, an inch or so, and walked appreciatively round the table. It looked festive and Christmassy but at the same time elegant and refined. 'Mister Goodman,' she sighed, and made sure the bell push was under his place.

She went to the bottom of the table and stood with her hands on the back of the chair facing Goodman's at the head. She hoped he would fit the part, not like the uncouth, aggressive young men who filled the City these days. She imagined him charming and distinguished, like Mr Simple, his manners exquisite. He would be courteous to his guests, a word to each to put them at their ease, a smile, a pleasantry to break the ice, a perceptive comment about the world economic situation to get the conversation going about the weighty affairs of the world.

'You're so right, Goodman.'

'Well put, Goodman.'

'Very perceptive, Goodman.'

But there would still be something missing, an attentive eye on the glasses and side plates and condiments to make sure everyone had exactly what they needed, a lightness, a delicacy. What this table needed was a woman's touch, not the sort of woman who came to lunch with a briefcase and pretended to be a man but a proper woman, refined and poised and feminine. She pulled the chair out and sat down, a wrist resting lightly on the table edge.

'Would you care for a . . .?'

She practised a charming smile, her hand on her throat.

'Would you care for some . . .?'

She laughed, tossing her head.

'Would you care for one of . . .?'

She nodded slowly and elegantly, her head slightly turned.

'Would you care for . . .?'

At the other end of the table Goodman caught her eye, a glance of complicity, encouraging each other, congratulating each other on how well the luncheon party was going.

'Would you care for a . . .?'

'Would you care for me, Nora?'

'You'd better take some coffee in to your new boss,' said Eddie, grinning in the doorway.

'What new boss?'

'Your new boss in there.'

'He's not here yet.'

'I know *he* isn't.'

'What are you blathering on about?'

'Goodman.'

'Who?'

'Our General Manager. The one sitting behind the desk in Mr Livery's chair.'

'I didn't know he'd arrived.'

'*He* hasn't.'

'What are you grinning about?'

'Your new boss. You'd better take *her* in some coffee.'

● ● ●

After lunch, when Percy and Harry had gone, the new General Manager closed the door of her office, flung her arms wide, executed a graceful pirouette and with the tentative glee of a child getting on a new bicycle sat down on the executive swivel chair behind the desk. The leather farted like a whoopee cushion. She made a mental note of her first executive decision: to order a new chair. She loosened the waistband of her skirt and made a second executive decision, to discuss calories with the cook.

'Hi boss,' she said out loud.

She sized up the symbols of her new status. The large desk, reassuringly empty, a fat red leather-bound diary, a pair of gold pens sticking out of an ebony holder, two telephones on a low credenza, a Reuter's screen, a personal computer, a weeping fig apparently growing in sheep droppings, a thick pile carpet, impractically pale beige. Behind the venetian blinds and padded door and outer office she was mistress of these things. She snapped the rubber band on her wrist. It would be very easy to hide behind them from the world outside.

'Miss Goodman, I can call you Elizabeth, can't I, I can see a bright future for Dividend Investments. It's a good little company and I want to see it go places . . .'

They had been so pleased with each other, Percy brash and chipper as an angler with a reservoir roach, Harry as modestly triumphant as a fly fisherman with a salmon, and she wriggling with pleasure on their hook.

'. . . your financial astuteness and management ability are just what we need. I can see a very bright future for you too with your expertise and commitment and energy and hard work . . .'

Management ability and financial astuteness, he said. Not bad for someone who had never written on a cheque stub in her life. She suppressed a tremor of anxiety with the thought that Wheeler had got where he was because he was a good judge of character. This was her last chance. This time she would show what she was made of, what Wheeler thought she was made of. No more losing her temper with bosses, no more sliding off to the cinema when she had nothing to do, no more doing the crossword when she should be looking busy. She would work hard but she would not let it spoil her. She would still be the warm-hearted, considerate, loveable Lizzie at heart.

'This company is going places, Liz. In six months, whoosh. Off like a rocket.'

'Absolutely. Whoosh.'

'Whoosh.'

She hugged herself. She was not a nothing in the City any more. She was a Something.

Meanwhile a two-tone brown Rolls Royce Silver Spur with the numberplate PW1 turned into Bishopsgate. Percy turned to Harry.

'Get to work,' he ordered. 'I want coverage on this. The first woman senior manager in the Dividend Group. The first in the City. Wheeler's golden girls. Equal opportunities.'

'But, Percy . . .'

'But what? She's perfect. Young, attractive, well-spoken.'

'What happens when you close it down?'

'Whose fault will that be? She's got her opportunity. Let her make the most of it. Not our fault.'

'But, Percy . . .'

57

'Everyone will have forgotten about her by then. You do the contract. No compensation if terminated in six months. No share options or anything like that until after the trial period.'

'Then what?'

'Then whoosh. Down the toilet.'

● ● ●

'How much did you raise?' asked the man from the Bank of England. He concealed his love of risk and double play behind an impassive façade.

'Ten,' replied Premium Insurance, gulping Perrier, not to keep a clear head but to regain one. He had been to a lunch and a private dinner at Lloyds that day. His crested tie bobbed as he swallowed.

'The big one, huh?' drawled the Bank of the USA. He sipped his bourbon and flipped a cigarette into his mouth from a soft pack.

'Well, well,' muttered City Limited, looking down at his hand. He was the youngest of the men, fresh and neat in a crisp blue suit and white shirt, like a professional footballer. He had an honest face and Eddie found him hardest to read.

'I'll go along with that,' he said, and tossed a handful of yellow chips into the pool of light in the centre of the green baize. The others folded. Premium saw him. Eddie stifled a grin and swept the pile of chips towards him.

'Not my night,' said the Bank of England. He picked up the cards and shuffled them.

'Fancy a bite lads?' asked Eddie, taking off his green eyeshade. The others had given it to him for his birthday and he still wore it as a host's badge of office after the joke had worn off.

They stood up. Eddie tossed the eyeshade on to the table and led the way from the ante-room into the dining-room. Bottles of red and white wine glowed among the glittering crystal on the table. The sideboard was laid out buffet style with cold meats and salads and delicacies left over from the week's lunches.

'Lucy's done us proud,' said the Bank of the USA, heaping up his plate.

Eddie turned the lights down a touch and flicked on the portable CD player on the sideboard. Frank Sinatra crooned gently as they helped themselves. City Limited cornered Eddie by the cocktail cabinet.

'I've got a gross of telex rolls need a home, Eddie.'

'I'll sign the requisition on Monday. Deliver Thursday?'

'Sure it's all right?'

'The ones we've got are useless. Blue copies don't come out. They'll have to be scrapped.' He winked.

'Thanks Eddie. I'll have the new copiers in next month.'

'The ones we've got are jamming already.'

'Great. I'll see you right.'

'I know you will.'

They filled their plates and sat down, Eddie at the head.

'What's the news lads?' he asked, forking smoked salmon into his mouth.

'Dai-Sushi's closing down its options department. They'll be telling the staff on Monday.'

'They're going to offer the Securities and Investment Board job to Smith.'

'Will he take it?'

'Dunno. He hasn't been offered it yet.'

'Our shares are on the slide,' said Premium Insurance. 'The Chairman thinks we'll be put into play.'

'Takeover eh?' said the Bank of England. 'I'll check with our insurance division.'

'Time to buy?' asked Eddie.

'I'd wait until the interims,' said Premium, 'they'll be pretty bad.'

'Your Dividend shares don't look too good either,' said Bank of the USA.

'Wheeler's got something up his sleeve,' said Eddie.

'There was talk of your new Manager in the Governor's suite,' said the Bank of England. 'They were wondering what Wheeler was up to. A woman for God's sake. Inexperienced. Job hopper . . .'

Eddie reached for the fruit bowl and nodded thoughtfully as he digested the information, adding it to the other morsels he gleaned from the grapevine that twined about the City, some of them green and unripe, some overripe and rotten, some fresh and juicy, all of them interesting. Salesmen, waiters, drivers, maintenance men, telephone engineers, builders and decorators, removal men and above all messengers gossiped in pubs and cafés and walking along the street and waiting beside paying-in windows and counters. They read telexes and memos and letters, listened at switchboards, browsed in the post-rooms, served drinks in boardrooms, waited at banquets, drove the boss home and picked him up in the morning, picked directors up from airports, the servants whom everyone ignored, invisible eyes and ears.

'Do you know the one about the Governor's wife and the Sheikh of Dubai . . .' said the Bank of England and inaugurated the cabaret part of the evening. Eddie fetched a box of Romeo and Juliettas from the humidor and they went back to the card table in the ante-room.

When they had all gone Eddie took a last look around the management suite. There was a lot of tidying up but the cleaners came in on a Saturday morning. Although they had not used it he walked into the general manager's office and looked thoughtfully at the vacant, executive chair. Something was not right. Something, as yet unclear, unformed, was threatening the even tenor of life at Dividend Investments. The sooner he got the measure of his new general manager the better.

●●●

Eddie came in weighed down with print-out as Nora, with an extravagant gesture of finality, pressed the print button on the keyboard. She folded her arms, her blood-red fingernails digging into her black satin sleeve as the laser printer behind her buzzed and hummed and excreted copy after copy of the same letter.

'Got you working already, has she? I bet she's a slave-driver. Women bosses. Tartars. She'll be cracking the whip, you mark my words.' He rolled his eyes in lasciviousness and terror, evoking little pictures posted up in public phoneboxes of women in underwear with whips and implausible pelvic postures.

'That's my letter. I wrote it,' she snapped.

Eddie craned over the desk and for once Nora did not stop him.

'Dear Sir, I enclose my curriculum vitae . . . what's this, Nora? Has she given you the boot? Already?'

'I'm resigning. I'm not standing for it. It can't go on. I'm as feminist as the next woman but I refuse to work for one. It's not right.'

'Come on, Nora. Give her a chance.'

'It's not going to work. I knew as soon as I stepped into that room. I said to myself this is not the general manager of a financial institution. There isn't a single other company in the City that's run by a woman. We'll be a laughing stock. I want no part of it.'

'It's only her first week.'

'And it's my last. I've put a lot of time and effort into my career, Eddie, and I'm not having it come to this. It's undignified.'

'You never know, she might do a good job. Wheeler's no fool.'

'He's picked the wrong one, that's all I can say. She doesn't know how to give orders. She's completely indecisive. She doesn't know her own mind. You've got to have someone who can take decisions.'

'Livery never took a decision in his life. Only about what to have for lunch.'

'It's not the same. He had authority. You know what she said? She asked me if it was good idea to have a management committee meeting tomorrow morning.'

Eddie recoiled in mock horror. 'She didn't! Power to the people. We don't have a management committee anyway.'

'I told her. I said Mr Livery didn't have a management committee. She asked how he took decisions and I said if he wanted something doing he decided and then we got on with it. She said she wanted a committee.'

'That sounds like a decision to me.'

'Yes, but she didn't come out with it like that. She asked me if *I* thought it was a good idea.'

'She thought a secretary might have an opinion?'

'I said that Mr Livery always used to say a camel was a horse designed by a committee. You know what she said? A camel's a lot more use than a horse if you're crossing the desert. She even asked me who I thought ought to be on it.'

'On the camel?'

'On the committee. Who did I think would represent all the staff, I ask you.'

'We'll have to stamp on this one, Nora. There'll be suggestion boxes next.'

'It's no way to run a business. You can't go round asking staff what ought to be done. There'd be chaos. They'd lose all respect. She's paid to take charge.'

The printer bleeped and stopped. Nora turned round and collected her letters from the hopper and tapped them on their side to even them up. A buzzer sounded and a red light on the front of her telephone began to flash. Nora ignored it.

'And another thing. You know what she wants? A dictating machine.'

'No!'

Eddie made a mental note to get some brochures from Office Supplies. It was time he passed them some more business in return for the Cup Final tickets. He would see if he could interest her in one of the scientific calculators they were pushing as well.

'I said I was quite happy to take dictation in the morning after coffee when she's had time to look at her post. Mr Livery always did his then. You know what she said? She said she wouldn't be giving dictation, that it was a waste of my time and hers. She said it was ridiculous in this day and age to have a scribe like in the bible. She would use the machine because it was more efficient.'

'Worse and worse, Nora. Lord save us from efficient managers.'

'I told her Mr Livery thought it was too impersonal. I told her I didn't fancy sitting down all day with those things on my head.'

'Shouldn't you be going in?' said Eddie, nodding at the red light.

'Let her wait. I told her it was quicker in the long run to take shorthand. I don't want to sit in front of that screen all day with her burbling on in my ears. Do you think she'd listen? Do you think she'd pay attention to my opinions? Oh no, not her. I mean there's two of us to consider, Eddie. She said she'd made her mind up and that was that. I'm not standing for it Eddie, I'm really not. I'm not going to be dictated to.' She put her letters in the top drawer of her desk, picked up her shorthand pad and with a toss of the head went into Liz's office.

Eddie tiptoed to the connecting door when it clicked behind Nora and put his ear to it. Goodman was either dictating or they were having a very stilted conversation. More than that he could not tell as she did not bellow like Livery. So Nora was unhappy. Good. He would lend her a sympathetic ear. Few sources of information were as useful as a dissatisfied secretary. But he did not like what he heard about Goodman's desire to change things, her ideas about consultation and communication. As long as it only meant chatty memos and heart-to-heart staff meetings it was all right. Nobody paid them any attention and she would soon get tired of it. If she started to poke her nose into what didn't concern her, really dig down to find out what went on in the office, it could cause everyone a lot of trouble. Interfering bosses got in the way of people getting on with their business.

His reverie was interrupted by Nora's phone. He picked it up on the first ring.

'Miss Truelove's desk. Can I help you?' It was the sergeant from downstairs announcing the arrival of a Mr Bibber to see Mr Livery. 'Please send him up to the fifth floor. Mr Fly will meet him there,' he said in fluent receptionese.

Bibber's thin, wasting body seemed bathed in nicotine, from the deep brown of his index and middle finger to the parchment of his complexion and the yellow streaks in his dull grey hair. Eddie ushered him from the lifts to the ante-room.

'Mind if I smoke, Mr Fly?' said Bibber, subsiding into the sofa and taking a packet of Players untipped out of his pocket.

'Not at all,' said Eddie, pushing an onyx ashtray in front of him. 'You had an appointment with Mr Livery.'

Bibber coughed and nodded.

'Mr Livery is no longer with us, I'm afraid.'

'That's very sudden,' said Bibber and inhaled the first drag deep with an inward sigh.

'A terrible shock.'

'Was it expected?'

'Out of the blue.'

'Under a cloud?'

'He's on one now.'

'I beg your pardon?'

'Mr Livery passed away. Passed on to his reward. His terminal bonus.'

'Oh I'm sorry.' Bibber lapsed into lugubriousness, the spark of interest kindled in Mr Livery's fate suddenly extinguished along with the match that he laid to rest in the ashtray. 'Are you a caretaker?'

'Sort of. I look after . . .'

'Permanent?'

'Yes. I've been here since we opened.'

'Congratulations.'

'Thanks. Who would you like . . .'

'I'm from the *Business Times*. I'm doing a piece on financial crime.'

'Insider dealing?'

'Fraud, embezzlement, anything.'

'And Mr Livery said he could help?'

'In a manner of speaking.'

'How?'

'We shall never know, shall we?' croaked Bibber, his face hidden behind a veil of grey smoke. 'Would you be able to spare some time?'

'I've got the post to do . . .'

'I won't keep you,' said Bibber, pulling a shorthand pad out of his suit pocket.

Eddie sat down on the chair at right angles to the sofa, the power chair with the telephone beside it. Mr Livery talking to the press about fraud? That was interesting. Wheeler had become very agitated when he thought Livery had been working late on the files.

'What did Livery tell you?'

'We hadn't got that far,' wheezed Bibber. 'Mr Fly, how does the new regulatory environment affect the way you do business . . . ?'

He was interrupted by Liz opening the door. She saw the room was occupied, muttered an apology, half-closed the door, remembered she was General Manager and made a second entrance. Eddie succumbed to a reflex. He stood up. Bibber, assuming that she was a secretary, did not. Eddie covered quickly.

'That's that then, Mr Bibber. We can talk again later. I'll give you a call. You didn't have a coat, did you? Oh, this is Miss Goodman. She's just joined us. I'm sure you'll be seeing her name here and there.'

Liz smiled and held out her hand to Bibber.

'What happened to Miss Truelove?' asked Bibber, standing up and putting his pad in his pocket.

'She's still around. Still, we mustn't keep you. I'll deal with the post when I get back, Miss Goodman,' said Eddie, ushering his guest out of the room.

'Nice-looking secretary,' said Bibber, stubbing his cigarette out in the ashtray by the lifts. 'Attractive girl.'

'It's hard to get good staff these days.'

'Listen Mr Fly, I understand you want to be discreet. Your Mr Wheeler doesn't like you talking to the press. Perhaps we can have a quiet drink one evening? Here's my card.'

Eddie went back to the post-room and stood looking out of the window at the courtyard below, tapping the corner of Bibber's card on his teeth. He was troubled, and the reason he was troubled, was that he felt troubled, an unaccustomed sensation. He should be feeling pleased with himself. He had passed off his boss as his secretary which, suitably embellished, would keep the lower bar of the Samuel Pepys entertained for a round or two. But he had to force himself to grin at his reflection in the window. She was not your typical boss. She was not fair game. For a start she was a woman and women had to be protected. And Bibber was right. She was an attractive girl. A very attractive girl. Now if she had just joined the typing pool . . . She had not joined the typing pool. She was the boss. He was a wage slave. He was the messenger and she was the manager, the class enemy.

● ● ●

Liz lit a cigarette and slumped back in her chair. Things were crowding in on her. She had never been busier in her life than in the past few days and was accomplishing nothing. How did people like Percy Wheeler find the time to run massive organizations? It wasn't just the in-tray that kept her chained to her desk. She had to choose the typeface and paper for her stationery and business cards, approve a press release, get her name in the *Financial Times* appointments column, send off an update to *Who's Who In The City*, have her photograph taken for the Dividend Group in-house magazine, draft a letter to be sent out to all the names in the business card file, go for a test drive in a Ford Granada and choose the colour and the accessories, fill out the BUPA forms, send in an application for the Contango Club, apply for a Company Diner's Club Card, and all the other time-consuming chores associated with shinning up the rungs of the ladder of success.

Nora came in with a Doulton cup and put it down on a coaster depicting a view-halloo beside the daily position report. This was a computer print-out six inches thick that listed all the deals currently outstanding.

'Where's my mug?' asked Liz, flicking the hair off her forehead and reaching for the packet of Camels.

'Your mug?' asked Nora, innocently.

'My mug. My Crystal Palace Supporters Club mug.'

'I couldn't find it,' said Nora, 'Rhoda must have put it in the dishwasher.'

'Why did it need washing up? You haven't let me use it since I've been here.'

'Sorry, Miss Goodman. Anyway, we always use the Doulton in the management suite.'

'I want my tea in a mug.'

'Mr Livery always had his tea in the Doulton.'

'I don't care about Livery.'

There was a sharp intake of breath. 'Yes, Miss Goodman.'

'Liz.'

'My name's Nora.'

'I know. I'm Liz. You're Nora.'

'I've got that straight, Miss Goodman.'

'Please call me Liz.'

'Mr Livery said we weren't Yanks.'

'Very observant of him.'

'So we didn't behave like Yanks.'

'What did he mean by that?'

'Yanks are Americans, Miss Goodman.'

'I know Yanks are Americans. What does not being American have to do with anything?'

'Yanks, I mean Americans, call everybody by their first names.'

'So?'

'We don't use first names for management.'

'From now on we do. Between us it's Liz.'

'Yes, Miss Goodman.'

'Liz.'

'Liz.'

'Nora . . .'

'Yes, Miss Goodman?'

'What can we do about all this bumf? I've been here less than a week and look at it. There's half a tree in there.' She pointed to her in-tray, piled a yard high with letters, internal memos, Dividend Group circulars, copies of the previous day's telexes, print-outs of the current trading position, the daily balance sheet, exception reports, deal tickets, daily profit forecast updates, absentee report, wages report, Reuter's telexes, stockbrokers' circulars, magazines, newspapers. For the past week she had come in at half-past seven, bleary-eyed, to try and deal with it. She spread it out over the desk and the floor, shuffled it into piles, signed some, threw some in the wastepaper basket, put some by for further reading, put some in the out-tray and some in the pending tray and still there was more by the end of the day than at the beginning. She looked balefully at the heap of paper.

'Dammit, if I'd wanted to be an in-tray jockey I'd have joined the Civil Service.' This was as far as she dared to go. She did not have the nerve to tell her new executive secretary that she thought that business was not about ploughing through forms and papers and print-outs but getting off your backside and doing things. She reached for her cup, playing for time, and sipped her tea. She was conscious that Nora was looking at her, sizing her up, waiting for her to be decisive, demonstrate her authority, tell her how she was going to run things. She stood with her shorthand pad at the ready, erect and severe and efficient, reminding her of her mother, waiting for her to explain herself.

'Mr Livery got through it without any trouble,' smirked Nora. She was not about to confide in her new boss that the Mister

Livery of revered memory thought that business was not about ploughing through forms and papers and print-outs but getting off your backside and doing things.

Liz lit a cigarette and sucked the smoke in deep, playing for time, trying to think of something managerial to say.

'Nora, I've been neglecting the staff. I have to make more time for them.'

'What?'

'I have to carve out time to meet the staff. Show myself a bit more.'

'You've been round the main office.'

'That was on my first day. It wasn't exactly a group encounter session.'

'You have to keep your distance. Otherwise they lose respect.'

'I want them to have respect for my performance, not my position, Nora.'

Nora sniffed and frowned and said nothing.

'I think they'd like some idea of what I expect of them.'

'They all know that. You expect them to get on with their jobs.'

'They need to feel that somebody cares what they do.'

'They knew Mr Livery cared. If they didn't do their jobs properly he came down like a ton of bricks. You should have heard him. Sometimes you could hear him right out in reception. He cared all right. He had grown men in tears.'

'I would rather they did their best for positive reasons. Not out of fear of being shouted at.'

'If you say so,' said Nora.

'This is to be open, positive management, communication, sharing. The open door.'

'Surely you don't have time for that. You've got a business to manage.'

'Exactly. And it's all down to people. What can be more important than creating a properly motivated and informed team? I'll start off with a staff meeting. Or didn't Mr Livery have staff meetings either?'

'Oh yes. Regular as clockwork. Every six months. What are you going to say to them?'

'Just what I told you. I want a properly motivated and

informed team. Our future is based on teamwork and co-operation, a striving for common goals in which the aspirations of every member of staff, from the highest to the lowest, is respected.' She reached for her pad and a gold pen from the ebony stand in front of her to jot down what she had just said before she forgot it.

Nora seemed unmoved by this declaration. Liz forced herself to look her in the eye. She had to put her foot down, start as she meant to go on, assert herself.

'In future, Nora,' she said decisively, 'I'll have tea and coffee in my mug. Unless I have visitors.'

'Yes. Miss Goodman.'

'Liz.'

'Liz.'

'That's better.'

'Will there by anything else?'

'No thanks, Nora.'

Nora stood up, flipped her pad shut and went to the door.

'Open or closed, Miss Goodman?'

'Liz. Closed please. I must finish writing this down while it's fresh in my mind.'

● ● ●

Three men stood inside the big main doors of the great and splendid medieval Guildhall, below the legendary giants of England, massive Gog and Magog, pop-eyed and gilded, who had stood guard above the door since 1953.

'They've got their man,' whispered the little one, nervously fingering the gold chain about his neck.

'Good show,' said the tall man on his right. 'Who?'

'Percy Wheeler.'

'Who?' said the tall man on his left.

'Made his money emptying dustbins for the council. He asked me the other day how he could get to be Mayor.'

The tall men chortled to themselves.

'He doesn't come under the Bank of England,' said the Governor, 'he comes under the Department of Trade.'

'So much the better,' said the Chairman, 'keeps our doorstep clean and drops a steamer on Whitehall's. Serve the buggers right.'

'Think we can do it?'

'Where there's a will. They've put someone on to it full time. An old pro called Bibber. He should rake something up.'

• • •

When Harry Simple suggested meeting at his club for lunch Liz looked forward to the RAC or the In and Out and was disappointed when it turned out to be the Colonial Bankers, in the shadow of the walls of the Bank of England.

'Jolly handy, the old CB,' he said as they waited for an antique lift in a dingy lobby. 'You can always get a table and the food's half-way decent. I take it you're partial to the old steak and kidders.' He seemed nervous, not looking her in the eye, as if they were on a first date and not a first business lunch.

'You belong to other clubs I suppose?' said Liz wistfully.

'I didn't want to drag you to the West End. Besides, the old Buffers has gone downhill since they started letting in w-w-w . . .'

She let him stutter for a bit. 'Weekend members?' she smiled, throwing him a straw which he gratefully grasped.

'Right. Weekend members. Nothing ruins a club like weekend members.'

On the first floor he slammed the rattling iron trellis behind them and ushered her into a large dining-room lit by frosted glass windows. The tables, wide apart, were laid with plain white cloths and soup plates. Some were already occupied by quartets of bankers in dark blue suits and white shirts and crested ties. Apart from the waitresses Liz was the only woman. Harry asked for one of the booths that lined the side. There was room for six round the table and they huddled against the wall facing each other as if they were waiting for others to arrive. Liz glanced down the menu and decided on Bucks Fizz, smoked salmon and a grilled sole.

'One of the few places left you don't get jostled by yuppies stuffing themselves with smoked salmon and Bucks Fizz,' said

Harry, looking about him approvingly. 'As I said I recommend the old steak and kidders. And how about oxtail soup to start?'

'Whatever. You order,' said Liz, mindful of her future career and of Wellington's advice: if you have to fight a battle make sure you choose the ground.

Over gin and tonic and soup they sent out the scouts and skirmished politely, Liz falling back each time. It was not until mounds of meat and pastry and boiled sprouts and potatoes were piled on their plates, and Harry had tasted the smoky claret, that they began the engagement proper.

'How are you settling in?' he asked.

She knew what to say. She had rehearsed it. 'Everything's fine. I'm on top of everything. I can really turn things round. Next quarter is going to be great. (Always next quarter. Never this.) I know I'm going to be very successful. The company will be successful. We're all going to be successful.' Whether you were supervising the post-room or running a division of General Motors you never took your problems to the boss. It wasn't what bosses wanted to hear. They only want to hear good news. But she felt disarmed by Harry, his charm, his frank and open face, his apparent lack of malice or guile. She needed an ally, a friend, a reassuring hand, a shoulder to lean on, someone to swap ideas with and give her encouragement. She toyed with the offal on her plate, laid down the crested fork and took a deep breath. 'I need help, Harry . . .' she started to say. Fortunately for her career prospects Harry was not listening. He was affecting the arthritic stoop that etiquette demands of a diner when an acquaintance comes over to his table, standing knees bent and shoulders hunched, holding a napkin over his crotch like a fig leaf.

'Sally!' he said. 'What a lovely surprise.'

Liz looked round, pleased that she was not after all the only woman in the room, but saw only a dark little man in a lightweight plain blue suit and pink bow tie. What he lacked in flesh and bone nature had compensated for with a luxuriant head of glistening black hair crimped and combed and artfully formed into an extravagant kiss curl over his forehead. There was enough left over for a pair of sinuous eyebrows and a moustache so perfectly trimmed and greased it looked stuck on.

'Hairy,' he said, not a description but a greeting, and shook Harry's hand. Harry subsided into his seat as if overcome by the cocktail of pommade and aftershave and toilet water that swaddled Sally in sweetness.

'Liz, this is Salvatore.'

Salvatore sniffed. He took her hand and kissed it. His moustache stroked the back of her hand like a moist paintbrush leaving traces of his scent.

'Enchanted. But Hairy, what a place to brrring a beautiful woman!'

'Miss Goodman's a colleague, old chap.'

'A colleague? She is on the payrrrroll? So you have learned something from us Panamanians after all. The Bank must be trrreating you well.' Gold glinted in his mouth as if to underline his creditworthiness.

'I'm not with the bank any more, Sally.'

'Trrruly? Who are you with?'

'The Dividend Group.'

Salvatore flinched as if he someone had mentioned alopecia in his hearing.

'Dividend?'

'A year ago.'

Salvatore displaced his surprise by grabbing for Liz's hand again. 'Congrrratulations, Hairy,' he sniffed, looking into her eyes, making clear what he was congratulating him on. 'But this is no place . . . you should be more discrrreet. Signorina, it was my pleasure,' and he gave her another sample from the scent counter.

'Sorry about that,' said Harry, when Sally had disappeared into a neighbouring booth. 'The old Latinos, you know. One-track mind.'

'Who is he?' said Liz briskly, stabbing a kidney with extreme prejudice.

'Old Sally's a lawyer in Panama City. He had lots of clients who invested money with the bank I worked for. He's very well connected. He comes from an old family.'

'Born with a silver spoon in his nostril?'

'Gosh Liz. He's probably just got a cold.' He took the wine

72

bottle out of its wicker cradle, filled their glasses, put it back to bed, dabbed his mouth, beckoned the waitress, straightened his pudding spoon, asked the waitress for water, and generally tried to divert her attention from the subject of Latin lawyers.

'So how are you settling in?'

'Just great. It's going to be very successful.'

'That's good. Percy's got his eye on you.'

'On me?' she preened.

'Dividend Investments.'

'I know. He's got plans.'

'But they're not very long-term plans, Liz.'

She hoped he would attribute her choking gasp to surprise and not the piece of gristle that had got the better of her.

'What do you mean?'

'Look old girl, I shouldn't be telling you this. Head Office. Sworn to secrecy. Lips are sealed and all that.' He clearly found his indiscretions as unpalatable as Liz found the pastry.

'Why are you telling me then?'

He struggled with another confidence, opened his mouth, closed it again and leaned forwards over his plate.

'I . . . er . . . think a lot of you . . . wouldn't want . . . you know.'

'What are his plans, Harry?' she put down her knife and fork with a decisive clunk.

'The jury's still out, old girl. DI is not doing well. It's inefficient and unprofitable. Old Livers falling down on the job attracted Percy's attention. He's dangerous when roused.'

This revelation was an ideal pretext for pushing her plate to one side. She took full advantage of it.

'So what am I supposed to do?'

He took a swig of claret and refilled his glass and leaned over towards her.

'You've got to show you can make it work, Liz. In double-quick time.'

'It'll take months, a year at least to get it on its feet.'

'I didn't say make it work. I said *show* you can make it work.'

'How?'

73

'Gosh, I don't know. Something dramatic. Show you mean business. Turn the place over. Fire someone.'

'I can't go round firing people to show what a great manager I am.'

'Why not? The others do.' He leaned over the table again. 'You've got to show you're tough, Liz. Tough as a man. Even tougher.' As if by association he looked reproachfully at her plate. 'I'm sorry it's put you off your steak and kidders,' he said, far too well brought up even to think of reaching over and helping himself.

'Do you want to know something?' She tried to keep her voice calm. She leaned over the table, further than him now her plate was mercifully out of the way, so their heads were nearly touching. 'It's not my style.'

Their heads were close together. His eyes were very beautiful, large and grey green, with lashes any girl would envy. She was vaguely troubled, vaguely excited, not only by his indiscretions and advice. The gnawing larvae of insecurity were metamorphosing behind her breastbone into large and gaily coloured butterflies, fluttering in the fragrance of his subtle, bittersweet aftershave. She tried to concentrate on business but other, more primitive, more pleasurable thoughts pressed unbidden into her mind. And, suddenly disarmed for a second time that day, she uttered words she should have left unsaid, words about herself, her life, her role as General Manager of Dividend Investments.

'Do you ever wonder if you're in the right place? That you've no business doing what you're doing? Taking advantage of people when you want to be on their side? That you're there on false pretences, pretending to be what you're not, wearing someone else's costume, someone else's mask, an imposter? That under the disguise you're really a different kind of person? Don't you ever want to be taken as you really are?'

She was undressing herself in front of him. She could not help it, nor could she help parting her lips and letting the tip of her tongue gently brush between them. His pupils widened. He abruptly sat up and she wondered if she had gone too far, given herself away, ruined her image as a capable manager with everything under control. But she had forgotten that, in an intimate

74

conversation between a man and a woman, the man usually assumes the subject is himself.

'I do, Liz. I think that all the time. How did you know?' He reached out and put his hand on hers. 'It's incredible. We've hardly met and you've seen straight through me. It's been so long since anyone really understood me. I knew you were special ever since I first saw you. I've been trying to think of ways to see you. Look, let's be silly. Let's give ourselves the afternoon off. We have to talk.'

'We are talking.'

'I mean somewhere else. Somewhere more . . .'

'Discrrreet?'

They had a full and frank exchange of glances. The panelled walls of the old CB had been silent witnesses to many propositions in their time but few that were given and received with such tingling anticipation. Liz took a deep breath. He fancied her. And she was beginning to fancy him. He was certainly very attractive, amusing even when he wasn't meaning to be, and he was the Chairman's right-hand man. It was an irresistible combination. Out of the turmoil of her own emotion she plucked words to inflame his passion, women's words, enticing, beguiling, seducing, and all the other titillations from love's thesaurus.

'Sorry. I have to get back to the office for a meeting,' she said.

Treat them mean to keep them keen, her mother used to say. And she wanted him keen. He could be very useful.

● ● ●

Eddie liked the Marie Celeste feel of the office at five past five. The lingering human warmth, half-drunk plastic cups of lukewarm coffee, brimming ashtrays, swirling smoke, sodden tea bags, spilling wastepaper baskets, humming screens, a ringing telephone, appealed to his sense of the dramatic. The place had been full of people going about their business. Suddenly they had disappeared, as if stricken by some mysterious disaster.

As soon as the stampede for the lifts was over he went into the back office and closed up for the night. He checked that the telexes were set up for the overnight messages, switched off the computer screens, patrolled the desks looking for papers left lying around. He tried the drawers on all the filing cabinets and the shutter on the Filomatic, the enormous cupboard with mechanically operated shelves that held the central files. Satisfied, he switched off the lights and went through reception into the management suite.

Liz was still in her office, the captain last to abandon ship, pouring over papers on her desk, the air thick with smoke. She looked up when he came in and swept the hair off her forehead. 'Working late again, Miss Goodman,' he said, cheerfully stating the obvious. She groaned and waved her hand at the in-tray.

'How did Livery ever get through all this?' she complained. He sensed after-hours camaraderie. All his best work with management was done after everyone else had gone home.

'Who said he did?'

'Nora.'

'He did and he didn't,' said Eddie, careful not to do Nora down until the most suitable moment.

'What's that supposed to mean?'

'You don't have to look at everything,' he said, sitting down on the visitor's chair.

'I'm in charge. I'm supposed to look at everything.'

'Mr Livery just looked at what was essential.'

'But how do I know what's essential and what's not essential unless I go through everything? And how do I know that what I think is essential is actually essential? It may be inessential. And what to me looks inessential may be essential. And what looks essential today may not be essential tomorrow. And what may be essential tomorrow doesn't look essential today. It clogs up my desk it clogs up my day it clogs up my brain it damn near clogs up the whole system. What am I going to do, Eddie?'

What am I going to do, Eddie? The appeal for help.

'Not listen to Nora for one.' She looked at him sharply. It was too soon. He should have cleared the ground before digging at Nora. He had to follow up quickly with hard information. 'Mr Livery didn't bother with the magazines. He said they were all advertising puffs.'

'Damn right.'

'They go to the coffee table in reception. The papers go on circulation.'

'Good idea. Bung up everyone else's in-tray. But how do I keep in touch with what's going on?'

'He said there was more than enough to remember in his *Telegraph*.'

'Sound man.'

'He liked the crossword too.'

'But what about all the post?'

'Mr Livery didn't bother with the post. Nora answered everything for him unless it was Personal or Private or Confidential. He'd read those first and then give them to Nora to answer.'

'How did she know what to say?'

'Yes to food and drink, no to requests for money, all the rest to the Chief Accountant or the Chief Dealer or the Head of Administration.'

'He was a sharp operator.'

'Standard practice.'

'But it'll still take me all day to get through the reports and the print-outs.'

'Mr Livery didn't bother with the print-outs and reports. He said green lines and little numbers gave him a headache.'

'But they still have to be signed by the General Manager and sent back and put in the file. It's an audit requirement. The accountants always check for it.'

'Nora or I signed those for him. Your signature isn't very difficult, is it? It looks quite easy except for the squiggle at the bottom of the G.'

'You forged his signature?'

'We certainly did no such thing,' he said indignantly. 'We reproduced it.'

'But that's terrible. That's dereliction of duty,' she slumped back in her chair.

'It's not for your benefit that the reports get sent to you. It's for the benefit of the people sending them.'

'What?'

'So they do their job properly. The boss doesn't have to read them. They just have to go back with your signature on them. And just because it's your signature doesn't mean that you signed it. But they don't know that and it keeps them honest.'

'I'm flabbergasted. I can't allow that.'

'Then you'll have to do them all yourself.'

'How did Nora sign his letters? PP and her own signature?'

'Oh no. That doesn't give a very good impression. People would think he didn't care.'

'She reproduced . . .'

'And many's the time I had to sign Livery's credit card chits when he was too pissed to hold the pen. Pardon my French.'

He had turned her off Livery now, he was sure, and Nora with him. Liz's indignant incredulity turned to baleful envy as she looked at the in-tray again.

'What about internal memos?'

'Mr Livery signed those.'

'I'm glad to hear he did something.'

'Only those he sent, which weren't very many. About one a month.'

She looked hard at Eddie for signs he was testing her, trying it on, kidding her along. He gave her his honest retainer look, humble but dignified, unsmiling but frank.

'Tell me, Eddie.'

'Yes Miss Goodman.'

'If Livery didn't read anything or sign anything how did he know what was going on?'

'I told him all he needed to know.'

'This is all preposterous. I don't believe it. And if it's true I'm going to change it. It's not how I'm going to run things.'

Eddie grinned. She'd learn.

'All right,' she challenged, 'what do you think I need?'

'A gin and tonic. Shall I get you one?'

●  ●  ●

Liz let herself into the flat just after nine. Fiona, who was lying on the sofa in a kimono watching the news, started as if she had been caught watching Neighbours or a porno video. She looked glowing and languid, fresh from the shower perhaps, her hair slicked back. Her look of guilty surprise changed to a frown of disapproval as Liz tottered in and threw her music case down on the floor and slumped into an armchair, kicking off her shoes. This was not the thrusting dynamic young executive setting the City on fire with youthful vigour and ambition. This was a work-weary wage slave simulating the aftereffects of lifting barges and toting bales and looking forward to getting a little drunk.

'I thought you were out for the evening,' said Fiona, accusingly, as if every waking moment had to be filled with gainful activity.

'I was working late. I hate missing the beginning of films. I'm not disturbing you, am I?' She spoke with her eyes closed, like a youthful medium possessed by an ancient and weary spirit.

'There's no need to take that attitude.'

'What attitude? I still live here until the end of the month. I'm going to look at a basement flat, by the way. I just have to get a mortgage.'

'Hundred per cent?'

'Hundred and ten I hope. I have to buy the curtains. Is there any vodka?'

'How should I know? You're the only one who drinks it.'

'Drunk it,' she said morosely, faced with the alternative tipple of Fiona's organic orange juice. She brightened. 'Hah. Emergency supplies. The bathtub gin.'

Fiona leaped to her feet like someone who has remembered they had left a tap running a long time ago. 'I'll go. Is it in your cupboard in the bathroom? You sit there.'

She had indeed left a tap running. Liz could hear it when the bathroom door opened. But she was diverted by Fiona's unaccustomed considerateness from speculating why anyone who looked freshly showered was running a bath. The clunk of the fridge door and the tinkle of ice fostered her hope that she had hit the bottom of her day and was about to crawl slowly back uphill.

'Here,' said Fiona, handing her the welcome glass. She switched off the television. 'You poor thing. Tell me about your hard day.'

This was not the pattern of Fiona's habitual conversational style. The usual gambit was a thorough review of Fiona's news before they got around to any other topic. Again Liz's resistance was so low that she did not question Fiona's solicitousness.

'My predecessor ran the place like a country house. He gave orders to the cook and the chauffeur in the morning and left the rest of the domestics to stop the place from falling apart. The computer system could have been put together by a Victorian sanitary engineer. It's clogged up with paper. It doesn't need an overhaul, Fiona, it needs demolishing and rebuilding.'

'Who told you all this?'

'I had cocktails with the messenger.'

Fiona looked at her as if she had joined a firm of football hooligans.

'He's the only one who talks to me. The rest all bury their heads and pretend to work when I go by. Except my secretary Nora who pretends I'm not there. I've learned more from an hour with Eddie than in the week I've been there.'

'You must be desperate.'

'He's nice. He's interesting. He sees things differently. He grew up in a Marxist family. He's about our age.'

Fiona humphed a humph that expressed her resentment at being categorized with a militant messenger on the tenuous grounds of being born in approximately the same year.

'My Aunt Alice ran off with a gardener. *Lady Chatterley's Lover* is still banned in our house. I'd be careful if I were you.'

'I'm relating to the staff. It's what you're supposed to do.' She buried her nose in her glass.

'Not with messengers and clerks and typists.'

'Why not?'

'They're not interested, are they? They just go to work for the money.'

'And for you it's a social service. Was that a bath I heard running?'

'I left the cold tap on. Would you like me to run one for you?'

'It's all right, thanks.'

'Let me just check to make sure I cleaned up,' said Fiona, already out of the door, leaving her flatmate to trudge behind in stockinged feet as if she had been slaving behind an ironing board all day instead of lounging around behind an executive desk.

But Fiona had not cleared up thoroughly enough. She had failed to see the stripey tie that had fallen down behind the heated towel rail and lay coiled on the skirting board like a snake ready to strike. Liz noticed it when she lay down full length in the bath. She reached out a dripping hand and picked it up. There was a numbness when it first struck. When the venom reached the bloodstream she got out of the water, flung a towel round her and walked into the sitting-room just in time to see David tiptoeing to the front door which Fiona was opening with the contorted, concentrated expression of intruders, elopers and other secretive door-openers.

'You're not properly dressed,' said Liz, very calmly, the venom turning her limbs cold. Fiona held the door open as a shield in front of her. David went bright red under his skiing tan.

'What a lovely surprise, David, how sweet of you to call.'

'Liz, I'm sorry, God, it's rotten. We were going to tell you. We didn't want to put you off your new job . . .'

She let him stutter on, curious to know what she would feel, what she would say, what she would do when all this sunk in. Right now she just felt drunk. His voice was booming. Wasn't there anything else to it? Whatever she did or said now would be inadequate, an anticlimax.

'You make a good pair.'

'Thanks, Liz,' said Fiona.

'Early morning runs together. His and Her rowing machines.'

'We want the same things out of life.'

'I hope you're in training.'

'Look, Liz . . .'

'It's why she lets you win at squash.'

'She does no such thing.' He gave Fiona a sharp glance.

'Oh yes she does.'

'She doesn't.' His frank blue eyes were anxious now.

'I don't,' protested Fiona.

'Any man she fancies she lets them win. I should have guessed. I thought she was letting you win because you were my man.'

'That's not true,' said the new lovers in chorus.

'She could wipe the floor with you on the tennis court too. And badminton. But she never will.'

'Liz, you're lying.' He was indignant now, and worried.

'I'm going back to my bath. Have a nice evening. And if I don't see you again, have a nice career.'

'Elizabeth . . .'

'I hope you'll be very useful to each other.'

She dropped the tie on the floor, a dead thing now, and discovered that turning on a wet bare heel is a lot more difficult than when you are wearing shoes. They were right, she had been lying about Fiona letting him win at squash, but it was the best she could think of on the spur of the moment. They would never have a decent game again. It was a little parting gift for their future life together.

● ● ●

When Nora came out of the station she wondered whether to catch a bus down to Pratts or to walk home for the exercise. She did not have to make a decision. A two-tone brown Rolls Royce Silver Spur with the number plate PW1 crawled along the kerb, the whitewall Avon 235s scrunching over the Macdonald's cartons and Heineken cans in the gutter beside her. She instinctively lengthened her lanky stride as the rear passenger window slid noiselessly down.

'Excuse me, I'm lost. I wonder whether you could . . . my goodness, it's Miss Truelove isn't it?'

She stopped and peered into the car. For a second she could not place the thin smile and the bushy black eyebrows, out of context in Streatham High Street.

'Fancy a lift? Hop in, dear.' The door swung open. She felt a sudden tightening behind the breastbone.

'Oh, Mr Wheeler. It's all right, I haven't got far . . .'

'Come on,' he ordered, sliding away from her along the seat and patting the cream leather he had vacated. With a glance round to see who was watching her step into the luxurious limousine she got in as she had been taught at college, bottom first and lifting her long legs together after her. In the nick of time she saw the chauffeur getting out and left the door open for him to shut.

'What a nice surprise,' purred Percy. 'Always nice to see a friendly face when you're lost. Especially a colleague. I hope you'll join me in my evening pick-me-up.' He lifted an open bottle of champagne out of the cooler in front of them and filled a flute so it

82

frothed over onto the brown carpeted floor. 'Happy days.'

Nora felt a bit dizzy. The inside of the car seemed twice as big as the old DI Humber. She was bathed in the scent of wealth and privilege, leather and Cuban tobacco and expensive aftershave. She sipped the champagne, and bubbles shot into her nose as they floated noiselessly into the outside lane. 'Colleague,' he called her.

'You'll have to do a U-turn,' she said, her voicy husky with excitement.

'Tell the driver where to go,' said Percy, pressing a button on the control panel by his side. The glass panel that divided them from the chauffeur slid open.

'Where are you going?' she asked.

'Your home first,' said Percy. 'Then you can tell him how to get to Streatham Hill, if you know where it is.'

'That's not far from me. You can drop me there.' She was riven by the conflicting desires to be seen by the neighbours getting out of this palace on wheels and not wanting Mr Wheeler to see the ordinary little house where she lived.

'Nonsense. Can't have that,' he said, gently but with the masterfulness of a man used to getting his own way. She looked at the back of the chauffeur's grey cap.

'Do a U-turn and take the second right after Pratts.'

'Yes Madam,' he replied and the panel breathed across.

'It's part of John Lewis's,' she said, trying to find some connection, however, tenuous, between the worlds in which they lived. 'Like Peter Jones. It's a very good store.'

'Such a shame about George,' he said, filling up her glass. 'He was a good man.' His tone was relaxed and confiding, two equals mourning a mutual friend.

'A wonderful man,' she sighed, 'and a wonderful boss.'

'You worked with him a long time.'

'Since he started.'

'You know him well then.'

'Better than anyone.' She could not resist a little smile, a playful glance. With older, richer, powerful men, such gestures were involuntary. They were stuck in a traffic jam now, outside the Odeon.

'You knew him intimately?'

'Intimately,' she breathed. She felt something loosen inside her head. She felt tears prickling her eyes. There had been no-one to talk to since that terrible evening when Georgie had died in her arms. Eddie was the only one who knew and understood but she could not share her feelings with him. He was beneath her. And he hoarded everything he learned for later use. But here, the sumptuous surroundings, the champagne, this authoritative and considerate man were breaking down her defences. Percy put his hand on her knee, consoling her. She left it there.

'He was up to something, wasn't he?' She closed her eyes and nodded. 'He was a naughty boy.' He stated it as a fact. She nodded again. 'He did things he shouldn't have done.' This time it was a reproach. She opened her suede executive case and took out a tissue from a packet in the pocket in the lid and wiped the corners of her eyes.

'Who says he shouldn't? You can't judge him. No-one can stand in judgement.'

'But he didn't want anyone to find out, did he?'

She sniffed. 'He never did anyone any harm. He needed . . .'

'What did he need?'

'He needed to feel he was still, you know, a man I suppose.'

'What about his wife?'

'She never suspected anything. He didn't want to do anything to hurt her. We were very discreet.'

'You were involved?'

'Who do you think?'

'How long?'

'Since the first week he started. I would do anything for him. Anything.'

'You were very loyal.'

'I loved him.' She put her hand over her eyes and sobbed while they turned right across the traffic and cruised slowly down the side of Pratts. He patted her knee.

'Who else was in on it?'

'Only Eddie.'

'Eddie? The messenger? He knew all about it? Who else?'

'No-one.'

'Who else?' he barked, roughly. His fingers tightened on her knee.

84

'Not a soul.'

'Just the three of you in bed together.'

'No! That's disgusting. It wasn't like that. It was Georgie and me. Eddie tried to stop it at first. He said I was being exploited. He said men like Livery just want use people like me. He said he was alienating me from my class. But it wasn't like that. I loved him.'

'Tell me exactly what he did.'

'I can't.' Percy squeezed her leg so it hurt. She looked down and saw his fingers pressing deep into the flesh under her stockings. The inside of her thigh tingled, all the way up.

'Tell me,' he commanded. His voice was hard and his face was stern and although he was still sitting back in his seat he seemed to tower over her.

'Not here.' She nodded at the chauffeur. As if by telepathic command the panel slid open.

'Is this the street, madam?'

'Yes. Let me out here.'

'I want to know everything about it. Now,' hissed Percy in her ear.

'Let me out now. You are hurting my leg. My relationship with George Livery was personal and private. You have a nice car but I am not overawed by it. Just because you are the founder and Chairman and Chief Executive of one of the fastest growing companies in the country you have no right to intrude on my private life. Or anybody else's. You think because you have money and power and success you can manipulate other people's lives. But you can't. All you want is my body. I will not be exploited by you. Thank you for the lift.'

This little speech flashed momentarily through her mind before it was submerged in a confusion of longing and excitement and grief, to surface in the conditioning of a lifetime.

'Number seventeen,' she said, barely disguising the tremor in her voice.

The street of thirties semis was lined with cars, except where the road was painted with white lines in front of driveways. There was not enough room in front of her house for the Rolls to park. Percy took the cellphone from its cradle beside him and ordered the chauffeur to drive around the block until he called. He held

Nora tight by the upper arm and steered her up the path as if one of them were blind. The house was indistinguishable from its neighbours, white stucco, a hydrangea, a glassed-in-porch, a little windmill on the patch of lawn, the front door studded with massive iron nail heads. She fumbled with her keys and opened it. A minute cairn terrier with a silver bow between the ears scuttled around their feet like a clockwork mouse, its yapping a frenetic squeak.

'Down, Sukie.'

He followed her into a through-lounge, stepping high over the luxuriant lilac shag rug, as if in long grass, and with the hope of landing a kick on Sukie. Now it was his turn to be taken aback by his surroundings. For a moment he forgot the purpose of his visit. Cream painted anaglypta embossed with roses, red velvet curtains, a tiger in a gilt frame peering through long grass, a hunting scene engraved on shiny copper, an electric fire with simulated coals, salmon pink tiles inset with blue triangles, ornaments on the mantlepiece, a three-piece suite in sculpted maroon velvet, a cream and brown pouffe.

'It isn't much,' she said, taking off her crisp white Burberry look-alike from Pratts and tossing it on an armchair.

'It's very nice,' he said quietly, almost wistfully.

The long wall facing the fireplace was covered with glass shelves dedicated to the largest collection of porcelain roses in south London, backlit and underlit and spotlit to show them off to best advantage.

'Very homely.'

It was like the house he owned in Bromsgrove when he was first married. He was twenty-one, a clerk in an insurance office. He would not have allowed Mary to work even if she had wanted to. She stayed in the house and made a home like this and changed her clothes and put on make-up before he came back from work and had his tea ready on the table and they flirted and talked baby-talk and chased each other round the sofa and went to bed early. Then he had tried his luck as a life salesman, door-to-door at first, out every evening and weekends, and never looked back. Except when he walked into rooms like this.

'Very homely indeed.'

Now he lived in houses furnished by designers, beautiful rooms with themes and styles and atmospheres, picked out of a glossy loose-leaf book or dreamed up by fashionable decorators to reflect his lifestyle and personality, a personality he could not admit to them he did not recognize. He was as much a stranger in his own houses as he was now in this one . . . Enough of that. Down to business.

'Right,' he said brusquely. 'Show me.'

'Wouldn't you like a cup of tea first? A drink?'

'I can't wait. Let's get on with it.'

She seemed nervous, which did not surprise him: he was used to dealing with nervous people, indeed he felt nervous if other people were not nervous in his presence, and she had a lot to be nervous about, as accessory to whatever Livery was up to. But she also gave the impression that she was enjoying the experience. Her face was glowing, her moist eyes were wide and frank, she smiled and bit her bottom lip, her nostrils flared as she breathed in, there was a tension, an electricity in the way she turned away.

'Come on then,' she said, walking towards the door. Her voice had become low and husky and she flashed him an enticing look over her shoulder. Puzzlement gave way to something else. She was actually a very attractive woman. He liked them mature, strong-scented, big-boned, well-built, meaty hips, long legs, big breasts . . . Enough of that. Down to business.

She went out into the hall and up the stairs. He stood at the bottom step, his hand on the bannisters, looking up, Sukie yapping at his feet.

'Where are you going?'

'I'm not showing you downstairs.'

She waited for him on the landing at the door of the back bedroom.

'Go on in. I'll be with you in a minute.' She put her hand on his shoulder and he felt a long fingernail brush the side of his neck, raising goosepimples and sending a tremor down his spine. 'Go on,' she said, picking up Sukie and closing the door on him.

At first he thought it was a study. It was sparse and uncluttered, decorated in neutral beige and brown. The fitted wardrobe was made of plain dark brown wood. A small weeping fig stood in a tub of what looked like sheep droppings in the corner beside the grey venetian blinds that concealed the window. The wall over the gas fire was covered with photographs in dark brown frames of serious men in suits. Some stood behind executive chairs, some sat behind desks with their fingers pointed, some posed with telephones, pictures from business supplements and annual reports. He recognized George Livery. Then he noticed that the leather-topped desk in front of the window was littered like a dressing table with bottles and jars and aerosols and a mirror. Last of all he noticed the biggest object in the room, a king-sized bed covered with a white satin bedspread.

'What . . . ?'

She had loosened her hair and brushed it in curling black tresses over her shoulders. She wore a long white cotton gown loosely laced up the front to the neck. She stood in front of him and watched herself unpick the laces over her breasts with her long red fingernails.

'What the hell do you think . . . ?' Her gown slipped down her shoulders and her large breasts spilled out. 'Miss Truelove . . .' She reached up and put her hands round his neck and pressed his face into her cleavage. He smelt scent and warmth.

'My baby,' she whispered in his ear, her lips tickling the lobes. 'My baby.' She pushed him back on the satin, his face still buried in her lovely soft flesh.

'Get off,' he protested, his voice muffled. He tried to push her away but she was very strong and lying on top of him and his body would not obey his commands.

'My little baby, my sweet, cuddly baby, my baby, baby, baby.'

'I didn't come here . . .' he started to say, gasping for breath, feeling her hand pluck his shirt out and glide up his chest to his nipple.

'Such a sweet little baby.'

'Miss Truelove, stop it. Let me go. Right now. You are hurting my leg. You have a lovely body and wonderful breasts but I am not giving in to them. Just because you are an attractive and experienced and passionate woman you think you can get round me. You think you can manipulate me with sex. But you can't. All you want is my money. I will not be exploited by you.'

This little speech flashed momentarily through his mind before it was submerged in a confusion of longing and excitement and nostalgia, to surface in the conditioning of a lifetime.

'Oh Nora,' he said, barely disguising the tremor in his voice.

● ● ●

The sweepers begin work early at the railway stations before the trickle of commuters swells to a torrent and makes their jobs impossible. The detritus is scooped into plastic bags or, if it is human, tipped into the street, unless it is too ill or drunk or argumentative or dead to move, in which case the transport police are called to dispose of it. Outside on the pavement the outcasts join others who have spent the night under bridges or in doorways or simply walking the streets, moved on by the police or too cold to rest. They mingle with the early passengers, parody their brisk and busy walk, their sense of purpose, looking neither right nor left, as if they too have something busy and important to do that day, which they have, if finding a meal and a bed for the night can be counted as important as the myriad tasks performed in offices. A few of them look like tramps and dossers and down-and-outs, caricatures of themselves, old men and women carrying parcels and paper bags of rubbish, wasted bodies made plump by layers of rags tied up with string, shuffling, grumbling, hawking, swearing, talking to themselves, poking in litter bins. But most of them are indistinguishable from those of fixed abode, young couples with pushchairs and suitcases, middle-aged men in clean collar and tie, housewives, senior citizens with bus passes, families, schoolchildren, employed, unemployed, all kinds of people, the only thing they have in common being that, for whatever reason, they have no home.

Liz walked with them. She had spent the night in a shabby little hotel near Liverpool Street Station. She had closed her eyes to the furtive couples she passed on the landings. She had closed her ears to the furtive creaks and moans from the next-door rooms. She had closed her mind to thoughts of Fiona and David. Which left nothing else to do but count the cracks in the ceiling until it was light enough to get up. She scrabbled around in a washbasin just big enough to submerge one hand, concocted an outfit from the clothes she had stuffed randomly into a sausage bag the night before, ran her fingers through her hair in the pale reflection of the window and stepped out to begin a new phase of her life.

'Elizabeth,' she said to herself on the pavement outside, and she knew it was serious because she called herself Elizabeth, 'things have got to change.'

She nodded to herself. She was ready. She was surprised how fit and strong and full of energy she felt.

'Yesterday,' she replied, 'I had a home and a friend and a lover. Today I don't. And I feel great, Elizabeth.' To prove it she danced a few little steps. 'It's amazing. I feel full of energy. And free. No ties.' She grinned at herself and sang. 'Nobody to hold me d-o-o-o-wn.'

'Elizabeth, how could Fiona ever have been your best friend? She was opposite to you in every way.'

'Good riddance. Get rid of her.'

'And that David. He was so feeble when he wasn't in front of a dealing screen.'

'Good riddance, Elizabeth. Get rid of him. They're all disposable.'

She ripped the rubber band off her left wrist and with an abandoned gesture threw it into the air. It landed in the gutter and a bent man in a long stained raincoat and a bundle of old newspapers under his arm scuttled to pick it up.

'Elizabeth,' she said to herself and stopped dead. A young man in a camel coat who had been dogging her footsteps jostled her and passed on. She had lost track of which Elizabeth had been speaking. 'Never mind,' she scolded, walking on, 'what were you going to say?'

'If you're not going to be a success in life,' she said, 'make lots of money instead.'

'Got any money?' said a different voice.

'I said if you're not going to be a success . . .' She stared at a girl walking by her side. 'What did you say?'

'I asked if you'd got any money. Will you give me my bus fare home?'

'Was I talking out loud?' asked Liz. She felt an icy tingling in her spine. The conversation. The little dance. The song.

'Not as bad as him,' said the girl, nodding to a bearded man haranguing his reflection in Dixon's window.

'Oh God.' She was about to tell herself out loud to pull herself together but stopped herself just in time. The girl looked as if she had been released from an institution which had shaved her head and denied her food and kept her in the dark. She wore a white satin ball gown under a denim jacket and Doc Marten's paratrooper boots.

'Spare the money for my bus fare home?'

'There are no handouts in this world. There's no free lunch. We have to look after ourselves.'

'You what?'

'Get a job. Self-reliance. Stand on your own two feet.'

'I only asked for my bus fare.'

'Get a job. Earn some money.'

'You must be joking. Who's going to give me a job?'

Liz opened her bag, took out one of her business cards and gave it to the girl.

'No handouts.'

The girl's pale face wrinkled in disgust and she melted back into the crowd. Feeling good, Liz walked on to confront the day.

• • •

*FIRST QUARTER*

Liz appointed Norman Foxwell, Freda Grafton and Larry Chivers to her new management committee. She knew that the first meeting was critical, her first opportunity to assert her authority and establish the way she was going to manage. She called the meeting for eleven o'clock in the dining-room. She sat at the head of the table with Norman on her right and the other two on her left. Norman sat slumped in his chair, brooding on a knot in the veneer, looking at his watch every few seconds. Freda sat bolt upright, her hands folded on the table, attentive and expectant, her eyes flickering around the room which she had rarely seen, let alone sat down in. With meticulous care Larry arranged three sharp pencils, a red and blue ballpoint and a fountain pen around a foolscap pad, like cutlery round a dinner plate, nervously adjusting them and avoiding everyone else's eye. Liz forced her right foot to stop jigging up and down, made sure her left earring was in place, pressed her hand into her rumbling stomach, took a deep breath and launched herself into positive management.

'Good morning everyone. Welcome to our first management committee meeting. I thought I'd start by . . . yes, Eddie, what is it?' Eddie padded across from the door carrying what looked like squares of hardboard.

'Lucy thinks you ought to have the cover on the table.'

'What cover?'

'The padded cover. The table's solid teak and she says it's very expensive to get scratches out.'

'Couldn't we have done this before?'

'You didn't tell me you were meeting in the dining-room. There was nothing in the book.'

'What book?'

'The book that says what's going on in the dining-room. Didn't Nora tell you about the book?'

Everyone lifted their arms and Larry scrabbled together his pens and pencils while Eddie put three sections of brown padded plastic in front of them.

'Do you want blotters?'

'No thanks, Eddie, this will do.'

'Pencils?'

'No thank you.'

'Paper?'

'No thank you.'

'All right then.'

'Thanks, Eddie.' Eddie left the room. Larry arranged his place setting. Norman looked at his watch. Freda noticed you could see the top of St Paul's from where she sat. Liz made sure her right earring was still in place and took a deep breath.

'I thought I'd start by explaining what I think the role of this committee should be . . . yes Nora?'

'Would you like coffee now?' Nora backed through the door and put down the tray she was carrying on the table and unloaded three Doulton cups and saucers and a Crystal Palace Supporters Club mug.

'Did we ask for coffee?'

'It's eleven o'clock. I thought you'd all need a cup of coffee. Shall I pour?'

'That's all right, Nora. We'll look after it. Could you make sure we're not interrupted?'

Nora made a gracious exit. Norman looked at his watch. Freda looked askance at the mug. Liz made sure her left earring was still in place and took a deep breath.

'I believe that it is impossible for a single person to manage a complex organization in a complex . . .'

'Shall I be mother?' said Freda, picked up the coffee pot. She knocked over the milk jug in the direction of Norman who jumped backwards to avoid the stream. 'Whoops. Ever so sorry.'

'I'll go for a cloth,' said Larry, brimming with helpfulness, and went out to the kitchen. He came back followed by Lucy with a roll of kitchen paper and the expression of a tyrannical play-group teacher. Norman stood out of the way, looking at his watch, while Lucy ripped off sheets of paper and scrubbed at the table and the carpet in silent fury. Larry gathered up his pens and pencils and Liz put the cups back on the tray so that Freda, blushing, could lift up the padded cover to get at the milk that had percolated underneath it.

'No use crying, is there?' said Larry.

'This carpet's ruined,' complained Lucy. She left muttering to herself and they all settled down again. Liz made sure her right earring was still in place and took a deep breath.

'I thought I'd start by explaining what I think the role of this committee should be. I believe we have to work together as a team. Obviously I haven't had time yet . . .' Someone knocked twice on the door. Liz ignored it but the other three looked round expectantly, '. . . to get my arms round the business yet . . .' Three knocks this time, loud and urgent. She ignored it. ' . . . which is why I'm going to have to rely on . . .'

'There's someone at the door,' said Larry.

'Come in,' she called. A head appeared, on its side, and a handful of fingers, clutching the edge of the door.

'The Deutsche Bank deposit matures today. They need instructions before twelve,' said a man's voice. The head disappeared as though it had been yanked on a chain. Without a word to Liz, Norman stood up and went to the door to confer with his assistant while Larry re-arranged his pens and pencils and Freda discovered that by raising herself from her chair just a couple of inches she could see a bit of the dome of St Paul's as well. Norman sat down again. Liz waited for him to say what he had decided but he slumped in his chair and stared at his coffee cup, eyelids drooping, as if he was falling asleep. She made sure her right earring was still in place and took a deep breath.

'Now obviously I'm going to have to rely on each of you a lot in the early days and I need to make sure we're functioning as a team. I have been assured by Mister Wheeler that he has serious plans for this company . . .'

She listened to herself with growing dismay. Where was the fresh, informal, sparky, inspirational, loveable person who had been so eloquent in the bath? What was this turgid corporatespeak blabbing out of her trembling throat, as if she were reading the chairman's report out loud?

'. . . set long-term objectives . . . increase productivity . . . seek out challenge . . . improve performance . . . problems are opportunities . . . all work together . . . common purpose . . . personal aspirations . . .'

But little by little, as she shared her hopes and ambitions, the others began to take notice. It started with Larry. He stopped playing with his pens and pencils, raised his head and looked curiously in her direction. Freda diverted her gaze from the picture of a Tongan parrakeet to a point somewhere by Liz's right ear. Norman shifted his buttocks and glanced shiftily towards her.

'. . . by sharing information and ideas . . . excellence is a common responsibility . . . we must be driven by quality . . .'

She suddenly found their attention more unnerving than their indifference. They were not nodding and smiling in agreement, they were looking through her, past her as if she did not exist, as if she was a talking head on television. Dismay at her own performance was replaced by uneasiness, a feeling that something was happening she was not aware of, that someone else was in the dining-room with them, that someone was creeping up behind her . . . paranoid anxiety, she told herself, the pressures of the first meeting, the stress of a new situation . . . above all she must not stop, she must not turn round, even though she could hear a creak behind her, a footstep . . .

She jerked round in her chair to see red-nosed Rhoda standing behind her on one leg, the other poised in the air, carrying a wooden cutlery tray. Suddenly confronted by Liz's astonishment she hopped on her supporting leg and simultaneously threw the contents of the box in the air. Showered with jangling silver she dropped the box to protect her head with her hands. The box fell on her foot. She hopped again, trod on a pile of forks and hopped again. Her impromptu sword dance was cut short by her losing her balance. She was saved by Liz holding out her arms over the back of her chair to catch her.

'I didn't want to disturb you, Miss Goodman, but I clean the silver every Tuesday morning . . .' She looked little and old and ridiculous, wringing her hands, looking down at the cutlery strewn over the carpet. She could have had a nasty fall at her age, she could have poked an eye out with a fork, cut her leg. Sit down, have a cup of tea, are you all right dear? That was a nasty shock. To her surprise all Liz felt was a desire to beat her over the head with the cutlery box.

'Please leave,' she said, crisply.

'Let me just pick . . .'

'Leave.' Liz stood up and Rhoda flinched and scuttled out of the room.

'Any other business?' she asked, sitting down. The others looked blank. Liz stared them out. She racked her brains for some way of finding out if they had taken in anything of what she had said. She searched for the phrases that would send them out of the room imbued with energy and team spirit, eager to spread the good news of the bright future she was leading them towards. But all she felt was disappointment with herself and impatience with the others. Didn't any of them have anything to say, anything to ask, anything to contribute? How could she have openness and sharing if they all sat like statues waiting for orders?

'What about the fleas?' asked Freda in a still, small voice.

'The fleas?'

'The fleas. There's a plague of fleas.'

'Rubbish,' said Norman, staring at the knot in the veneer.

'It's not rubbish,' bristled Freda, 'they don't show you the bites on their legs.'

'Vermin cover my flesh and loathesome scabs. My skin is cracked and oozes pus,' said Norman.

'They won't sit near the walls. Or the partitions. They say they live in that fuzzy wallpaper. Louise said she saw one hopping in the Filomatic yesterday. The girls say they're all over.'

'Is this the place to talk about fleas?' asked Liz. She felt a tickling at the back of her legs, under her thighs, in her scalp, her body was alive, if she scratched now it would be all over. . . .

'Where else can we talk about them?' said Freda. 'I thought this was a management committee. I've been asking the place to be fumigated for weeks. Does anyone do anything about it?'

'They don't exist,' grumbled Norman. 'They're a figment of your imagination.'

'Imagined or not, it puts them off their work.'

'Then get an imaginary fumigator.'

'Stop,' said Liz. 'I'll organize a fumigator. Is there any other business?' She had to retrieve something now or she would have lost control for good. 'Very well. This meeting is terminated. I want your job descriptions and an organization chart of your departments on my desk by this time tomorrow.'

'What for?' asked Freda.

'Some things around here are going to change,' said Liz grimly.

'Change?' said her committee in chorus, even Larry, the first time he had spoken.

She picked up her bag from beside her chair and walked out of the room, leaving behind a horrified silence.

● ● ●

Eddie went down the narrow lane from the underground garage into Capital Square and narrowly missed being run down by Liz. He thought of it this way although he was in the Humber and she was on foot. It would have needed a double-decker bus to crumple the zone of anger and frustration that enveloped her as she stormed across the cobbles. He did an emergency stop and was rewarded by a glare. He opened the window.

'Can I give you . . .'

'I have to be in Hackney in ten minutes.'

'No trouble. Hop in.'

She went round to the passenger side, gave the impression of slamming open the front door, plonked herself down on the leather seat and slammed the door for real. Eddie felt a wave of empathy for Boadicea's chariot driver.

100

'Fleas,' she growled with the acrimony that the Queen of the Britons reserved for Romans.

'You've been talking to Freda,' he said, nosing the car out into Bishopsgate.

'Management committee. You can't imagine.'

Eddie could well imagine. Larry Chivers and Norman Foxwell and Freda Grafton in conclave would challenge the chairperson skills of a cabinet secretary.

'I ask them to make a contribution to management, to take an active part and what do they do? Foxwell says it's a waste of time, Chivers fiddles with his pencils and Grafton talks about vermin. Fleas in the wallpaper.' She ran her fingers through her hair, scraping her scalp with her fingernails. The back of Eddie's neck began to prickle.

'I'll get the fumigators in.'

'You'll do no such thing. I refuse to pander to hysteria. And I refuse to pander to their antedeluvian ideas about management. They're going to work together as a team if I have to chain their legs together. I'm running a modern business, not a Victorian counting house.'

'A business isn't a democracy,' he said as they drove past a rampant City griffin into Shoreditch. 'We didn't vote for you. You can't expect us suddenly to behave as if we're all equal.'

'Everybody has something to contribute. Everybody has a commitment to the team. Everybody participates.'

'A company is a totalitarian state. Ever been to an annual shareholders' meeting? Single candidates, block votes, rigged motions, planted speeches.'

'I'm not asking for votes. I'm asking for ideas.'

'It's a dictatorship. Everything flows down from the top. Central planning. You're told what to wear and where to sit and what sort of carpet you can have and what to sit on and what car you can drive. You have to go through channels, follow the procedures. You can't expect people to behave as if there's a free market all of a sudden. Where are we going by the way?'

She rummaged in her bag, pulled out an estate agent's sheet and gave him the address. Eddie jerked the wheel with surprise but she did not notice, rapt in meditation on management style.

'That may be how it worked in the old days. But not any more. It can't. Everyone has a duty to contribute.'

Eddie let her have the last word. He had said too much already. In his experience passionate advocates of free speech did not like to be contradicted. They had left the clean and orderly streets of the City and joined the traffic jams through the shabby thoroughfares of Hoxton.

'This is a nice car,' she said, noticing her surroundings for the first time since they left Capital Square. 'Is it yours?'

'No. Yours.'

'What?'

'Yours. It's the company car. I'm taking it to be serviced.'

'The company doesn't have a car.'

'If you say so. But this is it.'

'Nobody told me.'

'You didn't ask.'

'I've seen nothing about it.'

'It's not in the books. It's written down to nothing.'

'But the insurance and repairs and petrol . . .'

'We put those through under miscellaneous.'

'It can't be economical. It's an extravagance.'

'That's why Wheeler banned all chauffeur cars except his own.'

'We'll have to sell it.'

'How will you explain selling something you're not supposed to have?'

'But we have to get rid of it.'

'Then you'll have to buy it first. And how will Larry account for us buying something off ourselves? Besides, you're not allowed to buy company cars.'

'We've already got one.'

'We don't. It's not on the books and if it's not on the books it doesn't exist.'

She leaned back in the seat and closed her eyes to escape from the unpleasantness of the day. Eddie glanced sideways at her and tried to choose between his conflicting feelings. One of the few pleasures in business life is to watch the boss wriggle around in hot water. But he had never before felt impelled to hold the boss in his arms and promise that everything would be all right. She snapped her eyes open again as if she were scared of lapsing into an even worse nightmare.

'If this is a company car I ought to be riding in the back,' she said.

Eddie knew exactly where they were going. He pulled up in front of a terrace of tall Victorian houses bristling with For Sale boards. It was opposite a housing estate inspired by the architectural genius of the Maginot line. Waiting beside an iron railing that cordoned off the basement entrance was a young, tall, fit, well-dressed, handsome Sloane, cream of England's manhood, oozing the disdainful self-confidence that passes for charm in the wine bars of Clapham. Eddie felt a twinge of jealousy.

'Miss Goodman,' he drawled through the driver's window, ignoring Eddie, 'I'm from the Estate Agency.' Eddie's twinge grew into a spasm as Liz brightened and smiled.

He stayed in the car for twenty minutes after they disappeared from sight into the nether regions of the area. He knew the street well. The houses had been built for managers and clerks. They could walk to the City in black frock coats and tall hats, sober and respectable men. When Eddie first knew the street it had gone down in the world; working men lived there and their wives walked to the City, to clean the offices when the managers and clerks had gone home to the suburbs. Eddie had played with the kids outside while his father went to interminable party meetings that lasted well past his bedtime, rewarded for his patience with a bob's worth of chips. When he was older he went to the meetings himself and listened to the famous men and wished he was back outside on the street playing football.

When Liz and the estate agent emerged from the depths they both indulged in mutual congratulation, lingering on the pavement and exchanging telephone numbers while Eddie beat a tattoo on the steering wheel like an impatient pimp. She came to the rear door and allowed the agent to open it for her.

'. . . I'll transmit the offer to the owner this afternoon. I think he'll take it.'

'Why shouldn't he? It's what he's asking.' She looked up over

103

the roof of the Humber to the concrete towers and terraces of the housing estate on the other side of the road. 'Is there much vandalism from over there?' she asked.

'No more than usual. London's so mixed now, you get it everywhere. Good source of cleaning ladies is what I always tell my clients.'

Reassured, she got into the back seat and ordered Eddie back to the City.

'You're buying a flat,' said Eddie, looking at her in the rear-view mirror. She had gone quiet and thoughtful again.

'Mortgaged my life away for three damp rooms and a view of a brick wall. It'll do.'

'Don't you own a place already?'

'I hated the thought of having property. Stupid, wasn't I?' she looked wistful at the memory of a carefree golden age. 'Now look at me. Riding round in the back of limousines lashing out a six-figure sum on a converted coal cellar. How do I make some money, Eddie?'

'Premium Insurance.'

'Uh huh.'

'Shares will be on the move.'

'Uh huh.'

'There'll be a takeover bid.'

'Uh huh.'

He gave up. She was looking out of the window. Whoever paid any attention to a messenger?

'Do you own a place?' she asked.

'No. I live in a council flat.'

'Where?'

'A tower block on the Bevan estate.'

'Where's that?'

'Opposite your new flat. Where the vandals and the cleaning ladies live.'

He should have taken pleasure from the remark. But he was surprised that he wished he hadn't said it.

● ● ●

104

'It's usually ten per cent,' stuttered the rep from Peabody Fine Wines. Eddie stuck his thumbs in his waistcoat pockets and looked down at his polished shoes. The rep shuffled his Hush Puppies.

'Ah,' said Eddie. 'Ah. I'm reviewing our suppliers.' He gave the rep his chairman-at-the-press-conference impersonation, staring at him over the top of imaginary half-moon spectacles.

'Mr Livery was always happy with our service.'

'I'm taking care of things now.'

'Fifteen per cent is a bit steep.'

Eddie took a deep breath. 'We could accept the discount in kind. Would that help?'

The rep brightened. 'What kind of kind were you thinking of, Mr Fly?'

'Black label?'

'No problem.'

'I knew we could do business.'

'Marked to your attention?'

'If it makes it easier.'

'To your home address?'

Eddie blinked in surprise. It was like plucking up courage to proposition a girl and she immediately replies, 'Your place or mine?' It was too easy.

'I don't think that would be right. It's for entertaining here.'

It was the rep's turn to look surprised. The toes of the Hush Puppies turned up like pantoufles.

'Mr Livery always had it delivered to . . .' He chobbled the end of his sentence.

'Where?'

'Nothing.'

'Invoice us in full for the wine. Attention of Miss Goodman,' said Eddie, reverting to his impersonation.

'Nod's as good as a wink, Mr Fly,' said the rep, scribbling on the order sheet. Nodding and winking he closed his briefcase and followed Eddie out of the ante-room to the lifts, where they shook hands.

Ti-tum-ti-tum. Ti-tum-ti-tum . . . Eddie did a little skip on the way back to reception. Livery had always kept the drinks account to himself. Now he knew why.

The doorbell rang as he was going back into the post-room. He turned to see an ash-blonde girl with her lips and her nose pressed to the glass door like a pig's snout. She wore a black tweed suit several sizes too big over a tight Hawaian shirt and red stockings and short black boots. She looked as if she had been released from an institution which had cropped her hair and denied her food and kept her in the dark.

'Who do you think cleans that off?' he snapped impatiently, head messenger again, as he opened the door. He rubbed the smear with his sleeve. She looked as if she would burst into tears and he was sorry. She had eyes like his Sharon, large and round and dark. 'What do you want?'

'I want to see the person in charge.'

He put his hands behind his back and looked her up and down. 'Oh yes?'

'I've come for a job.'

'There are no jobs.'

She looked as if she would burst into tears again.

'I spent five quid at Oxfam on this.' She lifted the hem of her jacket as if she was going to curtsey.

'Nice material. You could make it up into a suit.'

'But I was told there was a job.'

'No jobs.'

'Elizabeth Goodman told me there was.' To prove it she held out a dog-eared card. He took it between finger and thumb.

'Where did you find this?'

'She gave it to me.'

He stifled his annoyance. What was Goodman up to? He had seen no personnel requisition, no authorization, no vacancy notice. He stood aside to let the girl in and pointed to a visitor's chair. 'Wait there,' he said, and jerking on the lapels of his coat went into the management suite.

'She by herself?' he asked Nora.

'She's working on her speech to the staff. All about what we're going to do in the future. She must have written it ten times.

Why she just doesn't tell them to get on with their jobs I don't know,' Nora sniffed.

Eddie knocked and went in. Liz was poring over her desk, her head in her hands.

'How's the speech going, Miss Goodman?'

'Just great.'

'Traditional is it?'

'What do you mean, traditional?'

'The staff likes a traditional speech. The pep talk. Onwards and upwards, all pull together, shoulders to the wheel, we're all on the same team, I'll play fair with you if you play fair with me, grafters get promoted, slackers get the sack. Any questions.'

'Like school assembly.'

'Then they go back to their desks and forget about it.'

She looked up sharply. 'I'm breaking with tradition, Eddie. I'm going to tell you all what my ideas are, my plans are for the future. How we're going to make profits.'

'Ah yes. Another old favourite. The first-duty-to-the-shareholders speech. Their interests are our interests. They'll like that one too.'

'That's not what I'm going to say. And I don't think you're being very helpful.'

'Me?' He was puzzled, injured, the faithful retainer misunderstood.

'Yes you.' She looked down at the blank piece of paper.

'How about the people speech then?' he said, chancing his luck.

'What's that?'

'People are the most important asset in the company.'

She looked at him sharply again. He put on his innocent retainer expression. 'What's wrong with that?' she said. 'This is a people business. People matter most. It's people who make profits. People are our best assets.'

'Like an employment agency,' he muttered.

'Senior management has got to care about its people. There will be changes, change is a part of life, but people come first.'

'After the profits.'

107

'People make the profits. People come first. Open management.' She scribbled on the piece of paper.

'Very good, Miss Goodman.'

'Liz,' she said, still scribbling.

'Miss?'

'Liz. Relaxed and informal. Unless there's anyone around.'

'Liz?'

'Yes?'

'What if people are open and frank with you?'

'That's just what I want.'

'That opium of the people stuff doesn't mean anything. Tell them what they want to know.'

'What do they want to know?' There was an edge in her voice. It is uncomfortable to ask subordinates their frank opinions. It is even more uncomfortable when they come back with them. She sat back and brushed the hair off her forehead.

'Why do you think they come here in the first place?' he asked. He no longer looked the simple domestic, more the inquisitorial head waiter.

'A need to grow, to learn new skills, to feel they belong to a team, to make a contribution to a common goal, to feel pride in what they can do . . .' her eyes strayed to the management book on the corner of her desk.

'Money,' he said.

'People don't just work for money, Eddie. They work to fulfil themselves.'

'That's as maybe. But our motives are none of your business. There's no magic buttons you can push to make us work harder.'

'Thank you for your opinion, Eddie. I'll thank you to be more constructive in future. I'm the manager. I'm going to run this place my way. Now I have to get on with this.'

'Before I go, there's a young lady outside says you offered her a job.'

'Young lady? What's her name?'

He shrugged. 'School-leaver. Short dark hair, brown eyes.'

'I don't know anyone like that.'

'She said you gave her your card.' He held out the scrap of card.

She took it and looked at her name as if it was a stranger's. She cleared her throat.

'Ah yes. She's here, is she?'

'Sitting outside.'

'I'll have a word with Administration. They need someone.'

'You can't give her a job, Miss Goodman.'

'What did you say?'

'Sorry. Liz.'

'What can't I do?'

'Give her a job.'

'And why not?'

'You don't have authorization.'

She took a deep breath and ran her fingers through her hair.

'Eddie. I'll be manager. You be messenger. OK?'

'I don't mean authorization from me.'

'I am glad.'

'Head Office has to approve all new hires. Even replacements. And they won't. There's a hiring freeze.'

'I'll see about that with Head Office.'

'Shall I ask the young lady to wait outside while you fix it?'

'Yes.'

'I'll make up a bed for her.'

She chose to ignore him as she reached for the telephone. He struggled with his conscience. Was he going to let her make a fool of herself with Head Office? Certainly not. Always protect the boss.

'Liz.'

'Yes?'

'May I make a suggestion? Take her on as a temp for a week.'

'We can do that?'

'Of course. Book it under miscellaneous. And that way if she doesn't work out after a few days you can easily get rid of her.'

'But she would still come under the head count in the monthly returns.'

'You fire her the day before month-end and take her on the day after. No-one will ever know.'

'I can't do that.'

'You already are. We've got ten permanent temps already.

109

Have you ever counted how many people there are in the back office? And how many we log on the monthly head count? Wait until month-end and see how short-handed we are.'

She went very pale. She picked up her dog-eared card and looked at it as if she wanted to make sure who she was again.

'I'm going to get to the bottom of this, Eddie. I promise.' Her voice sounded very small and thin.

'Very good, Miss Goodman. Shall I take care of the young lady?'

'Do that please,' she said with authority and decisiveness.

'I'll send in a temp requisition for you to sign.'

She nodded.

'We're a people business, Miss Goodman.'

She nodded and picked up her pen and carried on writing her speech.

'Thanks Eddie,' she said as he went out.

● ● ●

When Eddie went back into reception he found the girl lying on her back on the floor in front of the visitors' chairs with her eyes closed and her arms by her side, pale and effigy-like. She had a very pretty mouth. Her eyes flicked open like a doll's.

'Oi. This isn't a doss house.'

'I was doing my yoga,' she said, scrambling to her feet.

'Not on the carpet, darling. You'll get bitten alive. Come into my office.' He led the way into the post-room and sat down behind his desk.

'Cor,' she said, awed by the bank of TV screens fed by the security cameras and the computer and the satellite dish on the roof, the panel that controlled the alarms and the air conditioning and the lighting, the auxiliary switchboard, the tall glass box with the tapes recording dealing conversations, the fax machine, the computer keyboard, the gadgets for weighing and franking and opening letters.

'I'm going to give you a job,' he said, and was taken aback when she threw her arms round his neck and kissed him on the cheek.

'Oi. This is an office. Save that for the Christmas party.'

'Sor-ree.' She bit her lip and shrugged her shoulders under the carapace of her jacket.

'Right. What's your name?'

'Carol Feely.'

'Do you have any experience?'

'Are you getting personal?'

'I mean what have you done?'

'Lots of things.'

'Like what?'

'I went to Ostend with the school once. And I've done all the rides at Alton Towers.'

'I mean work experience.'

'I was a roadie for a group for a bit. And I did the post at Christmas.'

'What sort of thing are you good at?'

She bit her lip. She furrowed her brow. She blew her cheeks out, as if she numbered blowing up balloons as one of her accomplishments.

'What about at school? Did they teach you typing? Office procedures?'

'Nah. That was boring. I did metalwork. Trouble is there was no metal because of the cuts. We all had to watch him do it.'

'Did they have computers?'

'Yeah we did that. That was good fun. You could draw circles and things. When you could get on it.'

'Have you ever been in an office before?'

'I been with my Dad to the social security. It wasn't as nice as this though.'

'Do you know the alphabet?'

'A B C D . . .'

'All right. That's a start. Filing.'

'Great. I did that in metalwork.'

Eddie considered whether to put her right but decided it would be more entertaining to leave Carol's education to Freda Grafton. He picked up the morning's payments for delivery. 'Come on, darling,' he said, 'it's time for a walk.'

Eddie did two walks a day. In the old days before electronic funds transmission, all payments were delivered by hand, drafts and cheques worth billions of pounds. But even in the age of the microchip there was still plenty of work for messengers. They bustled round the City, delivering and collecting payments and certificates and confirmations. The telephone and the terminal and the demise of the City lunch cut their masters off from each other but for the messengers the City was still a village in which they knew every street, every alley and short-cut, every new office, every new face.

Carol followed Eddie down a narrow side street of grimy Victorian terraces, dark doors with entryphones and shiny brass plates, waiting for the next Baedecker raid from the City fathers and their property-developing cronies. The tenants eked out a living on short leases. They were financial consultants, insurance brokers, news-sheet publishers, sucking-fish gaping for morsels from the bigger sharks. One of the doors was painted bright red and instead of an entryphone sported a cheerful notice saying 'MacKerel Personal Service. Come on up. First Floor.' With a quick glance right and left Eddie pushed the door open and they trudged up the worn wooden stairs. Half-way up they met a dumpy middle-aged man in a dark suit and carrying an umbrella. Sheepishly, eyes downcast, eyes flickering over Carol, he stood to one side to let them pass.

There was another red door at the top of the stairs. 'Don't be shy! Come on in,' it announced. They obediently went in to a room furnished with bright blue carpet tiles, half a dozen low chairs upholstered in red pvc, and a low table piled with magazines. Four of the chairs were occupied by pretty young women, artfully made up and attractively dressed, flipping through magazines. One of them, a black girl in a black leather suit and intricate beading in her hair, looked up and smiled at them. Eddie smiled back as he made straight for a frosted glass door. He knocked and opened it without waiting for a reply.

'Hello Mrs Mac.'

'Eddie love.'

The dinginess of the office, the threadbare carpet and heavy brown furniture and cream walls, were more than compensated for by the radiance of its occupant. She wore a vast and shiny peach coloured suit, the sort of garments brides wear for second marriages. Everything about her was effulgent: her patent shoes and handbag, her stockings shot with silver, her chunky costume jewelry, her busby of platinum hair, her glazed scarlet lips and sparkling eyes, illumined with eye drops. She looked like a middle-aged fairy godmother in a provincial pantomime. Here was a woman who believed in being gay and bright and life-affirming, a woman who believed in having a good time and getting the best out of life. She put down the telephone and stretched out both arms in greeting, pointing to the chair on the other side of the desk just in time to prevent her gesture being misinterpreted as an invitation to be clasped to her ample bosom.

'How are tricks? Plenty of new girls, I see.'

'Business is booming, my love. Lots of demand. I can't get enough, girls or boys. Best racket I've ever been in.'

Mrs MacKerel had set up the business when the escort agency she had run for ten years was the target of a hostile takeover bid from a rival concern run by a Maltese businessman in Soho. Until then the Maltese had been content to provide protection services to her staff: then he decided to expand by vertical integration and put in his own management. A dawn raid had left her with burnt out offices and the sort of threats that were outside even the permissive guidelines of the Takeover Panel. She decided against an appeal to the Monopolies Commission, even though two of its members were regular clients, and decided to diversify out of leisure services into daytime employment. Old friends like Eddie chipped in with start-up capital.

'This is Carol,' Eddie said, pointing to her standing in the doorway, fingering the hem of her jacket. 'Put her on the books for me, will you?'

'Come in, dear,' said Mrs MacKerel, her eyes penetrating now, sizing Carol up as she edged shyly towards her. 'Sweet. Very sweet, Eddie. I'm not sure I've got anything for her right now.'

'That's all right, Mac. I've got her fixed up at DI. I just have to run her through the books.'

'Typist?'

'Filing. Junior. Four pounds an hour?'

'That's steep.'

113

'Never mind. She could do with some new clothes. Bill us eight, I'll get it through.'

'You're a very lucky girl, Carol,' said Mrs MacKerel. 'Eddie looks after his people.'

'That reminds me. Give Louise a rise. She's a good girl. And add on something for yourself.'

'Thanks, Eddie.'

He told Carol to report for work at nine and left her to fill out the forms. He hummed his usual hum on the way back to the office, 'Ti-tum-ti-tum. Ti-tum-ti-tum', but not with his usual gusto. For the first time in his life he felt bad about putting one past the boss. Liz was so naïve and well-meaning. He caught himself wishing he was on her side. 'Pull yourself together Fly,' he scolded himself. All's fair in love and the class war.

● ● ●

By six o'clock the bar by the Stock Exchange was full of pasty-faced, overweight young men in shiny suits. Champagne corks popped. Giuseppe the manager made his rounds, smiling and nodding.

'Hey Juicy, whervey oysters?'

'No R in the mont', Vincent.'

'Wassa' gorrer do wivit.'

'Out of season.'

'Back to Tubby Isaacs fellers.'

'I'm not eatin' eels in these shoes Vince. Three hundred quid they were.'

Harry shepherded Liz through the crowd to a small table in the corner overlooking the garden. He ordered Chablis while she concentrated on reading the American Express leaflet on the table. She was feeling dizzy and disjointed. It had been a long day. Since they had last met at the Colonial Bankers she had been ditched by her man, walked out on her best friend, left her home, bought a flat, alienated her senior staff and been lectured in management by the messenger. She took out a Camel and let Harry fumble with the matchbook on the table before getting out her lighter.

'Had a good day?' he asked.

114

'Very good. Very successful. How about you?' She was impressed with herself. She should be sobbing on a shoulder or walking up and down Tower Bridge or sticking pins into a wax effigy of David instead of buttering up Head Office. She was tougher than she had ever suspected.

'Gosh. A day with Wheeler is like bomb disposal. It's not what you do. It's surviving that counts.'

They watched in silence until Giuseppe had finished the pouring and tasting rigmarole. She forced herself not to grab for a glass.

'You're not married,' he said. She held up her glass with her left hand so he could see the bare fingers. 'Do you have a, you know . . .'

'Lots. What about you?'

'Married. Sort of.'

'How can you be sort of? Are you separated?'

'Gosh no. Daff's a brick. Don't know what I'd do without her.'

'Do you talk to her about work?'

'I feed her the odd titbit now and then.'

'Is that all?'

'I don't want her to worry.'

'Isn't that what wives are for?'

'I mean worry like a dog worrying a bone. She thinks I should be planning my career better.'

'Should you?'

'I don't want to spend Sunday morning going over the appointments pages. In my experience life can't be organized and planned. It's no good pestering it to come with the goods. If you sit quiet and dangle your bait in the water long enough something will come along and snap it up.'

'Are you faithful to her?'

'Absolutely. I believe in marital fidelity. Nose clean and a straight bat. Play the game. Stick to the rules. My word is my bond.'

'That's the motto of the Stock Exchange.'

'Is it?'

'And look what they get up to.'

He beat a tattoo on the wine bottle with his fingernails, trying not to catch her eye. In the absence of a wax effigy Harry Simple would do.

'What's she doing now?'

'Who?'

'Daff. That's your wife's name, isn't it? Not the car she drives?'

'She has flying lessons on a Thursday.'

'How long has she been doing that?'

'Two years.'

'Is she going for a licence?'

'Transcendental meditation. They sit around on the floor and levitate. She hasn't got off the ground yet.'

'It's cheaper than hiring planes if you can crack it.'

'It does her good. She always comes back in a good mood.'

He emptied the bottle into their glasses and she swigged at hers. She felt the fatigue draining away. The bitterness and frustration and hurt of the previous twenty-four hours were being transmuted in his presence to something much more pleasurable. He waved the Chablis bottle at Giuseppe and she felt the empty smile on her lips filling with genuine pleasure. His looks, his manners, his breeding, his suave composure, his masculine self-confidence aroused something physical deep inside her. She snapped the lighter shut and sucked the smoke in deep. She had experienced it before but never with such intensity. The excitement of it made her catch her breath. It was raw and female and primeval. It was pure aggression.

'How do you know she's not seeing her boyfriend?'

His knee hit the underneath of the table with a sharp crack. A spasm of pain rippled across his face.

'Gosh. That was uncalled for.'

'Why? She might be having a nice chat in an oyster bar right now.'

'She doesn't eat oysters. They bring her out in a rash.'

'And you've always been faithful to her.'

'Absolutely.'

'Absolutely?'

'Absolutely. Well . . .'

Giuseppe brought the second bottle, uncorked it and sloshed it into the glasses without the tasting business. It was Harry's turn to snatch and swig.

'Well what?'

'Well, except for the odd DC.'

'What's a DC?'

'Doesn't Count.'

'Doesn't Count?'

'Capital D capital C. It's the initials . . .'

'. . . I understand the letters, Harry. I don't see why it doesn't count.'

'A chap has to once in a while. Releases the tensions. Keeps the hand in. Pick up the odd trick or two you can't learn from books.'

'Do you tell her?'

'Gosh no. DC ISDFO.'

'ISDFO?'

'Doesn't Count If She Doesn't Find Out.'

She laughed and shook her head. He smiled sheepishly. She filled his glass and her own.

'Tell me some more.'

'More what?'

'More DCs. More rules of your fidelity game.'

'DC BT.'

'Stop. Let me guess,' she said, reaching over and putting her hand on his sleeve. 'Doesn't Count . . . with Buxom Typists.'

'On Business Trips.'

'Ask me another.'

'Liz . . .'

'I said ask me another.' She squeezed his arm.

'DC EFE.'

'Doesn't Count . . . Every Friday Evening.'

'Especially in the Far East. Listen Liz . . .' He leaned over the table and would have gazed meaningfully into her eyes if the smoke from her cigarette had not made them blink. She knew the signs. The display of sincerity. The appeal for understanding. The speech about his feelings. Why did bloody men need to be taken so bloody seriously all the time?

'How about DC OMN? Get it?' she asked.

117

'Liz, listen.'

'Doesn't Count on Meditation Nights.'

'You've got the wrong idea. Since we had lunch I can't get you out of my mind. You understand me. You're a wonderful person. You're talented and attractive . . .'

'I knew it. You're giving me the sack.'

His eyebrows puckered. He filled his glass. She could not help smiling. He was so sweet and vulnerable when he was puzzled. And he seemed to be puzzled a lot of the time.

'Sorry old girl. I don't get the drift.'

'I get suspicious when people are nice to me. It means I'm being disposed of.'

'You're not a DC, Liz.'

'Glad to hear it.'

'You count very much indeed.'

Wine on an empty stomach and a sleepless head were making her dizzy and distant. She closed her eyes and strained her jaw to stifle a yawn.

'What are you thinking about?' he asked.

'Bed,' she whispered and was jerked into wakefulness by the sound of his other knee cracking the underneath of the table.

'Let's go,' he said, waving urgently at Giuseppe as if he were a long-lost friend.

'Where to?'

'A bite to eat first? Or afterwards?' He leaned over the table and held both her hands in his.

'I can't. Not tonight.'

His grip relaxed and the arrival of the bill gave him a pretext to disengage.

'Oh. Are you . . .?'

She nodded. He could infer what he liked. She had indeed been thinking of bed, with crisp white sheets and soft pillows and a firm double mattress. Failing that, even the lumpy hotel bed would do, as long as it was all to herself.

'Just a quick bite then. I know a great little place. You'll like their treacle pudding.'

An affair with Harry was going to leave her very slim and hungry.

'Sounds wonderful. And you can tell me how I can get staff increases past Percy Wheeler.'

• • •

Freda Grafton went in for mixed feelings. If there was cause for joy she would find reasons for sorrow and vice versa. Her feelings were mixed when Eddie brought her the approval, signed by Miss Goodman, for a temporary junior clerk, an interim measure pending a staff review. On the one hand she was pleased, since she had been complaining to Mr Livery for months that she was short-handed. On the other hand she was annoyed that Miss Goodman had chosen an incumbent for this position without consulting her. Her feelings on first being introduced to Carol Feely were likewise mixed. On the one hand she was dismayed at the appearance in her office of an insolent skinhead in outsized clothes and paratroop boots. On the other hand she was gratified that her opinion of the youth of today was so amply exonerated. To be fair, Carol did little to modify any of these feelings.

'They told me you had an office,' she said, flopping down on the visitor's chair, legs splayed and one arm dangling over the back. Carol had not meant this an affront. She had simply stated a fact. She was not to know that she had touched one of Freda's many raw nerves.

'This is an open-plan office,' she said, briskly. 'It is designed to improve communications and facilitate the accommodation of work-space to work-flow. Individual offices are not conducive to efficient processing.'

'Why is it all cluttered up with partitions then?' asked Carol.

The partitions were the focus of an unceasing underground and unspoken war of attrition. Freda's section, Administration and Personnel, occupied the middle ground of the back office. Dealing was on one side and Accounts on the other. In quiet moments, when she was alone, working late or over lunch, she inched her partitions outwards, imperceptibly enlarging her territory. After a few days her neighbours would notice they were being squeezed and inch the partitions back again.

'To keep down the noise. And to provide the privacy necessary

119

for concentrated work.' Why was she telling the girl all this? When people came into her office they waited to be spoken to, they said yes Mrs Grafton and no Mrs Grafton. Wait until she'd been there a week, she'd whip her into shape. She wasn't a bad looking child if you looked hard enough. She looked as though she could do with a few good meals. Nice skin, pretty face. Lovely eyes. Touch of Spanish or Indian in there. But if her Karen came home with a haircut like that and those clothes she'd take the stick to her, fifteen or no.

'Sit up straight please, Carol. Now, filing, do you have any experience?'

'Yeah.'

'Good. Where?'

'We did metalwork at school.'

Freda stubbed out her cigarette in the copper ashtray as big as a soup plate that was the centrepiece of her overloaded desk. Again her feelings were mixed. Resentment at being lumbered with this baggage was tinged with pleasure at the prospect of moulding the material to her will. In any case, management had hired the girl and hers not to reason why.

'What time did you get here this morning?'

'Ten past nine.'

'Anyone who works for me gets here at nine precisely if not before. And packs up their desk not before five to five.' She waited for acceptance of these terms but the little madam only pouted. Probably been up all night at one of the discos her Karen pestered her about. 'I look for punc-tu-al-ity, Carol. Come with me.'

Looking neither to right nor left, a novice master with a postulant, she led Carol through the office. Apart from those in her own section many of the desks were empty. People were still arriving, dropping their coats and bags on their chairs and going to the drinks dispenser. No-one said good morning, no-one smiled. They passed each other in the aisles like strangers in a cafeteria. Freda took Carol to an alcove about twelve feet wide and three feet deep. The long wall was made of grey metal.

'Carol,' said Freda, solemnly, 'I am putting you in charge of the Filomatic.' She waited for the significance of this laying on of hands to sink in. 'Here,' she intoned, holding up a key, 'is the

120

key. You will return it to my hands each evening. Do you understand?' She turned and inserted the key into a long, horizontal panel set into the metal wall. It slid up to reveal two shelves of files stacked vertically. 'There,' she said, as if no further comment was needed.

Painstakingly she explained Carol's duties. The Filomatic held all the customer files and dealing records. It worked like a paternoster lift. The shelves were twelve feet long and two feet high. Only two were accessible at a time, the other fourteen rolled out of sight. A green button set them revolving and a red button stopped them. Carol was their custodian. When someone wanted one of the files they had to sign a large red card which she put in its place on the shelf. She was never to leave the shelves open and unattended.

'Do you understand, Carol?'

'Yeah.'

'I'll come back later to see how you are getting on.'

Carol sat down on a typist's chair in front of the control panel. She played with the buttons for a few minutes. Then she swivelled the chair round, lifting her feet off the floor. Then she cleaned her nails with a cocktail stick she found in the jacket of her suit. From where she sat she could not see any other desks, only grey partitions, and she did not like to move off her chair in case it was against the rules. People walked past carrying papers or polystyrene cups but they must have been very busy because they did not notice her. A young Asian glanced in her direction and she smiled at him but he looked through her. She could hear telephones ringing and people talking. She would have liked something to drink but she did not know where to get it and in any case she had no money.

It was an hour and a half before someone wanted a file. An old geezer in a beige cardigan and suede shoes came up and without looking at her or saying anything pressed the M-O button. When the machinery stopped he took out a file, filled out a red card and put it on the shelf and walked away without saying anything. She might as well not have been there. She wanted a pee but she didn't know where the toilets were and if she was allowed to desert her post. She stared at the metal panel in front of her to see how long she could go without blinking. She looked at the neon lights and squeezed her eyes shut and looked at the patterns. She found that if she looked for long enough at the fuzzy grey material walls she could see hoppy little black and silver things out of the corner of her eye.

At twelve o'clock people began walking past with paper bags and cups or putting their coats on. She was hungry. She stood up from the chair and stretched and felt faint. She walked out into the aisle and looked round. All the desks she could see had been abandoned except for one where the old geezer in the cardigan sat reading a magazine and eating a sandwich. She walked over to him.

'Hey, where d'you get the sandwiches?'

He looked up at her blankly, as if surprised that he had been spoken to.

'Pardon?'

'Where d'you get the sandwiches?'

'I bring my own in,' he said and turned back to his magazine. Mindful of her responsibilities Carol went back to the Filomatic and sat down again.

So this was work. It wasn't what it was cracked up to be.

● ● ●

'Found another job yet, Nora?' chirped Eddie.

Nora pointed to the brimming out-tray without lifting her gaze from the word-processor screen.

'Thank you, Eddie.'

Her face glowed with August Peach again instead of Lily White. Her eyebrows had reappeared, circumflexed over round blue smudges. Her lips were transfused with crimson and her teeth were flecked blood-red. Her ears dangled with gold baubles above the upturned collar of an indigo silk blouse. She was back to her old self.

'How's your boss?'

'Fine, thank you.'

'What's she working on this morning?'

'I'm sure she'd tell you if you asked.'

122

She was definitely back to normal, prickly and distant like a mother to a son who has forgotten Mother's Day. Where was the complicity he had enjoyed since the night Livery had died? Where was the hold he had over her?

He knocked on Liz's door and went in with his sesame, the morning position report. She had changed too. Her hair was done up neatly and she was wearing a crisp white shirt buttoned up to the neck. She looked brisk and efficient. Eddie's antennae twitched. They reverberated when he saw what she was working on. The personnel files were piled on the floor beside her chair and she was poring over an organization chart, adding things in pencil.

'You were wrong about Head Office, Eddie. There's no ban on hiring. They just need proper justification.'

'What sort of justification?'

'Productivity.'

Eddie shuddered at the hateful word. It meant more work for the same money.

'Is that what you're looking at now?'

'I'm just making sure I know what everybody does.'

'You can't tell from those.'

'Thanks, Eddie.'

His heart sank. He recognized the symptoms. She was sickening for a dose of manageritis. While she incubated the disease she would shuffle names and draw charts and mumble about efficiency and through-put. If it was not halted in time it would erupt in a severe bout of reorganization. He put the report in her in-tray and hurried out, massaging his forehead.

'What's the matter. Have you got a headache?' asked Nora.

'She's going through the staff list.'

'Staff staff staff. It's all she thinks about. How can she run the business if she's thinking about the staff all the time?'

It was time to go on his rounds. First call was Larry, the Chief Accountant. As always he was sitting immersed in the VDU, green light glowing on his gold-rimmed tinted spectacles, as if it originated from his eyes and not from the screen in front of him. Eddie sometimes wondered who was operating whom.

| | |
|---|---|
| ENTER | 'Afternoon Larry.' |
| READY | 'Uh-huh.' |
| SELECT PROGRAM | 'How are things?' |
| ANY KEY TO CONTINUE | 'Uh-huh.' |
| FILE RETRIEVE | 'How do the figures look?' |
| EDIT | 'Uh-huh.' |
| ANY KEY TO CONTINUE | 'Pretty bad?' |
| RETRIEVE DATA | 'Uh-huh.' |
| ANY KEY TO CONTINUE | 'Down on last quarter.' |
| STATUS | 'Uh-huh.' |
| ANY KEY TO CONTINUE | 'Costs up?' |
| INQUIRY | 'Uh-huh.' |
| ANY KEY TO CONTINUE | 'Personnel?' |
| INQUIRY | 'Uh-huh.' |
| ANY KEY TO CONTINUE | 'Personnel costs?' |
| ESCAPE | 'Thanks Larry.' |
| QUIT | |

Freda Grafton was beavering behind heaps of files and piles of papers, a cigarette in the ash-tray and one in her fingers, a half-eaten egg salad sandwich under a mound of memos, squinting in the smoke, a telephone between her jaw and her shoulders, scribbling on a numbered pad.

'Goodman's going through the personnel records,' he said, offhand, trying not to arouse suspicion. She dropped the phone on its cradle.

'Why do you say that? What's up? What have you heard?'

'Nothing yet. But why would she do that unless it was for staff cuts?'

'It's market forces, Eddie,' she said, stubbing out a cigarette in the smouldering heap of ashes and filters beside her telephone.

'It's always market forces when somebody else gets it. One man's market forces is another man's victimization. What will you say when it's your turn?'

'It's not for us to usurp the role of management.'

'What sort of management is that? They stumble on from one month's end to the next and suddenly there's a crisis. Whose fault? Market forces. Who pays? Not the managers. Oh no, their bums don't shift off their leather seats. We're just another resource, Freda, human resource, raw materials, use them and then chuck them away.'

'That's the way it is. It's a hard world.' She opened a manilla folder and started to count a sheaf of oblong tickets.

'It doesn't have to be.'

'I don't come here to collect appearance money. I work hard, Eddie, I have no right to a job, I earn it.'

'And everyone else is a layabout.'

'Not everyone. Some. The drones.' She lit a Silk Cut from the plastic lighter that hung round her neck on a chain.

'And who decides who's a drone? Liz Goodman has no idea what any of us does all day. We're lines on the salary sheet to her.'

'It's about time they made an example of someone,' said Freda, peeling the paper off the top of a roll of mints.

'Example? Example of what?' said Eddie. 'We do what we're told to do. Nobody tells us to it different or better. Suddenly it's time for a purge. Cut costs. Chop out the dead wood. Your turn to be liquidated. Bullet in the back of the head. Back to work the rest of you.'

Freda got up from her desk and crooked a finger. She walked a few steps to the partition that divided her corner of the room from Dealing. She squinted through the crack between two panels and then made way for Eddie. 'See for yourself,' she whispered.

There were half a dozen desks in Dealing. A thin girl sat at a desk covered with print-outs and little piles of confirmation tickets held together with rubber bands. Her mouth was open and her long tongue wiped salaciously back and forwards over her bottom lip in concentration. Next to her a spotty youth was engaged in similar work. In front of them a fat girl entered numbers from a schedule into an electronic calculator that spewed a long paper ribbon, like an outsize flypaper, over the back of the desk and into a loose coil on the floor. One desk was unoccupied, heaped with massive print-outs bound in blue plastic. Supervising them, at right angles to where Eddie spied, his back to a partition, sat Norman Foxwell.

The front of his desk was lined with ornaments. It looked like a mantlepiece at home – a brass statuette of the Needles lighthouse

125

with a thermometer fixed to the front, a six-inch high mermaid made of seashells combing her hair on a large clam, a wooden Whitstable oyster boat with parchment sails, crewed by fishermen made of pipe cleaners, a fretwork pipe-rack, a white tobacco jar decorated with blue dolphins, a brown carved wooden elephant with a prosthetic tusk made out of a matchstick, a little Dutch clog, a silver-plated effigy of a man swinging a bowling ball, his free hand on his bent knee. Behind, hooked on the top of the partition, was a coat-hanger with a dispirited dull grey suit jacket obscuring a collage of picture postcards, featuring light blue skies and dark blue seas, stapled into the furry brown fabric.

'So?' whispered Eddie.

'Look at him,' whispered Freda.

Apart from the ornaments, a Reuter screen and two telephones, his desk was completely clear. He sat upright in his chair, his hands folded on the desk top around a pipe, grey woolly cardigan ruckled around his shoulders, staring at a point somewhere above the fat girl's head. He was quite motionless.

'So?' whispered Eddie. 'He's finished dealing for the day.'

'He finishes at ten in the morning. Sometimes he has ten deposits maturing, sometimes he has none. What do you think he does the rest of the time?'

'What?'

'Nothing.'

'What's wrong with that, as long as he's done what he's supposed to?'

'One day management is going to find out that a clerk could do that job in half an hour a day.'

'And what happens to Norman?'

Freda shrugged. 'Don't try to stave off the inevitable, Eddie. It's not worth the energy.' She led the way back to her desk and sat down.

'You're just going to let it happen? Like the rest?' said Eddie, unable to keep the irritation out of his voice.

'Everything happens for the best.'

'People don't matter, do they? All that matters is pushing numbers around.'

'Perhaps all that matters to you is pushing the people around.'

Eddie picked up the contents of her out-tray and took them back to the post-room, deep in thought. Freda had strong opinions about how Norman's job should be done. And she would take the first opportunity to share them with management. There was no time to be lost. Mindful of the crack in the partition he waited for her to go to lunch before paying Norman a visit.

'Goodman's on the warpath,' he confided, sitting down on the visitor's chair beside his desk. Norman looked wearily at him.

'Costs is it?' he asked.

'I think so,' said Eddie.

Norman sighed and examined his pipe as if it were the first time he had seen it. 'Memos about turning off the lights and not wasting toilet paper I suppose. It'll pass.' He had seen it all before.

'It might be more serious than that. She's got the job descriptions out. She's talking about productivity. And you know what that means.'

Norman pushed his bottom lip out and sucked his moustache, the closest he ever came to exhibiting inner turmoil. Deep in thought he contemplated what Eddie had just said, mulling it over in the light of a lifetime's experience. 'What does that mean, Eddie?' he finally asked.

'She'll be cutting staff. It means we have to look busy. All of us.'

'Busy busy.'

'Busy busy busy.'

Norman sucked his moustache again. He squinted down the bowl of his pipe and tapped it on the heel of his hand. ' ''Is not man's life on earth nothing more than pressed service, his time no better than hired drudgery?'' What we need is a study,' he said.

'A study? What good will that do?'

'Never do anything without a study. After the study a report. After the report a plan. After the plan a conference. After the conference an implementation programme. And by the time that's ready the situation has changed so much we need another study. I've seen it all before.'

'You'd better hurry up and suggest it.'

'I'll bring it up at the next management committee. She wanted ideas.'

'Who's going to do the study?'

Norman leaned over the side of his chair, opened the bottom drawer of his desk and with two hands heaved up a black loose-leaf binder six inches thick. It thunked down on the desk. 'Remember the nephew Livery gave a summer job to? Business school chap?' He squinted at the cover. 'Relationship Analysis and Projected Business Plan. It should keep me going for a few months. Eh?'

'What if she's already got it?'

Norman shook his head. 'Only copy. Livery chucked it at me. Plans are all right, he said, as long as they don't interfere with the business.' He patted the tome. 'There's nothing new under the sun, Eddie.'

● ● ●

Percy Wheeler drove the Rolls up the ramp from the garage and listened for the reassuring thunk as the automatic doors closed behind him. There was a parcel on the seat next to him, prettily wrapped, and he was dressed to visit his new mistress, in a pink and blue striped golf sweater and tartan trousers. This was not the way he dressed to see girlfriends, sharp suit and silk shirt, or his wife, dark suit and white shirt, or his mother, blazer and flannels. He was always careful to dress for the occasion and Thursday was the one night of the week when he relaxed. Nevertheless he used the time in the car to make a few phone calls he preferred to make in privacy. Switchboards have ears. He checked on a couple of share prices with his personal broker in New York, checked on the agenda of the council meeting with his contact at the town hall – yes, the privatization of the cemeteries was up for approval – checked on his wife with the matron of the nursing home, do you want to speak to her – no just say I called – checking that everything was under control, going to plan. The disembodied voices filled the car like his own thoughts. He let them talk, knowing his own silence would make them nervous and talk more, not knowing if he was disapproving, giving away more than they intended. You learn a few tricks when you get this far.

He turned off Streatham High Street opposite the Odeon and through an estate of identical thirties houses, semi-detached. In the fading light he parked under a tree beside the common. There was a greater risk of a break-in but it was more discreet than parking outside the house. He put on a shiny silver golf jacket, set the alarms, picked up his parcel and walked back along the road to Nora's house. He let himself in. 'Yoohoo, I'm home!' Sukie with a shiny green bow between her ears scuttled yapping around his feet like a clockwork mouse.

'Down, Sukie,' said Nora, coming out of the kitchen with her arms wide. She wore a pink linen skirt that clung to her ample hips and an indigo silk blouse. She put her arms round his neck and pecked him on the lips.

'Has my baby had a tiring day?'

He pushed the parcel into her hand and watched her unwrap it, a yellow capodimonte rose on a silver stem. He liked the way her scarlet lips make a perfect circle when she said oooh, reminding him of blowing out birthday candles.

'I know you haven't got it because it's a new one, just out,' he said, taking off his golf jacket and hanging it on a wrought iron hook beneath a marquetry depiction of Malaga.

'Percy, you shouldn't, you're too good to me.' He patted her bottom and followed her into the lounge, trudging through the luxuriant lilac shag rug. While she gently jostled the porcelain roses round on their shelves to find pride of place for the new addition he sat down in the armchair by the fireplace and took off his shoes, Sukie sniffing at his socks, and replaced them with the furry brown slippers warming in the glow of the artifical coals.

'Nice cup of tea?'

'Love one. Be a pet and take the dog.' She went to the music centre on the other side of the fireplace to put on the Best of Aled Jones. She picked up the dog and went out swaying her bottom in time to the music to please him. He laid his head on the antimacassar that protected the sculpted velvet and gazed into the fire, soothed by the flickering of the spinning propeller behind the black and red plastic. Hubby for an evening, he twiddled his toes in his slippers and felt the tension of the day oozing into the warmth and comfort of a real home. He helped himself to a Rothmans from the onyx cigarette box and lit it from the blazing tongue of a silver-plated City griffin, activated by pressing his tail at the back.

Nora came back from the kitchen with a Charles and Di wedding mug and a jaffa cake on a Wedgewood saucer.

'Only one, you're having your meal in a minute.' She put them down on the table. He sipped the tea and grunted with pleasure, just how he liked it, and settled back on the antimacassar again.

'What's for tea?' he asked.

'Fish fingers and baked beans, your favourite, and tinned peaches and ice cream.'

'Lovely.'

She pulled a moroccan leather pouffe, red and yellow segments, closer to his chair and put her hand on his knee and gazed into the flickering fire with him. He put his hand on top of hers.

'So how's my office doing?' he asked, casually.

'Terrible,' she sighed. 'That Goodman is the worst boss I ever worked for. She can't make up her mind. You need someone who can put their foot down. She lets the staff walk all over her. If it wasn't for me they'd be in and out of her office all day. They've got no respect for her, you know. She thinks she's in charge of some sort of commune. Always asking people what they think. People want to know where they stand. You can't run a business with opinion polls. I mean what's the point of having a boss?'

'Don't worry. It won't be for long,' he mused, gazing thoughtfully into the flickering coals.

'You're getting rid of her? Good riddance I say.'

'That's not what I said, pet.'

'Everybody would thank you for it. Thinks she can turn the whole place upside down. Even Mr Foxwell was moaning about her the other day. He's got to do a study of all the business we've done with our customers. She calls it a relationship study.'

Percy's eyebrows fluttered and swooped.

'What for?'

'I don't know. It came up at one of her management committee meetings. She says it's for a strategic plan. Mr Foxwell says it will take him months to do. Anyway, you don't come here to talk shop.'

She brought the fish fingers and beans and instant mashed potato into the lounge and they ate watching the snooker, Sukie nestling between them on the sofa. When he had finished a second helping of peaches and Neapolitan ice cream she moved to an armchair so he could stretch out on the sofa and doze. During the break in the ten o'clock news she made two cups of cocoa. He yawned and stretched when the news had finished and took off his slippers.

'Put the milk bottles out, baby. The blanket's on.'

'Sorry pet, I can't stay tonight.'

'Oh baby,' she exclaimed and pressed his head into her bosom. His voice was muffled.

'Early start tomorrow. I'm looking at a racehorse. I've got to be in Battersea at seven.'

He struggled free and found his shoes.

'Do they keep racehorses in Battersea?'

'No. They keep helicopters, though. The horse is in New-market.'

'What do you know about racehorses?'

'They cost money.'

'I'd love a share in a racehorse.'

'Which bit do you want?'

'Is it a stallion?'

'No, a filly.'

'Then it's got nothing I'm interested in.'

He chuckled and patted her bottom. She helped him on with his shoes and kissed him on the forehead. He put on his silvery golf jacket and pecked her on the lips as she opened the front door.

'Percy. Are you doing something with Dividend Investments?'

'Now don't you worry your pretty little head about that.'

'What did you mean about Goodman not having very long.'

'Nothing. Careless talk costs lives.'

'I think I have a right.'

'Don't worry. You'll be all right. Next week same as usual?'

'Of course, baby. We'll have sausages.'

'My favourite.'

She stood at the open door, holding Sukie, and watched him walk bandy-legged down the street in his silvery golf jacket and tartan trousers, bald patch glistening in the street light, a little middle-aged man in a street of thirties semis, and felt a pang of affection, a desire to hold him in her arms and pat his head. She still waited after he had disappeared from view, until he reappeared at the wheel of the Rolls, like a baby in an old-fashioned perambulator, his little head low behind the steering wheel. She toyed with the idea of buying him a cushion to sit on when he drove it himself but decided he might be offended. When he had finally gone she closed the door and went inside to the kitchen. She scraped her fish fingers and beans into the waste disposal, poured her cocoa after them and put the plate and mug in the dishwasher with Percy's. She slipped a tin of smoked oysters into the automatic opener, took a bottle of gin out of the cupboard next to the fridge and went into the lounge to watch the late-night film, deliciously alone, happy to have spent an evening with a lover who wanted her for her company. And nurturing a very interesting piece of information. Goodman didn't have very long.

Percy too was content. He drove back over the river whistling tunelessly and tapping the wheel in time. He felt restored and refreshed by his evening of sensual indulgence. He could have girls at any time and often did, paying them to do his unfettered, and occasionally fettered, bidding. But Nora satisfied other needs. She pandered to his masculine craving for simple domesticity. It was nice to enjoy it without the tensions of sex or guilt. The evening had not been wasted either. What was Goodman doing getting Foxwell to study business relationships? He had told her plainly enough what he wanted her to do. It was time to cut her down to size. He had to nip this manageritis in the bud. His fingers drummed on the arm-rest as if they were trying to bring up a vein in the soft, dead leather. It was a pity he let slip to Nora about DI's short-term future. Still, Nora would forget about it. And if she didn't, what harm would it do? She was only a secretary.

• • •

# *FULL MOON*

Whispers echoed under the low vaulted ceiling of the Guildhall crypt. For such a cellarous place it was warm and comfortable with clever concealed lighting that made it at once mysterious and soothing. Men in dark suits, wearing various insignia, stood around in groups talking in hushed voices, not necessarily out of secretiveness but because the acoustics were especially sensitive. Three men, two of them tall and one of them short, all three wearing blue ribbon collars making a V on their chests, huddled beside a marble pillar.

'How's it going?' one of them asked the little man.

'Not too good. Bibber hasn't come up with anything yet.'

'He'd better hurry up. Wheeler's approached Premium Insurance. Old Pansy Browning's in a funk. He was just telling me there could be a full bid.'

'If he gets his claws into Premium it'll make even more of a stink.'

'Are we sure we want to go through with this?' said the tallest man, flicking his fingertips over his little lambskin apron.

'Who ran squealing to Downing Street when you suspended his shares?' said the little man.

135

'Who's always shooting his mouth off about the Takeover Panel?'

'Who's too big for his boots?'

The little man nervously fingered the point of his blue ribbon collar.

'You're sure he's not on the square?'

'A murky past,' sighed one of the tall man, shaking his head.

'A murkier future,' said the little man.

'We just need one thing to pin on him.'

'You never know, this Premium business may be our chance.'

'I've heard that . . .'

But the little man was cut short by the rap of a gravel. The conversations stopped and all the men in the room silently took their places for the meeting.

● ● ●

Five men sat in a large black Bentley parked in a side street off London Wall, two in the front and three in the back. They wore dark suits and white shirts and sober ties.

'Premium Insurance has hit bottom,' said the man in the front passenger seat, casually.

'They were up ten pence at the close.'

'Someone's in the market,' said the man in the window seat behind him.

'Think there'll be a bid?' asked the man in the middle.

'Could be. I took the Chairman to a secret extraordinary board meeting yesterday. At Claridges. Hush hush. I was waiting two hours. Browning was pissing himself on the way home. Kept on swearing he hadn't worked all his life to end up in a dust-cart.'

'Worth a call to Cayman?'

'Buy now. While stocks last,' said the front passenger. The other laughed politely.

'Here we go,' said the man in the driver's seat, nodding in the direction of the building on the other side of the street. 'Yours isn't it, Eddie?'

'Cheers lads,' said Eddie, turning round to the rear shelf and picking up the five chauffeur's caps. 'Mind how you go.' He passed round the hats and the five men put them on. Four of them got out of the Bentley, leaving its driver, and went over to their own cars, which were also parked in the side street.

Eddie negotiated the Humber out of its parking space and joined the queue of black limousines moving spasmodically past the entrance to Plaisterer's Hall. He did not have time to get out to open the door. Liz jerked on the handle as he stopped and threw herself in the back seat as if it were a get-away car. She ran her fingers through her hair and gave a massive sigh as Eddie eased out into London Wall.

'Thank God for that. Are we as boring to the Japanese as they are to us? I'm up to here in raw fish. I can feel them wriggling around. Even the crisps taste of seaweed. I don't trust that Suntory whisky either.' She sighed again and looked out of the window. 'That place is like an enormous boudoir. Pink walls and fancy plaster.'

'Was it your first reception?'

'Yes. What a waste of time. See and be seen. You never hear anything useful. You must be fed up waiting too.'

'It's not so bad. You have a natter with the other lads. Where to?'

'Covent Garden please.'

He turned towards St Pauls and switched on the radio. The financial news came on as they drove down the Strand past the City's silver griffin sticking out its spiky red tongue at the law courts.

'That Premium Insurance sounds interesting,' mused Eddie. 'There's going to be a takeover.'

'You think?'

'I'm sure. They've already been approached.'

'How do you know?'

'Word gets round.'

'Do you play the market, Eddie?'

'Not me,' said Eddie. 'It's immoral.'

'How is it immoral?'

'Making profits you haven't earned. How about you?'

'I've still got my British Telecom. I'll have to sell them to buy furniture. They'll stretch to a kitchen table if I'm lucky.'

He glanced at her in the mirror. Since she started wearing her hair up she looked tense all the time. When she spoke to him now she always seemed to be thinking of something else.

'What opera are you seeing?'

'Figaro.'

'What's that about?'

'A count who wants to sleep with his servant's fiancee.'

'The class war, eh? I hope the servant has it off with the countess.'

'No. He doesn't.'

'Pity.' He glanced in the mirror but she was looking out of the window, thinking of something else.

He nudged slowly between the taxis and limousines and drew up as close as he could to the front of the opera house. It was milling with people, in furs and anoraks and cashmere coats and woolly sweaters. He got out to open the door but Harry Simple beat him to it.

'Gosh. Pretty smart timing.' Harry held out his hand and she let him help her out. He was in dinner jacket and black tie, suave and elegant and slightly stooping.

'What time shall I come back, Miss Goodman?' asked Eddie.

'You shouldn't do that,' said Harry to Liz. 'They charge the devil at night.'

'Oh, it's not hired,' said Liz, airily, 'it's the company . . .'

'Company Contract Rental,' chipped in Eddie, pulling the peak of his cap down over his nose. Harry looked at him, surprised that he spoke. Eddie took a card out of his top pocket and handed it to him. *Luxury Limousines – 'Your Fly Awaits You' – Weddings and Airports a Speciality.*

'I say, haven't I seen you before?' said Harry, pocketing the card.

'Me, sir?'

'Perhaps not.' He took Liz's arm. 'All these drivers look the same in their grey caps.'

'Thank you, sir.'

'You needn't wait,' said Liz, looking over her shoulder. 'Thanks, er . . .'

He got back into the empty car and watched them go inside,

drumming his fingers on the wheel. He was surprised by a surge of anger and resentment. It was partly jealousy, the mirror image of love. And it was partly something much more malignant. It rose out of the gulf between officers and men, gentlemen and players, public schools and comprehensives, royalty and commoners, people like us and people like them, Oxbridge and redbrick, management and staff, staff and workers, drawing-rooms and lounges, dining-rooms and canteens, all the dichotomy of privilege and deference and snobbery and obeisance and condescension at the heart of English life. He knew that it was envy and he hated himself for it.

Figaro. He wondered if it was on video.

● ● ●

In the interval Harry found a quiet corner beside a pillar. Liz sipped her champagne with a silent prayer that it would accommodate itself to the Suntory and raw fish. She offered Harry a Camel. He took the lighter out of her hand and employed it with great concentration and when he gave it back let his fingers linger on hers.

'I've never been here before,' she said.

'It was better before they spread it around that you didn't have to wear the old soup and fish.'

'You're wearing evening dress.'

'Rearguard action.'

'I bet the rot started when people stopped buying their own tickets. When you've lashed out your own money it feels like more of an occasion. When you're on a corporate freebie it's only like staying late at the office.'

He folded his arms defensively across his pleated shirt.

'There's nothing wrong with corporate hospitality, Liz. It keeps places like this going.'

'As long as they clap in the right places it doesn't matter I suppose.'

She had better make amends. Although they were company tickets he was still in charge of doling them out.

'Thanks for inviting me. Doesn't Daff like opera?'

139

'Gosh yes. But I thought you needed a bit of unwinding.'

'An evening of farce and adultery does take the mind off the office.' She sipped her champagne. 'Perhaps not.'

He grinned and topped up her glass. He was much more at ease here than at the office. He was in his element among the chandeliers and champagne and the gold card set.

'How are you getting on?' he asked.

'Just great. I had a very successful day. Has Percy still got his eye on us?'

'I haven't seen a lot of him recently, thank God. I think he's got a deal brewing.'

'I've got a quarterly financial review next week. What should I do?'

'Know your stuff.'

'Who will be there?'

'Apart from Percy? Spight, the Finance Director. And me. I'll give you moral support. Listen, why don't we have a run-through at the weekend?'

'Are you sure? That would be wonderful. At my office or yours?'

'I thought we could do it at my place. Do you fancy a trip in the country?'

'That would be nice. I'd like to meet Daff.'

'I'm afraid she won't be there. She's away on a meditation course. They're all going off with the guru.'

'Flying again?'

'They're going by train. We'll have the house to ourselves. Will you?'

He pleaded like a little boy, a shy smile on his mouth. She wanted to ruffle his carefully brushed hair. She felt a sudden tightening behind the breastbone, a fluttering in her stomach, a tremble in her knees, a flush in her cheeks. Was this love? Or was it raw fish and Suntory and champagne? She considered her reply very carefully.

'Listen, Harry. I think you're very sweet and very attractive. I suspect you would be a very considerate and amusing lover. I know your marriage is not my business but I wonder if it's really in the doldrums. I wouldn't like to be the one who blew it on to the rocks. I am trying to get over a broken relationship. I'm not sure I am ready for another yet. My new job is draining me dry at the moment. A weekend in the country would do me good I know, but I've set aside Saturday to look for a service flat until I move into my own place. You're Personal Assistant to the Chairman and I'm not sure it's a good idea to mix business with pleasure.'

'I'll bring a toothbrush,' was what she actually said.

● ● ●

'I'm fed up,' said Carol, slamming the post-room door shut. Eddie looked up from the cardboard box he was slitting open on the floor.

'What's the matter, darling?'

'It's like an asylum in here. Nobody talks to each other, nobody laughs, nobody acts natural at all. What are they like when they go home?'

'Just the same as everybody else.'

'The only time anybody talks to me is to give me orders or give me a bollocking. That Grafton's the worst. God help her kids.'

'She's probably as nice to them as your mum.'

'I wouldn't wish that on them.' She sat on his desk with her arms defiantly folded. Eddie stood up, Stanley knife in his hand.

'You're making the same mistake everyone else does,' he said. 'They think that the office is just an extension of life outside. You just do different things. Well it isn't. As soon as you come through that front door you're in another world. It's got its own rules and its own way of doing things.'

'I wish someone would tell me what they are.'

'Ever see stuff on telly about how they used to live in the old days? The big house and the servants and the butler and the cook and the gardener and the maids?'

'Yeah?'

'It's like that. Know your place.'

'Great. Hey, what are those?' She pointed a paratroop boot at the open box.

'Gas masks.' He lifted one up. 'I've got a mate in the fire brigade.'

'What on earth for?'

141

'Never you mind. You'd better get back to the Filomatic or she'll be after you again.'

'It's my lunch break.'

'Help me down to the basement with these then.'

He picked up the cardboard box and put it in her arms. From under the post table he took out three large transparent polythene bags. Each contained a copper canister, a length of plastic hose, bits and pieces of plastic tube and a bundle of straps.

'What are they for?'

'Spraying fruit trees.'

'You're up to something, aren't you?'

On top of the box she was carrying he put a large can wrapped in a brown paper bag.

'I said never you mind.'

'You're a fixer, aren't you? What happens if you get found out?'

'What do you mean, if I get found out?'

'All your little fiddles.'

'They're not fiddles. I do the job I'm paid for. Anything I put in over and above that belongs to me.'

'Real little capitalist, aren't we?'

'Taking out what other people put in is capitalist. I only take out what I put in. Come on. I'll open the door.'

● ● ●

Harry was waiting for her at the station on Saturday afternoon. She hesitated between a kiss and handshake and gave him her overnight bag instead. She kept her bulging music case. After a lot of thought she had decided to wear her hair up. With a crisp white shirt and tan skirt it sustained the fiction, for the time being, that this was a business meeting. He was wearing a tweed jacket with patches on the elbows and tan cords and a Vyella shirt and highly polished brown brogues. He looked like a country solicitor. When he smiled, shy and excited, she was glad she had come.

'Ah, the country,' she said, taking a deep breath as he fiddled nervously with the lock on the passenger door of the company Granada. It was a beautiful late spring day, warm and fresh. In the cloudless sky above a microlight buzzed like a chainsaw. In the vast flat fields, swept of woods and hedges and ponds, a chugging tractor sprayed a fine green mist over sprouting rape. The scent of nitrates wafted on the air. A grader ploughed the rich red soil of a new motorway slip-road.

'Makes a break from the city,' he said.

They dawdled along a country lane behind a Range Rover towing a horsebox before getting on to the fast lane of the M25 where they dawdled behind a petrol tanker.

'Contraflow ahead,' he said, breaking the silence. 'That's why it's all clogged up.'

'You have quite a commute in the morning,' she answered, to keep the conversation going.

'That's not my station actually,' he said. 'Mine's the next one down the line. I thought this one was er, you know.' She noticed that the tips of his ears went pink when he was embarrassed, as if they had been boxed.

'More discreet, as your Panamanian friend Sally would say. Don't worry. Say when and I'll duck down. You can cover me with a blanket.'

'You know the country, Liz. Village life and all that. People gossip. They get the wrong idea.'

'Pity. You could have dropped Daff off and picked me up on the same trip. It would have saved petrol.'

He glanced over to see if she was smiling or bitter. She kept him guessing with a poker face.

They left the motorway and drove through more country lanes, Harry humming nervously under his breath whenever they passed a car coming the other way or slowed down at a busy junction. At last they drove through a gap in a wall of leylandii and down a gravel drive. He parked in front of a double garage.

'What a pretty house,' she said.

It was half-timbered, the other half white pointed brick, with a low tiled roof and tall chimneys and gables and eaves and leaded windows and a clematis round the front door. It was a truly English house, Tudor and Restoration and Georgian, roast beef and ale and cucumber sandwiches and summer pudding. The year it was built was chiselled on the old stone lintel over the door.

MCMLXI. He fumbled with the door lock and let her go first. The inside was pretty and cottagey, chintz and beamed ceilings and low lintels. She realized why he sometimes affected a stoop.

The drawing-room seemed very familiar. She puzzled over the big china elephant and the flowery patterned sofa and the chandelier wall lights and the pictures of horses until she realized where she had seen it already. It was straight out of the country magazines that Fiona and her friends left lying around their flats in the Barbican. Daff had been meticulous. Everything toned and matched, everything was just right. She had copied the model so accurately that she had somehow succeeded in imprinting her own personality, like an anonymous medieval craftsman. It was immaculately clean and tidy, the sort of room that made Liz want to scatter old newspapers and drop cigarette ash and play loud rock music. The only sign of a personal life were two colour photographs in silver frames on a small round table. One showed a young and dashing Harry in a military uniform standing beside an English rose in a wedding dress looking as though they were about to be chopped into small pieces by a score of upraised swords. The other was of two boys in ties and Fair Isle sweaters and tweed jackets.

'Nice boys,' she said. 'Who's looking after them this weekend?'

'They're away at school. Jamie's eight and Roddy's nine. How about a spot of tea?'

She dropped her music case on an armchair.

'Not just now thanks. Let's get down to business.'

An hour later they stopped for a break.

'I didn't think men who said gosh did all those things,' she whispered, running her hand across his smooth chest. He kissed her gently on the forehead.

'What did you expect?'

'A clean nose and a straight bat.'

'You're a pretty useful tail-ender yourself,' he said. She pursed her lips and peeked the tip of her tongue out, upside down. He jerked and shuddered.

'How do you do that?'

'A woman's secret. There's more.' She bent down towards his chest.

'Let's have that spot of tea first.'

'And my quarterly presentation.'

He sighed and looked solemn.

'You're very single-minded, aren't you, Lizzie?'

'I've realized that I like to get what I want.'

'What do you want?'

'Right now I want to be the best manager in the Dividend Group.'

'Once upon a time there was a pond full of frogs. One day a visiting frog asked them who their queen was. "What's a queen?" they asked. 'Everyone has to have one,'' said the visitor. So the frogs pestered God for a queen. The next day there was an enormous splash in the pond. It frightened the frogs away. When they came back they saw a large log bobbing up and down on the water. They were very happy and jumped up and down on the log and boasted they had a queen at last. Then they got tired because the log didn't do anything. It was ugly. It only moved when they moved it. It said nothing. It had no charisma. So the frogs pestered God again. The next day there was a big splash and when the frogs came out they saw the most beautiful and noble queen standing in the middle of the pool. She had charisma all right. She was tall and slender and dignified and elegant and wore lovely feathers. She was a stork. She looked down her long, aristocratic beak and, one by one, ate them up. Is that what you really want to be?'

'I'll take that risk. Besides, it's what the frogs wanted.'

He got out of bed and put on a red silk dressing-gown hanging behind the door. He tossed another one on to the bed, daffodil yellow.

'No thanks. It's all right.' She drew the line at wearing Daff's clothes. She followed him naked downstairs to the hall where he had left her bag. She put on jeans and a sweater and found her cigarettes.

While he was busy with kettle and cups she unlocked the kitchen door. Hanging on a hook on the back of the door were two pairs of earphones, the sort that airport ground crew wear. When she stepped outside she realized what they were for. The noise made her flinch. She put her hands over her ears. It was a remorseless, reverberating thrumming. It came from the M25 which ran along the bottom of the garden. She could not see the vehicles that caused it because this stretch of the carriageway was raised on stilts. The noise seemed to come from all round, descending from the sky like the music of the spheres with the volume too loud, in four-part harmony, the booming bass of diesel trucks, the throbbing tenor of cars, the alto hum of tyres on concrete, the soprano sussurations of slipstreams, interspersed with virtuoso klaxons and sirens and horns.

'Daff always wears these for gardening,' he said behind her, holding out one of the pairs of earphones.

They walked down the garden hand in hand like two hi-fi buffs.

'It doesn't disturb our privacy,' he shouted, 'they can only see the top of the roof. We've still got the view.' He pointed between the concrete pillars to the featureless countryside stretching away to a distant town. 'It does block out the sun, but only for a few hours a day. Less in summer when the sun's high. And we get a second sunrise and a second sunset over the eastbound carriageway.'

'It's very handy,' she said, struggling for something to say.

'That's true. We can always see what the driving conditions are.'

'Easy access.'

'It's only ten miles to the nearest junction.'

'What about lead poisoning?'

'It's no worse than central London.' He pointed to a pillar. 'The potting shed used to be there. It would be great for wisteria if it didn't face north.'

They kissed and turned back up to the house. The garden was lovely – the trees and shrubs were a bright, fresh green, apple and pear and cherry were in full blossom, the yellow flowers of early spring were mixed with blue, the lawn was neat and stripey. He led the way into a triple-glazed conservatory built against the dining-room French windows where he had laid a tray of tea and tuck-shop buns on a low rattan table. They took off their headsets and sat side by side on a wooden garden seat, surrounded by pots and trays of peaty brown compost.

'Why don't you get 'phones with a radio in them?' she asked

146

when they came in. 'Like they have in factories.'

'Daff likes the peace and quiet.'

'It's what living in the country's all about.'

She poured the thick brown tea. He handed her a plate.

'Have a bun.'

'Have you lived here long?' she asked, picking currants off the dough in search of something palatable to fill the growing void inside.

'It was one of my great deals. That's what Daff calls them. I bought it from a county councillor a week before they announced an alteration to the proposed motorway route.'

'Didn't you sue him?'

'I threatened legal action all right. He gave back some of the money. And we got quite a bit from the compulsory purchase.'

'But you kept the house.'

'I invested the cash in an Australian mining share. It crashed two days before we were to exchange contracts on the new place. Spot of bad luck actually. At least we've got a roof over our heads, I told Daff. Two, she said. It'll be like living under a railway arch.'

They laughed and Harry slapped his knee and swigged his tea and took a bite of bun. Liz put her hand on his shoulder. She needed to touch him.

'Not my most spectacular disaster though. At least we came away with something. Compared with others it was relatively minor.'

'What sort of others?'

'Let me see. Retirement homes in Florida. Airships in France. Borzoi breeding in Wales. Commodities in Chicago. To name but a few. Never be frightened of failure. That's my motto.'

She felt chill and snuggled up to him.

'It's all laughter and champagne to start and tears and gin to finish. And debts.' He grinned. 'But you have to learn from your mistakes.'

'All you learn from making mistakes is how to make mistakes.'

'You sound like Daff.'

'Doesn't she go along with your ventures?'

'She used to. In the old days. Not any more. I don't know why. The hormones perhaps? The cares of motherhood? She's

147

much more cautious than she used to be. Downright suspicious most of the time.'

'I wonder why.'

'Can't think. I suppose I've given her a hard time. I've lost all her money as well as mine. I stick to the stock market now.'

'You ought to buy Premium Insurance.'

'It's a dog, isn't it?'

'There's going to be a takeover.'

'Gosh. How do you know?'

'The board has had secret meetings with the buyer.'

'How on earth do you know that?'

'My messenger told me. He knows people at Premium.'

She expected him to laugh and slap his knee and pat her on the head. But the light of hope came into his eyes and he put his arm round her.

'One day I'm going to make it, Liz. I promise.'

She pursed her lips and peeked her tongue out upside down. She felt him shudder as if she had touched a nerve-end.

'Let's go inside,' he said, half lifting her.

'What about my quarterly presentation?'

● ● ●

'Morning, Lizzie.'

'Morning,' said Liz, running her fingers through her hair.

'You're looking good today, Lizzie.'

'Feeling good too, Lizzie,' said Liz, tightening her floppy bow tie and adjusting the visitor's pass clipped to her top pocket so it was exactly horizontal.

'A bit nervous? A touch of the old butterflies is a good thing. Keeps you sharp. You can handle him. He's no smarter than you are, Lizzie. Keep your wits about you and you'll be OK.'

'Be natural, Lizzie. Feminine but not sexy.'

She was feeling only slightly nervous as she rode up in the lift to the top floor of Dividend House, the West End headquarters of the Dividend Group. She had spent the weekend, at intervals, going over the accounts with Harry. They had picked every nit out of the accounts with the finest of fine-toothed lice combs. She

148

was prepared, poised, confident. In tiny writing in the margins of her copy she had written explanations for all the entries and reasons for the two or three obvious changes between this quarter and last quarter. On the back page she had jotted down the essential stand-bys of a board presentation, the decoy, the red herring, the spurious problem and its spurious solution. Not that she thought she would need them. She looked forward to a pleasant chat about the generalities of the financial markets with Wheeler in his chrome and glass office, a quiet drink and perhaps a spot of lunch before heading back to the City.

'Remember he's an ordinary little man, Lizzie. A successful, rich and important ordinary little man but still an ordinary little man. I bet his bathroom at home's like this . . .'

The inside of the lift was panelled with smoked glass mirrors illuminated with yellow pea bulbs in the ceiling, which was also mirrored. Liz was not alone. She was surrounded by other Lizzies, murky and fragmented. In the corners she could see, darkly through the glass, an infinite regression of identical Lizzies, a gynaecocracy of Lizzies stretching back through time, elegant, poised, self-confident, erect, well-groomed, dressed in a dark blue interview suit. She waved and the line of Liz's waved back, drilled like a line of guardsmen, wishing her luck. Encouraged, the last of the line gave them a confident smile, threw back her shoulders and stuck out her chin and stepped out of the lift at the top floor. The doors closed on all the other Lizzies and they were taken back down.

She was met by a beautiful young woman in a dark grey career suit. With her was a man in his early thirties, everything about him from the Next mail-order catalogue except his round, jowly face and his pot belly and his soft, pink, fingers. Under the artificial tan his face was deathly white. His permed hair had gone limp and there were beads of moisture on his balding temples. He looked as though he had been thrown from a horse or turned down for a gold card. He pushed past Liz without waiting for her to come out, dropped his calfskin executive case, personalized with gilt initials and a Concorde tag, ripped off his visitor's pass, threw it viciously on the floor and headbutted his reflection in the back wall. A myriad corporate executives banged heads all round him.

149

'I say,' said Liz, hopping out between the closing doors, 'are you all right?'

If there was a reply it was swallowed by the rubber-edged jaws of Leviathan closing on the despairing victim, already downwardly mobile.

'What's the matter with him?' she asked the beautiful young woman. She shrugged.

'Quarterlies,' she said, as if it explained everything, the male equivalent of the monthlies perhaps. 'Quarterly review. The hung, drawn and quarterlies we call them.'

The beautiful woman's job description included making coffee, answering the telephone and making photocopies, but her primary task was to meet visitors at the lift and lead them down the long and narrow carpeted corridor in a stately conga, showing off her pert little bottom, to the chrome and smoked glass doors of the executive suite. The walls were decorated with photographs, framed in aluminum, from the front of the Dividend Group Annual Report and Accounts. Groups of happy smiling people posed in front of office blocks and housing estates and dust carts and oil rigs and computer screens. Some of them were obviously employees, in crisp new uniforms and caps and hard hats, others were contented customers. Like the buildings behind them they were as nice and clean as a bright new pin. This was a people company, the pictures said, it's not bricks and mortar and machinery and money we care about but the people who work for us and who we work for: people, people, people, happy smiling people.

Unlike on her first visit, when Wheeler was interviewing her for the job, she was not ushered straight into the office with the white leather armchairs and the cocktail cabinet behind the Canaletto, sit down, have a drink, what will it be? The receptionist showed her into a small, windowless room furnished with a round chrome and glass table, half a dozen chrome and black vinyl chairs, and closed the door on her. The hessian walls were decorated with photographs of smiling dustmen in pristine uniforms posing proudly in front of their Garbage Gorger trucks. She opened her old leather music case and took out the accounts. There were three sets, bound in fancy brown plastic covers with spines like rows of pointed teeth. She knew them inside out. She had pored over every single figure, including the date and the page numbers in the top right-hand corner. She had read each word backwards to make sure there were no spelling mistakes, she had checked each copy three times to make sure there were no pages missing. But here, in this windowless, airless room, they looked completely alien. She felt, with an onrush of panic, as if she had never seen them before. They had taken on a life of their own.

The figures, typed on paper, bound in a book, were all that really mattered. The number for Fixed Assets did not relate to chairs and tables and computers and waste-paper baskets and her weeping fig and Nora's card file. It related only to the number for Long-term Liabilities on the other side of the page. The number for Cash did not relate to the three-month Barclays Certificate of Deposit, watermarked with an eagle, that Norman Foxwell had bought last Tuesday morning and had had delivered to Eddie Fly that afternoon by their messenger. It related to the number for Deposits under Short-term Liabilities on the other side of the page. Only the numbers connected, only the numbers made sense, only the numbers had pattern and logic and meaning, Assets equal Liabilities, Gross Profit less Tax equals Net Profit . . . The people and things had faded away into the past, forgotten, a tissue of confused impressions and half-formed memories.

The beautiful young woman came to fetch her. 'Mr-Wheeler-will-see-you-now-would-you-care-to-come-this-way-please,' she intoned in management suite singsong. Liz shuffled her papers into the music case and followed her across the reception area to the boardroom. This was furnished in town hall traditional with a long, narrow oak table and tan leather chairs with the Dividend Group logo embossed on their tall backs. Percy was sitting in the centre of the long side facing the door on a throne with a higher back than the others and arms that prevented him pulling it close to the table. He sat on the edge of his seat, hunched up with his elbows on a blotter, his shiny grey suit perfectly tailored but apparently not in touch with his body, like a suit of armour. On his right sat Harry, lounging back with a sheaf of papers as if he were studying the racing form. She caught his eye and he raised an eyebrow. On Percy's left sat austere Mr Spight the Finance Director, large head and thin body, looking grim in dark blue suit and dark blue tie infected with measles spots, poring over a massive tome of computer print-outs spilling out of their blue plastic covers. He looked in acute need of an indigestion tablet. Next to him, identically dressed, was a fresh young man with pink cheeks, sitting bolt upright, as if allowed for the first time to join his parents' dinner party. At one end of the table sat a grey-haired woman in a cream dress with shorthand pad and pencil poised. At the other end was a slide projector trained on a screen suspended from the ceiling. Percy looked Liz in the eye, expressionless, and pointed to the chair immediately opposite him.

'Sorry, I didn't bring the snaps,' said Liz, nodding at the screen and broadcasting her most charming smile. It fell on stony faces. Harry looked at his fingernails. She opened her music case and took out the three booklets. 'You've all seen the accounts, haven't you?' she asked. Spight pressed his lips together as if he was forcing a belch. Percy continued to look at Liz, expressionless, waiting for something. 'Good. Any questions?' said Liz.

All except Percy looked down at the table in front of them. No-one moved. Liz wriggled on her chair and made a loud squeaking noise on the leather. She seemed to be missing something. She felt she was the only one without a script. Finally Percy spoke, not in the confiding, nasal Midlands drawl Liz was used to but in a thin, icy monotone, full of menace.

'Miss Goodman. You are here to present the accounts to the finance committee appointed by the Board of Directors. You are here to present them in such a way that there are no questions. You are here to demonstrate to the full and complete satisfaction of the Board that the company it has entrusted to your management is meeting the performance objectives laid down for it.'

'Right,' said Liz, 'you want the full dog and pony show.' Thank God she had done her homework with Harry.

'Exhibits?' asked Percy, holding out his hand. Liz handed him two of the booklets. Percy kept one and handed the other to the young man. Spight heaved over the pages of his print-out and picked up a sharp pencil. Liz opened her copy of the accounts and for the first time felt the clammy, spine-tingling clutch of fear.

'Er, right, let's start at the top, er Cash . . .'

If the accounts had seemed like independent, alien things in the waiting-room, here they were objects whose existence she had never even dreamed of before. The pages were thick and heavy and stuck together when she tried to turn them. They were not in the order she remembered them. The numbers had got transposed, turned upside down. The words made no sense. Her mouth felt full of novocaine with thick tongue and swollen lips and dry throat. They let her have her say, stumbling and confused. She looked to Harry for moral support but he was doodling with a pencil. Then judge Wheeler nodded to prosecutor Spight who, in calm and modulated tones, tore her evidence to shreds. There was no animosity in his words, no passion, only a meticulous attention to detail and a cold, remorseless patience acquired in years of ticking off, adding up, searching out, tracking back, checking through, the frustration and resentment and boredom of the wasted auditing years of his articled youth transmuted into clinical detachment and forensic indifference.

But the worst was yet to come. Hanged by herself, drawn by Spight, Liz was now ready to be quartered by Wheeler. Behind his glittery gaze, beneath his querulous brummy, rising in pitch as he became more heated, boiled rage. It was not directed simply at Liz's incompetent presentation, her shortcomings as a manager, her inadequacies as a businesswoman. It was directed at her very presence in the heart of the Dividend Group. Percy had shaped the company in his own image. It was founded on the virtues of self-respect, self-reliance, self-interest, self-motivation. Those who out of ignorance or malice or stupidity denied these self-evident truths had no place in the Dividend organization . . .

At one stage during Wheeler's tirade Liz contemplated telling Wheeler to stuff it and walking out of the room. There were sound practical reasons why she did not, such as not wishing to be unemployed. But was it worth this? Was it worth being bullied by this little man whose only achievement in life, whose only claim to attention and respect and admiration, was the accumulation of large amounts of money?

'Are you clear about this?' said Wheeler, finally. All those on his side of the table nodded. Liz tried to catch Harry's eye but he was still examining his fingernails, the tips of his ears bright red. Liz struggled to find something to say, not that it would make any difference. She was perspiring, her hands felt clammy, her stomach churned, she felt her face burn. She expected to feel anger and indignation but instead was surprised by a much stronger, rawer, and pleasurable emotion that took her back to childhood. Since then she had forgotten about it, but now it came flooding back: the mixture of shame and humiliation and subservience when she had been shouted at by teachers, smacked by her father. It was the delicious sensation of being subject to authority.

'Right,' she heard herself say. 'What do you want me to do?'

'I want the bottom line doubled by the end of the next quarter.'

'But rates are falling, sterling's rising, there's nothing happening in the markets . . .'

'Cut costs. Cut waste. Cut overheads,' said Wheeler, his voice grating like steel shears.

'How . . .'

'What's your biggest cost?'

Liz fumbled for the accounts and found the profit and loss statement.

'Telephones.'

'Look again.'

'Magazine subscriptions?'

'Bah,' said Wheeler, 'you'll be telling me toilet paper and the Christmas dance next. Your biggest cost is people. Cut them.'

'We don't have enough to cut. They're all essential.'

'Nobody is essential. Cut.'

'This is a people business.'

'Exactly. And what costs us money? People. People's salaries. People's national insurance. People's benefits. People's sick pay, pensions, holidays, cars, luncheon vouchers, toilet paper, soap, stationery, pens, pencils, waste-paper baskets, a hundred and fifty square feet of floor space at fifty pounds a square foot, personnel officers, administration. It's people who are sucking us down. People who are bleeding us dry. Give me that.' He reached over the table and snatched the booklet out of Liz's hand. He turned to the organization chart at the back. 'Look at all these people. What do they do all day? I'll tell you. They cost us money.' He stabbed his finger at the page. 'Here. Chief Dealer. Norman Foxwell. What does he do to justify his existence?'

'He's the Chief Dealer.' She fumbled for a more comprehensive job description.

'And he's got an assistant. Why does a little shop like yours need two dealers?'

'To keep track of the deals . . .'

'They've got a computer haven't they? Let me tell you something, Miss Goodman. When personal computers came in they were going to make us more efficient. Everyone said buy me a computer and we can cut down on the people. So what do we have? The computers *and* the people.'

'I'll transfer his assistant then.'

'Why do that? Just get rid of one of them. Foxwell. He costs us more.'

'Norman's fifty-two.'

'There you are. Early retirement. It will reduce our pension cost too.'

'He's in the middle of a study for me.'

'Study? What sort of study?'

'A relationship analysis. For a business plan.'

'We have a business plan, Miss Goodman. It is to make more profits next quarter than this quarter. That's all we need to study.'

'But . . .'

'Foxwell has to go, Miss Goodman,' threatened Percy. He stared at her. 'And if he doesn't, someone else will.' He looked at his watch and tutted. 'Who's next?'

'Er, Dividend Car Rental,' said the eager young man, quick as a flash, on the ball, sharp as a tack.

'Send him in. Thank you, Miss Goodman.'

She stood up to go and looked at Harry, who lowered his eyes.

• • •

Eddie knew something was up when he went into Liz's office and saw three volumes of the procedure manual open on her desk and the other three heaped on the floor beside her chair. They covered everything from the organization chart (A01) to the design of application forms for season ticket loans (Z34). They were revised every three years or so and, according to procedure V23, constantly updated. Yet they had as much relevance to what actually happened in real life as a timetable on a bus stop. Procedure manuals were meant to be written, not read. Their function was to provide a tick on the auditor's report in the section marked 'Written Procedures Established'. The volumes, bound in numbered sets of loose-leaf leather binders, adorned shelves in the offices of the general manager and the head of administration, and were referred to only slightly more frequently than the collected works of Victor Hugo and Thomas Carlyle which adorned the bookcase in the dining-room.

He closed the door and walked round beside her to see what she was reading. M012 Employees, Holiday Pay, Administration of. She swept her dishevelled hair from a care-lined forehead.

'Can I help?' he asked.

'No you can't,' she snapped. 'Sorry, Eddie.'

'Yes, Miss Goodman.'

'Liz.'

'You won't find anything useful in the procedures.'

'Everything but what I need,' she said, slapping the book with her open hand.

'Funny that, isn't it? They never have shrively toes in the medical dictionary either. It's the commonest ailment among messengers, especially on humid days. It causes a lot of anxiety, I can tell you.'

She slammed the procedure manual shut with a bang.

'Are you sure I can't help?'

Liz looked at him, through him, and shook her head. 'I don't think so. Thanks, Eddie,' she sighed, swivelling her chair round to contemplate the venetian blinds.

● ● ●

'What's going on?' asked Eddie in Nora's office. 'She looks like she's come back from a funeral.'

Nora contemplated the middle fingernail of her left hand, emery board at the ready. 'She's been like that ever since she came back from the quarterly meeting yesterday,' she complained. 'I don't know what's got into her.'

'I'd take away her letter-opener.' He gave his impersonation of ritual disembowelling. 'Keep your ears open. There's something going on.'

• • •

It was Eddie's open ears that discovered what was afoot. That afternoon he was at his desk in the post-room, sorting confirmations for mailing, when he saw the switchboard light button flash on under the number of Liz's private outside line. This line by-passed Nora's extension and, in theory, the switchboard. A decent bottle of twelve-year-old malt to the telephone engineer at Christmas had corrected this intolerable disregard for the head messenger's responsibilities for effective communication. He picked up the receiver, holding his palm over the mouthpiece.

'. . . I wonder if you could help me out . . .'

'Help? What sort of help?' Eddie recognized the precise, diffident voice of Mr Spight, the Group Finance Director.

'It's about how we handle staffing changes. It came up at our meeting yesterday.'

'We expect the subsidiaries to run their own businesses.'

'There are aspects . . .'

'You're the chief executive, aren't you?'

'Absolutely, but . . .'

'But what? We're just the holding company. Are you telling me you can't take decisions about your own company?'

'Of course not. But you wouldn't have me contravene corporate policy, would you?' Eddie stifled a yawn at the ritual banter, stag-butting he called it, like adolescents jostling in the playground, that characterized conversations between corporate executives. He waited for them to get to the point. When the point came he was wide-eyed, wide awake.

'It's about redundancy procedures. What the package is, that sort of thing. We've never had any head office guidelines.'

'Not the sort of thing we shout from the rooftops,' admitted Spight, grudgingly, 'You'll have to talk to the head of Human Resources.'

'Can you transfer me?'

Eddie listened to their conversation and waited until she had hung up before replacing his own receiver, so she would not hear a click on the line.

• • •

Word began to spread. Nobody spoke the victim's name but somehow, from scraps of information collected and disseminated, it got into the air. At first it was nebulous apprehension, drifting through the office like a cloud of invisible viruses circulated by the air conditioning. Slowly it took shape: a vague, scarcely perceived ectoplasm of rumour, winding, twisting, forming into the protoplasm of speculation; there'll be changes mark my words, moves, cuts, reductions, until, suddenly, the solid fact was there for all to see. Norman was for the chop. One of the few who did not see it was Norman himself. He carried on oblivious of the fate in store. It was as if he had cancer or AIDS and no-one had the courage to mention it. People were cheerful in his presence, which they avoided if they could. Some who had not spoken to him for months started talking about foreign holidays, the pleasures of gardening, new banks that had announced they were setting up in the City. The colleagues he spoke to every day were cautious, embarrassed, too busy to chat.

• • •

At ten to five Norman was putting his ornaments away in the drawers of his desk when his phone rang. It was Nora. Could he step along to the General Manager's office please? Norman scowled and looked at the clock, ten minutes to five, what a nerve, still, it couldn't be anything important at this time. He took off his broken suede slip-ons and put on his Houndsditch Warehouse Allweather City Slickers, shiny as galoshes under the light patina of dirt, grunting with the effort of bending down into the well under the desk. He took off his woolly cardigan and put it carefully on the hanger behind him, fastening the two leather buttons that remained out of the six with which it was originally provided, to keep its shape, if the amorphous glob to which it had

158

degenerated could be called a shape. He put on the tired grey jacket, shook down his shirt cuffs and hitched up his trousers, making all these preparations not for the interview with the General Manager but so that he could go straight from the management suite to the lifts. He took his gabardine flasher's mac with him, to leave on one of the chairs in reception. Foxy Louise and Fat Mona looked up at him and then at the clock as he went past.

'Early night Norman?' said Mona.

'Got to see the big white chief,' he said in a glum voice.

'Taking her out for a drink, are you?' chirped Louise and then looked at Mona, wishing she had kept her mouth shut.

● ● ●

'Hel-low Norman,' said Liz cheerfully, standing up. She held her arm out straight, fingers outstretched, so Norman thought she wanted to shake hands until he realized she was pointing to the visitor's chair. Norman's heart sank. It wasn't a quick in and out, he was going to miss his train. He sat down on the edge of the chair, feet and knees together, hands on his knees, ready to run as soon as Liz gave the signal.

(Oh Gosh he's taken his woolly off and put his jacket on, he knows this is a formal meeting, he knows, he's sitting on the edge of the chair waiting for the worst, he looks so seedy and beaten already, how can I do this to the poor little shit, don't forget, I mustn't knock his confidence, it's the job we're getting rid of not the man.)

Liz sat bolt upright behind her desk, playing here's-the-church-and-here's-the-steeple-open-your-hands-and-there's-all-the-people, and don't forget we're a people company.

'How are things, Norman?'

Norman's heart sank. What a time for a confidential chat, a manager's heart-to-heart. She must have been on a course. Let's all relate to each other. I'm OK you're OK. Management by motivation, pestering us a minute a day, prowling round our desks, asking questions. Fine, it only lasts a couple of days until they go back to their old ways but why does she have to start at

159

five o'clock? The cats will be prowling outside the kitchen window, the dogs waiting by the door, the turtles scrabbling in their tank, the budgies pecking at their empty dishes, all his babies waiting for their dinner.

'I'm getting on well with your special project, Miss Goodman.' It was true he had made progress. He had drawn a brand-new pocket file from stationery and labelled it 'Relationship Profile'. He had photocopied the first five pages of Livery's nephew's report and stuck them in.

'Good. You've been here a long time, Norman. Since we opened for business.'

'And never missed a day since.'

'Super record. Super. You've been doing a terrific job.'

'Thank you.'

'You've been a lynchpin of the organization.'

'I've done my best.'

'You've got a lot to offer, Norman.'

'Very kind, I'm sure.'

'A bright future.'

Norman felt a click somewhere in the back of his head, a tremor in his bowels. This wasn't a pep talk, this wasn't the result of reading some damfool management book, this was a real talk, a serious talk, his future. The special project was only a beginning. He was being promoted. After all these years, head down, fair day's work, no fuss, no bother, never late, never missed a day, he had come to his reward. He told the young ones, desperate for advancement, ambitious, job hopping, it's the tortoise who finishes first. I shall die in honour, my days like a palm tree's for number.

'You're a very marketable person Norman, someone of your skills and experience.'

Buying everybody drinks would be expensive, never mind, it didn't happen very often, and the first month's pay-rise would take care of that.

'Have you ever thought of other jobs?'

'I've been very happy where I am.'

'Great.'

What job? Was Larry moving on? Leaving? Oh Lord, the

computer, the damn thing scared him to death, he left it alone, never touched it, he wasn't like Larry, he didn't understand computers, even on the keyboard he was all fingers and thumbs, Louise would have to help him out.

'There's a lot of scope these days for people with experience and common sense and a bit of initiative.'

Administration? Was Freda leaving? They wanted a steady hand on the wheel, don't rock the boat, stick to policy and procedure, the mature approach.

'The problem is, Norman, er, that, er . . .'

Fifty-two years old and he thought he was past it, washed up, dead end, waiting for retirement, and here he was being promoted. He would write to his son in Vancouver. If only his mother was alive to tell.

'. . . we're having to cut back and we're reorganizing the dealing operation, company policy, and consolidating it and, er . . .'

How much? It had better be a decent rise.

'I'm afraid we're having to make you redundant.'

A thousand a year? About seven hundred after tax, fifteen pounds a week, that would come in handy. What did she say?

'Redundant?'

(There it was, out on the table, the worst was over, a nasty moment, not nearly as bad as she thought it was going to be, once you'd done it a couple of times it was probably a piece of cake, don't know what the fuss was about really, the next time she wouldn't beat around the bush.)

'But my project? My report?'

'I found I didn't need it after all.' She picked up a large white envelope and handed it over the desk. 'There's all the technical stuff. I don't think you'll have any reason to complain, you'll find we've been pretty generous, one month's pay for each completed year of service. That's ten months. Not so bad eh?'

'Ten years.'

'To the end of this week. There's some holiday pay as well.'

Norman's face had gone very pale. He sat hunched in his shabby grey suit looking down at the envelope in his hands, struggling to find something to say. Liz had expected to feel sorry for him, expected to feel embarrassed and guilty and glad she was not on the receiving end, which she did. But she was also surprised by another stronger, rawer, more pleasurable emotion. As well as sympathy she had a heady, exciting sense of power over this little man. It was the delicious sensation of imposing her authority.

He stood up and held out his hand, looking her in the eye. 'Thank you, Miss Goodman,' he said quietly, turned round and left her office. For the first time since she had joined Dividend she felt she was a real manager. In charge. And she was beginning to like the feeling. She was still wallowing in it when Eddie came bursting in.

'You can't do it.'

'What can't I do, Eddie?'

She was precise and efficient. Her desk was clear except for the file she was reading. Her hair was neatly combed back over her head. The ashtray was empty and she was chewing gum. He stood in front of her desk.

'Fire Norman.'

She looked at him like a mind-reader's stooge.

'Why can't I fire Norman?'

'He's been here ten years. He'll never get another job.'

'That is irrelevant.'

'He knows the accounting system backwards. It'll fall apart without him.'

'Mr Chivers is perfectly competent.'

'Larry only knows how to work the computer. The system is a white elephant. Norman knows all its wrinkles. He's the one who sweeps up behind. Larry only sits on top and pokes it now and then.'

'We've got procedures.'

'Hah,' said Eddie, even he was lost for words at her ingenuousness, and again, 'Hah.'

'I have let Norman go because his job is redundant. That is my decision. As a person I regret it but it's my job to run this company efficiently. It is my prerogative. Managers have the right to manage.'

'Who put you up to it?'

'How dare you?' she blazed.

It was time to try a different tack. He went round her side of the desk and sat back on it, facing her. She frowned at his familiarity.

'Sorry, Liz. Let's not get het up. Let's discuss this reasonably.'

'There is no trade union or staff association in the office. There's nothing to discuss, Eddie, especially with you. You are the messenger.'

'You're making a big mistake.'

'You're making the mistake, Eddie.'

'You can't do it on your own.'

'Eddie, let's get one thing straight. The staff look to me to provide firm leadership. Even if it means some of them have to fall by the wayside the majority will thank me for it. If this organization is not efficient and productive and successful we'll all be redundant.'

'The greatest good for the greatest number.' He smiled, although there was little merriment in the puckered corners of his mouth.

'Perhaps.'

One last try. 'Liz . . .'

She stood up, sending the chair clattering back against the venetian blinds behind her.

'I am not Liz. I am your General Manager. Now if you will leave my office I have work to do.'

'Just one . . .'

'If you don't get out now I shall fire you as well.'

'What for? You have to give me a verbal warning and a written warning first.'

'Insubordination.'

'I've disobeyed no orders.'

To prove it he buttoned his jacket and left the office. He stomped through the management suite and reception and into the post-room where he punched his palm and looked out of the window and slammed his cupboards shut. He had made a serious error. He had confronted management. The first rule of dealing with management is to agree. He had backed her into a corner. He should have sounded her out first, found out if it was her decision or it it came from above. With authority you finessed, you weasled, you manipulated and manoeuvred, sniped and ambushed and sabotaged, like a guerrilla, always avoiding the pitched battle.

Carol came in and stood behind him as he stared out of the window. 'You're wanted in the back office, Eddie,' she said.

'What for?' he said wearily.

'What's got into you all of a sudden?' she asked, putting her hand on his shoulder. 'Norman?' He nodded. 'There's nothing you can do about it.'

'If it was Goodman's doing we might be able to do something. It would be internal. But it's not. She's only been here a month. Someone's put her up to it.'

'She's the boss.'

'So?'

'She's in charge.'

'Carol, this is serious. We can't afford romantic delusions. We have to be realistic.'

'What do we have a General Manager for then?'

'Why do we have a Queen? Why do we have a Lord Mayor? You think they take decisions? They're figureheads, Carol. Human beings need someone to grovel to. They take orders like everyone else. If you want something done you have to look for who's pulling the strings. And it's not Goodman.'

'Mr Wheeler?'

'Could be. But not necessarily. Someone pulls his strings too.'

'It's not as bad as that. Come on. Norman wants you in the back office. And cheer up. You'll make everybody miserable.'

'Cheer up? What am I going to say to Norman? He's wondering what he's done. How can I tell him it's what he hasn't done. He hasn't bought a new suit in years, he hasn't made work for himself, he hasn't sucked up, he hasn't looked busy, he hasn't done unnecessary overtime, he hasn't played the right game. So he gets the bullet. Liquidated.'

'Don't take it so personal, Eddie.'

'That's what they tell you. It's not personal. It's the job that's going. And it wasn't personal to them. For them you're just a line on a staff list. But it is personal. It's personal to every single one of us.'

'Come on Eddie,' she cajoled, and slipped her hand through his arm.

'You're right. It doesn't help to get upset. It's an ill wind. I'll get Norman on Mrs Mackerel's books. When Goodman goes on holiday I'll have him back at his old desk as a temp. Then he can threaten a case at the industrial tribunal for wrongful dismissal, as the job is necessary after all. She'll have to reinstate him. Or give him compensation as well as his redundancy.'

'You old fixer.'

He thumped his fist again. It was little consolation. With heavy heart he allowed her to lead him to the back office.

'Eddie,' shouted Norman as he went through the door. 'I have a feeling in my heart like new wine seeking a vent and bursting a brand-new wineskin. Join the party.'

Norman loomed above the partitions. He was standing on his desk with a litre of white in one hand and his tie in the other. He was red-faced and grinning. A girl's voice urged him to go for it and he did a little jig. Someone clapped. The contents of the base of a two-hole punch showered him in confetti. There was laughing and cheering.

'It's turned his brain,' said Eddie to Carol and rushed to the rescue. He found the dealing area packed with people. Norman skipped off his desk on to his chair and on to the floor and pushed through the revellers around him with his bottle and a polystyrene cup. He looked fifteen years younger, more like his actual age.

'You'll have to share with Carol,' he said as he filled the cup. 'You won't mind that, will you. She's a little darling.' He put his wine-bearing arm round her shoulders and kissed her on the cheek. Carol kissed him back.

'Norman. Are you all right?'

'Never been better. Cheer up, Eddie. This isn't a wake. It's a party.'

'Listen, Norman. I can get you a temping job. No problem.'

'Job? Who wants a job? I've got early retirement and a year's pay. I've been working for this all my life. I never thought I'd do it. I thought I was going to have to stick it out to the end. I've finished with jobs, Eddie. I feel like a Russian with an exit visa. I'm going to do something worthwhile with my life.'

Eddie looked into his bright eyes and tried to decide if it was the drink or the future that made them shine.

'What are you going to do?'

'The house goes on the market tomorrow. I'm going to Canada to stay with my son for a bit. And then I'm going round the world. Yippee!'

His yell brought a momentary silence on the gathering. Then, in a fruity baritone, he began the conga. Da-da-da-da-da DA DA. Tripping lightly on his toes he danced round the desk. Carol grabbed his waist. The spotty temp grabbed hers. Soon most of the staff were weaving round the desks and partitions. Da-da-da-da-da DA DA. Only a handful of people remained aloof. Larry Chivers was engrossed in his screen. Freda Grafton pulled on her coat and fled, grim-faced. Several did not want to miss their trains. The rest packed up their desks and joined the snaking dance out of the door into reception and cheered when Norman gave their destination as the Samuel Pepys where the drinks were on him. Eddie promised to follow when he had locked up for the night.

'Yippeee!'

Attracted by the noise Liz watched them go from the door of the management suite. Nora peeped over her shoulder.

'Morale seems pretty good tonight, Miss Goodman,' said Eddie.

● ● ●

'What's for tea?' asked Percy.

'Sausages and baked beans and potato croquettes.'

'Lovely. My favourite.'

He finished his tea and put the mug down on the breakfast bar. The motif of the kitchen decor was tropical. The tiles featured pine-apples, the wallpaper was woven from simulated palm leaves, the furniture was made of rattan. Nora opened a can of baked beans on an automatic opener.

'Any little jobs I can do for you, pet?' asked Percy, hubby for the night.

'You can put a new plug on the kettle. It's there, by the custard powder.' He poked around in the cutlery drawer for a screwdriver and sat at the breakfast bar humming to himself while she cooked the meal and told him about the pair of shoes she had taken back to the shop at lunchtime because the buckles were badly sewn and how she made a fuss and got her money back.

'You wouldn't like to do a little job for me would you, pet?' he asked. 'If I asked you to bring me a couple of files from the office you'd do that for me, wouldn't you?'

She dropped the grill pan on the bar with a clatter.

'You still think Georgie was up to something, don't you?'

'I've got to make sure. You know I have. To clear his name.'

She wiped the corner of her eye with the back of her hand and took a deep breath. He moved round beside her and put his arm round her waist. 'Nobody else will know. I wouldn't do anything to harm George's memory. It'll be our secret. Will you?'

She nodded. He went back to his work on the plug.

'I bought a boat today,' he mused.

'That's nice.'

'Bought it off Rookham. Got a good deal. I helped him raise his bail. It's moored in Antigua. He's got an apartment down there.'

'Are you buying that as well?'

'All the property's in his wife's name. He had the plane and the boats and cars.'

'The toys.'

'What?'

'Nothing.'

'They're no good to him now. They've taken his passport away.'

'Poor lamb.'

'Do you ever feel you'd like to get away from it all?' he mused.

'Oh yes, Percy.' She tried not to show her excitement.

'Just drop everything. Lie on a beach all day?'

'Oh yes, Percy.'

'I can't understand it myself. I'd get bored in ten minutes.'

She was glad she had controlled her excitement. She put the pan of sausages under the grill and came round to his side of the bar. She stroked the back of his podgy neck.

'Percy?'

'Mmm?'

'You wouldn't get into trouble, would you?'

'What do you mean?' he snapped, hubby no longer.

'All these City types going to jail. You wouldn't get mixed up in anything like that?'

'What do you think I am?' There was a menacing edge in his voice.

'Sometimes I'm not sure.'

'What's that supposed to mean?' Aggression joined the menace. She had touched a sensitive spot. Knowing she should change the subject, she took a deep breath.

'It's hard to know what you want. You've got everything. You can have anything. I wouldn't want to see you throw it away.'

His wiry body tensed and his hands balled into fists.

'What do I want? I'll tell you what I want. I want a bit of respect for a change. Starting with you.'

'But, baby . . .'

'I'm Chairman of a public company. I own ten per cent of the equity. Everything I've got I've got because I've earned it. You know what I started with? Nothing. You know what those City types started with? Silver spoons. The best schools. The best education. The fancy houses. The clubs. The old boy networks. I worked my way up the ladder while they stepped on the escalator. And if you think I'm going down the same snakes they're going down you're mistaken.'

'Baby . . .'

'Hard work. Graft. It isn't only who you know that counts. It's what you know. I've known the hard times. I've known what it is to have my foot stamped on when I stuck it in the door, I've know what it's like to be jeered at and looked down on, the brummie nouveau riche from the secondary modern, the little spiv, and still I've made it, on my own, because I wanted it and I still want it and no-one's going to stand in my way, you watch, do you think they'll change their tune when I'm Sir Percy and Mayor Percy and Lord Percy, when I can buy them all out, not on your life, they'll still snicker about me behind my back but in front of my face? Never. It'll be yes, Sir Percy and no, Sir Percy. That's what I want, I don't care what they do behind my back, it's to my face I care about.'

There were flecks of saliva in the corner of his mouth. He gripped her shoulders and shook her.

'B-a-a-a-by . . .'

168

'And if you think I'm going to let them find a way to do me down, drag me through the mud, trample me in the dust, you're very much mistaken. Oh they'd like to, I know. But I'll get them. I'll get them by the short and curlies. They'll dance to my tune.'

'B-a-a-a-by I'm so-o-o-rry . . .'

'You'll be sorry all right. Am I in any trouble indeed. I want some respect. Starting with you.'

She let him shake her although she was quite capable of picking him up and throwing him across the kitchen. He was not very strong and he soon got out of breath and she was an old hand at relaxing and thinking of something else and simulating entreaties for forgiveness and forcing some tears and all the rest of the charade.

'Let that be a lesson to you,' he panted. She pretended to snivel.

'Oh Percy, you're so masterful,' she whispered in his ear, and wondered what he was so afraid that someone would find out.

• • •

*LAST QUARTER*

Liz was hosting her first in-house lunch. The preparations had started on her second day when she had spent a couple of hours going over with Nora the list of guests who had been invited in the past year and the schedule for the coming three months. Nora picked out the few they did business with among the host of George Livery's friends, cronies, old colleagues, relatives, golf partners, bridge partners, chaps from the club, and those, the majority, whose only justification for being invited was the quality of the reciprocal entertainment. Like many of the City's venerable institutions, lunch, or luncheon as the traditionalists called it, was undermined by change, fashion and transatlantic business methods. And like them all it was fighting a gritty rearguard action.

'Things are changing, Nora, new ways. Big Bang, twenty-four-hour trading, mergers, mobility, new management styles. There's no place for the three-hour lunch any more.' Liz glowed with good news.

'Mister Livery said luncheon kept the wheels oiled.'

'Well-oiled. But I don't want all these spongers in my dining-room. There has to be a point to them, Nora, I'm not running a social club. I'm all for the ebb and flow and cut and thrust of lively business conversation but it has to have a theme, like the future of the nuclear industry or what the deutschmark's going to do.'

The theme of her inaugural lunch was how well Elizabeth Goodman had done for herself. She invited Warwick Kingmaker and her former boss from the high street bank and David's boss from the Merchant Bank of Switzerland and the manager of the broker they did most business with. Nora phoned their secretaries, sent out the confirmation cards with a little map printed on the back, put the names in the diary, checked in the guest book if they had been before and, in the case of Herr Löffli, who had, in the menu book to see what he had eaten.

Nothing remained to be done until the day itself. There was a buzz of excitement in the management suite from ten o'clock. It began with Lucy coming in to discuss the menu. She sat with sharpened pencil poised, her mouth twisted into a wavy thin line, as if the very mention of food was abhorrent to her.

'Scallops in butter and madeira sauce, goose in calvados with dauphin potatoes, creamed broccoli, petits pois, tossed salad with avocado, cream caramel or mango pavlova, cheese.'

'Bit rich isn't it? Couldn't we have something a bit more nouvelle?'

'I'll give you a couple of prawns and a lettuce leaf, see how your guests like that.' Lucy fixed her with a glittering eye and smoothed her dress over her thigh. She was wearing scarlet snapdragons today.

'No, it's fine; sounds a bit heavy on the cholesterol, that's all.'

'That's what the men always say. Then they wolf the lot.'

'You won't mind if I peck at it, will you?'

'Mister Livery never held back.'

'And look what happened to him.'

'Are you accusing me of anything?' Lucy crackled.

'No, certainly not. Go ahead. That's fine. What about the wine?'

'Eddie looks after that.'

Lucy left looking pleased with herself, like Lucrezia Borgia after a planning session. She gave the menu to Nora to type on gilt-edged cards at the same time as the place cards and the seating plan. Years of experience had given Nora a courtier's nose for protocol and precedence.

● ● ●

Harry arrived an hour before lunch, elegant in medium grey flannel and plain shirt and striped tie and a purple rose in his lapel and a red one wrapped in tissue that he tried to keep hidden.

'What's the matter, Liz? You don't return my calls, you're never in, I've been going potty.'

She made an effort to transform the involuntary thrill on seeing him into invective. This was not the hostess who was going to imbue her guests with good humour and light-heartedness.

'Why didn't you warn me about the quarterly review? I felt such a fool,' she snapped.

'That's Percy. You got off light, old girl. He's usually worse than that. It wouldn't have helped to tell you. It would have made you nervous.'

'And where was the moral support you promised?'

'Gosh Liz, what did you expect me to do? You handled it beautifully. Token resistance followed by complete cave-in. That's the way to deal with Percy.'

She slumped back in her chair.

'I did what I was told. I fired Norman Foxwell.'

'Ah. The first time's the worst.'

'It was a nightmare.'

'Did he cut up rough?'

'He couldn't have been more thrilled.'

'Seriously?'

'Seriously.'

'So you made a right decision. What's wrong with that?'

'Can you imagine how I feel? What sort of manager does that make me? My staff can't wait to get fired.'

He leaned over the desk and put the red rose on her blotter. It might as well have been a memo to file for all the effect it had. 'Listen,' he said, 'I've got some news.'

'It had better be good.'

'Daff's leaving me.'

175

Liz closed her eyes and hoped he would interpret it as sympathetic dismay. She couldn't take any more complications in her life.

'Because of me?'

'Gosh no. She doesn't suspect a thing. It was the meditation.'

'She finally took off with the guru?'

'She wasn't meditating. She's been having an affair with a dentist in Godalming. She's moving in with him.'

'I'm sorry Harry. I really am.'

He shrugged and sighed.

'I knew it was coming. One usually does.'

'Stay for lunch,' she said. It was the only consolation she was prepared to offer.

'Can I? Thanks.'

'It must have been a blow.'

'It's all for the best. It's made me think.'

'Gosh,' said Liz.

She tried to find the sympathy she knew was in her somewhere. But this was the wrong place, the wrong time. She had the position report to go through and a new organization chart to draw and lunch to think about. Harry's marital problems did not belong in her office, even though she was one of them.

'Yes. It's made me think. About my whole life. The City's not for the amateurs any more. It doesn't owe us a living. I'm an endangered species. Like the lion and the meadow moth. If I carry on doing what I've always done I'll end up stuffed. I'm getting out.'

'You mustn't do anything impulsive Harry. I know it's a blow . . .'

'Hear me out. This isn't a new idea. I met a chap who runs courses for foreign executives who come to this country to work. Americans and Japanese mainly. How to handle the knife and fork, how to find your way round Harrods Food Hall, you know. Life in England. He owns a house in the country with a paddock and a pond and he teaches them how to shoot and fish. He wants me to buy it off him and live there and handle all that side of it. It's a great investment Daff . . . Liz.'

'Where is it?'

'On the M4.'

'On or under?'

'I'm serious. It's a paying proposition. You make the money from selling them the togs. The Japanese snap up the tweed plus-twos.'

'Harry, I think you ought to wait a bit. Let everything cool down. She may come back.'

He stood up and jiggled his hands in his trouser pockets.

'I don't want her to come back.'

She picked up a letter from her desk and gave it her full attention. Her hand reached for the phone. He reached over and gently put his hand on hers, resting on the receiver. He took the letter out of her other hand and turned it the right way up.

'You've got to think about the commitment, Harry.'

'It's for ever, Liz. I lo . . .'

'I mean the financial commitment.'

'I can do it. Thanks to you. Those Premium Insurance shares have gone up a quid in three days. I went in big. Options as well. Daff can have the house and I can pay cash for the other.'

'She'll get that too if she has a decent lawyer.'

'I put the shares in another name. She'll never find it. I can sniff this one, Lizzie. This is the one that's going to work.' He came round the other side of the desk. She swivelled her chair to look up to him.

'I want you to be a part of it, Lizzie. I want you to come in with me. Partners.'

'I don't think I'd be very good fitting Japanese for plus-twos.'

'I'll do that. You look after the garden.'

'Me? That's like putting a vegan in a butcher's shop.'

'This has given me a real leg-up. I've proved myself. I don't mind telling you now I was feeling trapped. Can you understand that, Liz?'

'About feeling trapped?'

'Nowhere to go. Do you see?'

'I see,' she said.

'All these years I've pottered along trying to be happy in the third team while other chaps got the good jobs and the money and the kudos. And now I'm making money and I've found you. A fresh start.'

He grasped her hands in one of his and with the other stroked

177

her hair, pressing her head to his chest. All men experience rebuff at some time in their lives, even those as beautiful as Harry. He misinterpreted the resistance in her neck and her attempts to extricate her hands and pressed his suit even harder. They would have been locked in this wrestling hold indefinitely had a peremptory knock on the door not been immediately followed by Eddie. He looked coldly on this tableau of office life.

'See?' said Harry. 'Feels better already, doesn't it? Nasty thing a crick in the neck. I should stay out of the draught.'

'Yes, Eddie?' glowered Liz.

'The wine for lunch, Miss Goodman,' said Eddie, reflecting back her glower with a polished shield of officiousness. 'There's a very nice '84 Bordeaux will go with the goose and I think you'll like the Muscadet with the scallops, crisp enough to cut through the sauce. I would think Muscatel rather than Sauternes with dessert and how about a tawny port with cheese?'

'I don't think so, Eddie.'

Eddie blinked. 'Beg pardon?'

'I don't think so. What else is there?'

'For the menu, nothing.'

'We've got nothing else?'

'Plenty but . . .'

'Where do you keep it? Stacked in boxes next to the boiler I'll be bound,' chipped in Harry, 'or do you run round to the off-licence?'

'Mr Livery was very particular about his wine . . .'

'I choose the wine from now on,' she said. 'Give me the list.'

'The register is in the cellar.'

She sighed and turned to Harry. 'Would you mind choosing the wine?'

'Gosh no. You've got a lot to think about. I'll get out of your hair.'

'Thank you, Harry. Show him the cellar please, Eddie.'

Silent and smarting, Eddie led the way out of the office and into the lifts and down to the basement and through the car park and down a narrow corridor to a steel door which he unlocked and threw open.

'Good Lord,' said Harry. 'Is this ours?'

178

Eddie did not deign to reply. Harry wandered like Aladdin through the warren of interconnecting arched cellars. There was a workshop with a fully equipped workbench, a stationery store with shelves loaded with reams and rolls and forms, a dead-file store with documents going back several years, a large alcove with a carpet and a couple of armchairs and a dartboard and a television and a video, storerooms full of furniture and pictures and boxes, and finally, in the deepest recesses of the basement, the wine cellar. From floor to ceiling one wall was lined with racks, carefully numbered, cork seals glowing in the subdued light like jewels, deep dark ruby red through scarlets and pinks and greens to opal white. The register was on a mahogany table beside tasting glasses and a large corkscrew. Eddie pointed to a thermometer on the wall. 'We're far enough from the boiler,' he said frostily.

'What's in there?' asked Harry, pointing to a mahogany cupboard against the far wall. Eddie opened it to reveal shelves of brown boxes, most of them with Havana in the label but a few representing Honduras and Jamaica and Brazil and Virginia.

'Mr Livery was very particular.'

Harry pulled out bottles at random and squinted at the labels, puffing dust off the more venerable.

'These would look good in the old Habitat wine rack,' he said. 'My father had a wine cellar like this, only bigger. The butler looked after it. Once a month the chappie from Peabody Wine called for a tasting.'

'Try the claret,' said Eddie, reaching for a bottle, 'it ought to breathe before lunch anyway.'

'Let me do that,' said Harry, taking the corkscrew out of Eddie's hand. 'It's important to do it right.'

He sipped the wine while he examined the racks, had another glass, and another. He poured one for Eddie.

'I say, Eddie, haven't I seen you before?'

'I'm sure. I've been with the company ten years.'

'I mean somewhere else.'

'Try the Saint Emilion sir.'

'Right. Don't get this in the wine box, do you?'

Harry browsed through the register while Eddie fetched an armchair and a tin of smoked oysters and some cheese crackers from the stationery store. They shared these over a Muscadet Ligoté and went back to the claret. Eddie reached into the back of the humidor, behind the Jamaicans.

'You ought to try these. Davidoff's Specials.'

'Thanks, Eddie,' said Harry, putting his feet up on the table while Eddie expertly trimmed the end off the cigar. 'This is the life, eh? Old man Peabody was a character. Always wore a morning suit. He came to see my grandfather in an old Rolls sitting in the dickey seat with the cases under cover inside. Sample this, Sir Harry. The good old days, Eddie.'

'For some.'

'The old manor house is a community centre now. Plonk in the middle of a housing estate.'

'What a shame.'

'Don't get me wrong. I don't stand in the way of progress. But why cover the old house in graffiti? What's happened to standard's? It's a yobbocracy, Eddie, bullies and bovver boys. Decent people get squeezed out.'

'Victims of the class war?'

'That's the word. Spot on. Exterminated by the proles. I say, this Beaune isn't bad.'

'It wasn't the proles. It was the bourgeoisie.'

'Bourgeoisie? The Frogs had nothing to do with it.'

'The bourgeois revolution created the economic and social conditions necessary for capitalism to function freely.'

'You know what my old man used to say to Peabody? I've got a Beaune to pick with you. Ha ha. B-E-A-U-N-E. Good eh?'

'They abolished the monopoly of legal rights of the privileged landed minority and created institutions which were not dependent on birth.'

'He liked his port too. Any port in a storm he used to say. Get that Eddie?'

'The former feudal class, deprived of power and property by the middle classes, were proletarianized.'

'What are you blathering on about, Eddie?'

'The revolution, sir.'

'What revolution?'

'The next revolution. When the working class replaces the

middle class by abolishing private property.'

'Are you a Trot, Eddie? Are you a red under the bed?'

'Do I look like one?'

'You sound like one. That stuff sounds great but it's all blather when you look at it. Damn good cigars these. You can't beat a Davidoff, that's a fact. Now let me tell you something about a good cigar . . .'

Eddie, perched on the desk, nodded and sipped and opened more bottles and kept Harry's glass full and listened to the life history of the tobacco leaf. When it was time to go up for lunch he steered Harry through the cellars to the car park. Waiting for the lift he brushed the brick dust off Harry's coat, where he had staggered against the wall and helped him fasten the top button of his shirt that seemed, to Harry's fumbling fingers, about three sizes bigger than its hole.

'Jolly good set-up. We'll do it again.'

'Yes sir.'

'Look, call me Harry when we're by ourselves. We're all democrats now aren't we? You said so.'

'Did I?'

'You know why your revolution will never work, Eddie?'

'No sir.'

'Because your average prole would rather be a watchemacallit.'

'Bourgeois.'

'It's nicer being a bourgeois than a prole.'

'Yes sir.'

Harry made several stabs at the lift buttons before Eddie could select the right one, with the result that they stopped at every floor. Each time the doors opened he lurched forwards against Eddie's restraining arm. On the fourth floor he got half-way out and fought the chomping rubber jaws until Eddie dragged him back in. He leaned back on the wall, breathing deeply, focussing hard on the numbers and counting them out loud. At the fifth floor Eddie had to hold the doors open and coax him out.

'Make up your bloody mind, Eddie.'

He tumbled through the door of the management suite as Nora was taking the coat of a small, dark, precise little man with rimless spectacles. She looked at him in dismay. His suit was decorated

181

with cobwebs and brick dust and cigar ash and evidence of his heroic tussle with the lift doors. His cheeks were flushed bright pink and there was a watery gleam in his eye.

'Löffli, you old Swiss Cheeseli,' he bellowed, pumping his hand and slapping him on the back. 'What a useless man for bun-fighterli. Skeleton at the feasterli. Anyway as you're here, come and have a drinkerli. We've had a bit of a head start so you can stop looking as though you're sucking a lemon and join the party.' He pushed Löffli ahead of him into the sitting-room, where the rest of the guests were waiting.

'Where have you been?' hissed Nora at Eddie, performing the clever trick of speaking through a mouth buttoned so tight that her lips had disappeared. This was not ventriloquism. There was no doubt where the voice was coming from. Behind her from the sitting-room was a crash of breaking glass and a guffaw from Harry. Rhoda scuttled out and into the kitchen and scuttled back with a sponge and a roll of kitchen paper.

'Not my fault,' said Eddie. There was another roar of merriment from the sitting-room. His day was getting better. He would take Carol out for a pizza to celebrate.

● ● ●

After he came back from lunch Eddie picked up a pile of reports and set off for the management suit. He went to the kitchen first.

'I've never been so humiliated,' said Lucy, slotting knives angrily into a block, ramming the hilts home like a practising matador. 'They had Rhoda drinking brandy Alexanders.' She pointed with a peeler at Rhoda sitting on a chair with her head back against the side of the fridge, legs splayed, conk aflame. 'She's the last one to encourage. She's thrown up twice.'

'She should lie down in the ante-room. That's the emergency sick room.'

'His lordship is in there,' she said, 'out cold. Serves him right.'

'Must have been a great lunch.'

'He'll need a new pair of trousers.'

'Did they debag him?'

'Rhoda was presenting the goose on the platter. Mr Simple

182

pinches Rhoda's bottom and she jerks round. 'That looks good,' says the American. The bird slides straight off the plate into Mr Simple's lap. 'Feels good too,' he says. And he plops it back with his hands.'

Eddie grinned.

'It's not funny,' she scowled, 'it set Rhoda off. She comes straight in here and downs a whole tumbler of sherry. She goes back and puts gravy on their salad and vinaigrette on the meat. There was nothing I could do. And the cream caramel. Don't talk to me about cream caramel.'

'Tell me about the cream caramel.'

'Here am I serving pavlova to Miss Goodman at one end of the table and there's Rhoda at the other serving Mr Simple out of the big dish.'

'Don't tell me that went over him.'

'Not him. She tilted the dish away from him and the bald one with the moustache got the syrup in his lap. He didn't notice until he stood up to go. You should have seen his face.'

Again Eddie found it hard to participate in the affront to Lucy's professionalism.

'They even had that Swiss telling dirty jokes. That was after the argument about how to chuck a bread roll.'

'There's lots of ways.'

'Not when they're loaded with petits pois. Nora's in a state. She had to clean them up to go home. You'd better get the steps out as well. My mango pavlova's all over the ceiling.'

'Perhaps you put too much madeira in the sauce.'

She wrenched open the dishwater and threw in a saucepan.

'The sooner they clog up their arteries the better. Good riddance.'

Eddie looked in the ante-room. Harry was spreadeagled on the sofa as if he had fallen from a great height – the top floor of Head Office for example. The satisfaction he felt was only an aperitif for the pleasure he anticipated in Liz's office. He adjusted the pile of reports under his arm and went in to test the temperature. From the titbits he had gathered from Lucy, and from those he saw for himself on the dining-room ceiling, and from the sight of Harry on the sofa, he expected it to be outside the temperate zone but was not prepared for the chill that greeted him when he went in. Liz stood up and fixed him in the eye, jaw set, knuckles white as they pressed down on the edge of her desk. Even Livery, famous for his Genghis Khan impersonations, could not have matched the repressed fury that she exuded. Eddie had planned to take the initiative by asking how lunch had gone, wide-eyed and innocent, but thought better of it.

'Why didn't you tell me about the cellar?'

'You didn't ask.'

'I want the keys.'

'But Liz . . .'

'I want the keys. And I want an inventory. Mr Simple tells me there's a fortune in wines down there.'

'He should know. He tasted most of them.'

'That was your doing.'

'You asked him to.'

'Let me get one thing clear, Eddie. I'm in charge here. Do you understand?'

He nodded. She was coming out in her true colours. Never confront the boss.

'I say, got an aspirin?'

If it was time for coming out in true colours Harry participated in various shades of green and white. His clothing too had become variegated in the course of the morning – brick, burgundy, portwine, avocado, olive, peagreen, caramel, cream and the indefinable hue of goose decorated his grey flannel suit. He stood in the doorway of the ante-room, gripping the door-handle and sucking in air through his nose as if it were the finest ozone. He examined the office with care, his eyes trying out various focal lengths to make sure that the evidence was indisputable, namely that the double vision in front of him indeed consisted of two people.

'Liz,' he said, 'wonderful lunch. Best ever.' He fixed his gaze on Eddie with the tentativeness of a blindfolded partygoer pinning the tail on the donkey. 'Haven't I seen you before?'

'He'll run you to the station,' said Liz crisply. 'Wait outside please, Eddie.'

He did as he was told and grinned at Nora on the way out. He fetched a step-ladder and a bucket and a cloth from the kitchen and went into the dining-room. He pulled the table to one side, set up the ladder and got to work on the ceiling. He wet the cloth and attended to a lump of meringue encrusted with a kiwi fruit. As he scrubbed he dislodged a ceiling tile from its aluminium rail. The cavity between the tiles and the concrete floor above was full of cables and ducts and the sound of conversation. He could hear Lucy in the kitchen berating Rhoda and clattering plates. He could hear Nora talking on the telephone. And he could hear Liz and Harry as well as if he were standing in her office.

'. . . Liz, I want to apologize for lunch. It must have been something in the goose that upset me. I've been under a bit of stress the past few days. I know things got a bit out of hand in there. Everyone had a good time, you have to admit. I didn't think old Löffli had it in him. The Swiss are innoculated against that sort of thing at birth.'

'I did not have a good time. I had a very bad time. It was the sort of male behaviour that turns women into wimmin.'

'I don't get it. Women into women . . . ?'

'Forget it. I'm going to build a successful business here, Harry. I'm knocking this place into shape. I thought I could rely on you.'

'You can. One hundred per cent. I won't let you down.'

Eddie heard the farting noise as she flopped down into her swivel chair. He heard a sniff. He heard Harry say 'Here,' and the sound of her blowing her nose.

'Come away with me, darling. This isn't for us.'

'I want to finish what I've started here.'

Eddie listened hard. Harry must have gone round to her side of the desk. He had to strain to catch what they said.

'I've never been so embarrassed.'

'I'm sorry. I really am. Give me a little smile. There, that's better. Will you think about it?'

'All right.'

'Darling Lizzie.'

'Will you do something for me?' she sniffed.

'Mmmm?'

'Find out what Wheeler's up to.'

'And if I do?'

'I'll think about it. Now you'd better go.'

'Do that thing first.'

'What thing?'

'The thing with your tongue.'

'. . . Now go.'

Eddie replaced the tile and folded up the ladder. As he came out of the dining-room Harry came out of Liz's office and took a couple of deep breaths.

'The car's downstairs, Mr Simple.'

'Thanks er . . .'

'Eddie.'

● ● ●

Carol put the phone down.

'Was that you?' Freda's face appeared over the top of a moveable partition, wide-eyed with outrage. Seen for the first time it was an impressive sight, eyes staring, cheeks quivering, wire-wool hair electrified, smoke pouring from her nose. No-one forgot their first reprimand from Freda. Or their second. But after about twenty the effect was diminished. Outrage was second nature to Freda, a permanent state of dissatisfaction with her own and other people's performance. She was the only one who would not admit that her standards were unattainable. You always knew where you were with Freda, metaphorically pinned to the floor, and once, in the case of a petty thief in search of unattended handbags, literally.

'I should like a word, please, Carol.'

This was not Carol's first reprimand. After a week she was into double figures and knew what to expect. She had begun to enjoy them as she enjoyed encounters with her social worker. Anything was better than filing. She stepped behind the partition which delineated the extent of Freda's personal territory. Freda had gone back behind her desk but remained standing, gulping in smoke from a fresh Stuyvesant and stubbing out its predecessor in a heap of butts in her copper soup plate, re-igniting a few yellow nub-ends as she did so.

'Who was that on the telephone?'

'Dunno. Someone wanted Mr Chivers.'

186

'And you informed him that Mr Chivers had gone to the lav.'

'That's where I saw him go. Sorry. I should have said toilet.'

'You should not have said toilet, Carol, nor lav, nor loo nor gents. What do you say?' giving her one more chance of mitigation. Carol looked puzzled: indeed she was puzzled. It was yet another little mystery of working life to go with not being able to talk to anyone outside her section, or whistle or hum while she worked, or look over people's shoulders to see what they were doing, or have a coffee when she felt like it, or ask what the point of her job was. She had learned to look busy when Freda or Norman or anyone from outside was looking, to chant Dividend Investments can I help you? in a sort of rising singsong when she picked up the phone, to say 'Miss Goodman' or 'Management' in a hushed and reverent voice, to say 'Thanks Eddie' when he dropped a load of filing on her desk instead of 'Christ not another lot.' She sensed that the details of etiquette which she was discovering day by day obscured much deeper, significant differences between life at work and life outside. For a start you were always on the receiving end, but of what she was not sure.

'He's gone for a pee?' The stream of smoke from Freda's nostrils would have done credit to a real dragon, not just a human one.

'He's not here?' she added quickly, as a peace offering.

' "I'm sorry, he's at a meeting," is what you say, Carol,' fumed Freda.

'Who does he meet in the lav?' asked Carol, innocently.

Freda sucked on her cigarette, drawing the smoke down to her diaphragm. 'Do you want this job, Carol?' she demanded, part threat, part hope of a negative reply.

'Course I do. Wouldn't be here otherwise.'

'Then let me give you one word of advice. Only one. Attitude.'

'Attitude.'

'Attitude.'

'What's that supposed to mean?'

'You work hard in your own way and you do as you're told, I'll give you that. But your attitude is all wrong.'

'I still don't know what you mean by attitude.'

Freda sucked and puffed and snorted.

'You don't give the impression that what goes on here is very important to you.'

'How can I if I don't know what does go on? It's all a bloody big mystery to me. No-one I've asked seems to know either. Sort this, file that, add up the other. Dead boring. Chimps could do it. You don't learn anything. Nobody would do it if they didn't need the money.'

Suck. Puff. Snort.

'This is what I mean, Carol. Your attitude.'

'I do the work. What more do you want?'

Suck. Puff. Snort. The phone rang. Carol heard Nora say that Miss Goodman would see her now.

'We'll continue this conversation later, Carol, I have to go to a meeting.'

'So do I. I'm busting.'

When she came back from the lavatory Eddie was dropping a batch of papers into her in-tray.

'Cheer up, darling,' he said, 'it's nearly Friday.'

'It's nearer last Friday than next,' she grumbled. 'If I didn't need the money I'd tell that Grafton what I think of her.'

'What's she been on at you for this time?'

'I told somebody on the phone that Mr Chivers was on the lav. It's true. He's always in there. He must have prostate trouble.'

'Nah. He likes to be alone. He reads his computer magazines. Stick it out, darling. You'll get used to it.'

'I don't want to get used to it. You're lucky to get a job, they all say. I'd rather be in a squat sniffing glue.'

'Where does that get you?'

'Where does this get me?'

'It's work. We're working class. We work.'

'Nobody even knows my name. I'm the temp in filing.'

'I know your name.'

'You're the only one. How do you cope with it all?'

'You don't let yourself be exploited. Be your own boss. You do what they pay you to do and no more. The rest is for you.'

'That doesn't stop the way you're treated. There's that cow from the other office. She helps herself to the files as if I'm invisible. Never signs for anything. Real snot-nose.'

'Which cow is that, Carol?'

'I dunno. The bossy one.'

'Miss Goodman?'

'Not her. The other one in that office.'

'Big girl? Red lipstick? Dangly earrings?'

'Yeah.'

'What files did she take?'

'How do I know? She never signs for them.'

'She takes them away? For how long?'

'She hasn't brought them back yet.'

Eddie bit his bottom lip and frowned. There were no files lying around Liz's or Nora's office. And he had collected none from their out-trays.

'Listen, darling. Stick it out. I'll get you moved on to something else. There's a requisition for a telex operator. I'll get you trained up and we'll get someone else for this. But first I want you to do something for me.'

'Oh yeah?' She picked up an emery board and concentrated on her middle finger.

'There's a card index of all the files. I want you to go through every one and check it's there or that there's a sign-out card for it.'

'That will take me ages.'

'What else have you got to do? And if Nora comes back for more files make a note of which ones she takes. Will you do that for me?'

'Why?'

'Please. For me.'

'Nobody ever tells me why I'm supposed to do anything. What's all the mystery? And what's it to you anyway?'

'I don't know, Carol. Honest. I just like to keep an eye on things. I tell you what. I'll buy you a drink after work.'

'A cocktail?'

'If you like,' he said, making for the lavatory.

● ● ●

He had the uneasy feeling that ever since Livery died there had been something fishy going on, something swimming around in the depths which he knew nothing about. The journalist Bibber had called him three times since his first visit, trying to make an appointment. Eddie had put him off, not wanting to admit he was just the messenger and not the manager. But why was Bibber so persistent? Pensively he bent down and opened the door of the library, the cupboard where the Harpic and the soap and the toilet rolls were kept. Tucked at the back were back copies of *Playboy* and motorcycle magazines and racing papers. He took out the *Daily Mirror* and went into the middle cubicle, his favourite because the centre light was directly above it. He lowered the seat and his trousers and sat down. He flipped through the paper but could not concentrate. He noticed consciously for the first time details which he had always taken for granted – the two holes in the back of the door where the coathook had been unscrewed, the little blackened ashtray on top of the toilet-roll holder, the burn marks in the formica, the scratches around the screws in the lock where the screwdriver had slipped, the tracery of cracks in the blue plastic tiles beneath his feet, the six-inch gaps under the walls and the door. It was all so temporary. The structure in which he sat, so ordered and private, was nothing but sheets of chipboard and formica bolted crudely together, held up with a handful of thin little screws.

● ● ●

There was a goggle of tourists outside the Mansion House on the evening of Liz's first Lord Mayor's dinner. They would have been as surprised as Liz at how small and crowded the dark panelled entrance hall was, how unobtrusive the security, how narrow the stairs up to the reception room. They would have been as nervous in the waiting queue on the landing and one or two might have made the *faux pas* of offering their hand to a portly man in tails instead of whispering their names to him before he turned on his heel and shouted them out loud to three distinguished gentlemen standing in a line, the little one in the middle in a velvet suit with knee breeches and silk hose and a lace cuffs and lace jabot and the other two in white tie and tails. But none would have been so poised and elegant as Liz Goodman, who strode across to allow her hosts to welcome her into the halls of privilege and power.

As halls go they were certainly impressive. A lofty room,

brilliantly lit with massive crystal chandeliers and wall lights, creams and pinks and peaches, ornate plasterwork gleaming with gilt. It deserved a more colourful, more extravagant and joyful throng than the wake of black suits and white shirts standing in knots and gaggles, talking rates and yields and markets, the yoke of fiduciary responsibility lying heavy on their shoulders. Lone fish cruised among them, pretending they had friends on the other side of the room or standing disconsolate by the pillars, tended by subservient women with trays of drinks. Spouses were not invited to the Annual Mansion House Dinner of the Institutional Investment Dealers Association, INSIDA, and there were only a handful of women diners, aping the men in sober evening gowns. Liz had been careful to distinguish herself from the waitresses by flaunting a long gold lamé scarf.

'How did you get here?' demanded Percy Wheeler, looking up at Liz from inside a double-breasted dinner suit that looked as if it could have been wrapped round another half turn and buttoned at the back. His tie, in contrast, was a tiny black moth hiding from the light under his protective jowls.

Why did Percy Wheeler's clothes always look too big for him? Why did he look like a schoolboy on the first day of the year, a child dressing up, the last customer at the dress hire shop? It was certainly not the fault of his Savile Row tailors, who had dedicated their finest minds and most skilful craftsmen to the problem. His insistence on styles more suitable for a bigger man, compounded by his tendency to rise on the balls of his feet and puff his chest out and throw his shoulders back and lift his chin whenever he was in front of a mirror, may have exaggerated the tape measurements taken by the tailor, caused the rasping blue chalk to err on the generous side at fitting time, but could not have made more than half an inch of difference. Closer examination showed that although of generous cut his clothes fitted perfectly. She realized that their apparent voluminousness was an optical illusion in the eye of the beholder whose inner voice whispered that here was a man too little for his boots and determined to grow into them.

'I was invited,' she said, piqued. She did not reveal that the invitation was addressed to George Livery and that Nora had spent a considerable part of an afternoon on the phone having it transferred. Nor did Percy reveal a mental note to have his secretary call the Mansion House invitation office and have Goodman taken off the lists. The less visibility the doomed Dividend Investments had the better.

'How are things?' he asked, his mind not on the question, his eyes darting round the room in search of more important people to talk to. She had to nail him now as he would be lost for the rest of the evening, working the room until dinner was announced.

'Fine, fine. It's going to be very successful. No problems. What about you? Are you happy with Dividend Investments?'

'It's not making enough money. It's had poor returns. It's your job to increase them. The search for excellence.'

'What about the quality of its investments?'

Suddenly she became the most important person in the room. He turned to face her instead of standing alongside her.

'What's that supposed to mean?'

'The investment policy. The people we do business with.'

'Why? What have you heard?' All his attention was on her now. Although he was shorter than her he gave the impression he had grown and was looking down at her. The trick was to hold back his head and look down his nose, his eyes small and sharp and unhooded.

'Nothing. I thought I was responsible.'

'Responsible? What for? What have you done?'

'Nothing. I mean I'm in charge. That's why I wanted a full-scale review of our relationships . . .'

'That's not what I hired you for. We'll do that. It's a headquarters matter. You just run the business.'

'But that is running the business . . .'

'We'll hold a full review in six months time. Meanwhile leave the investments as they are. You concentrate on cutting costs. Make the operation efficient. Cut waste. Raise productivity. That's what I hired you for. Understand?' It was uncanny how he seemed to have grown. His belly had risen into his chest, he filled out his suit, his massive head seemed to tower over her.

'Well . . .'

'Understand?'

'Yes.'

He subsided to his normal size and looked round the room again. 'Get me a scotch and water, will you?' he said, 'champagne gives me the burps.' A lesser person would have run obediently off to find the bar, a greater one would have told him to get lost and find his own drink. Liz merely raised an eyebrow to one of the several waitresses who had been ogling from a distance and, when she bustled over, invited her with a subtle movement of the hand to take her Chairman's order. Percy, sensing the danger that in this environment he might be on even ground with his employee, excused himself and went to congratulate a new member of the Securities and Investments Board.

'Super to see you here,' said Harry Simple mellifluously into her ear, softly gripping her elbow. She felt the tremor behind the breastbone, the sensation of mild electric shock, that she expected now when she met him. He made his conventional evening dress looked raffish and elegant, as if he had was about to sit down to roulette instead of brown Windsor and overdone beef. 'The City at play,' he said and laughed as if it was the wittiest thing to be heard in the room, which, given the company, it probably was. She laughed gaily back. He didn't look over her shoulder all the time to see who he should really be talking to. He gave her the impression that she was the only other person in the room.

'The City at work you mean. Our boss Wheeler doesn't let the grass grow under his feet.'

'Absolutely. Always on the lookout for a deal. If you've got a grandmother to sell, Wheeler's your man. He'd rather you privatized the family silver though.'

'What did you find out about DI?' she asked. He looked over her shoulder, he flicked out his shirt-cuffs, fumbled with the jet studs down his shirt front.

'Nothing old girl. Absolutely in the clear.'

'He jumped when I mentioned my relationship study. Nearly bit my head off. What is he hiding?'

'Look, Liz.'

'Yes?'

'Do you forgive me for the other day?'

He looked so handsome and dashing and at home in these splendid surroundings and yet so vulnerable. He had worked his way if not into her heart then into the palm of her hand and she did not have it in her to reject him. She pursed her lips and peeked her tongue out upside down. He convulsed and nearly threw his glass over himself and looked round the room.

'Don't do that here,' he hissed.

'How's Premium Insurance doing?' she asked.

'Up like a rocket. It's in play. Listen Liz, half of it's yours, you know that. As soon as I get sorted out with Daff . . .'

'Have you found where you're sitting?' she asked.

They joined the crowd in front of the seating plan pinned up on an easel by the door into the Great Hall and peered through the heads of loiterers suddenly afflicted by an inability to recognize their own names. She discovered that she had drawn an end seat with no-one on her right and a Japanese on her left. She consoled herself with the thought that this was the first of many such occasions in her blossoming career and that she would work her way up over the years.

'My lords, ladies and gentlemen . . .'

Concealing disappointment or pleasure or indifference at their distance from the top table the guests filed in to take their seats in the Egyptian Hall, even more ornate than the reception room, more gilded plaster, ceremonial plate, gleaming crystal, marble statues as solemn and prepossessing as the footmen in scarlet livery. They all stood expectantly behind their chairs until, with a roll of drums, a band struck up the march from Handel's *Scipio*. Those in the know began to clap in time, followed by the rest, not the slow handclap of impatience but ponderous applause for a stately procession in measured, weighty step. In a stately waddle they processed to the Lord Mayor's throne. Above it hung the crest of the City of London, a white shield with the red cross of St George and in the top left quadrant the dagger that slew Wat Tyler, the poll tax rebel. Most of the guests felt their chests swell and their eyes grow moist, as they did at the Trooping of the Colour and the State Opening of Parliament and Founder's Day Service at school, thanking God that all the old decencies were still alive, and if they sometimes seemed dead and gone, murdered by yobs and trade unionists and trots and immigrants and trendy intellectuals, it was only because they were in hiding, gone to ground, nurtured by the few who cared. Above all, the pomp and majesty assured them that their life's work was not just buying cheap and selling dear, not the greedy pursuit of wealth and material success which socialists and do-gooders and left-wing journalists made it out to be, but noble and dignified and honourable.

• • •

'Who dropped the loving-cup?' asked the Governor. The tradition of passing it round at the end of dinner did not include dropping it on the floor with a cries of 'Oh shit.'

'Made a hell of a mess,' said the Chairman, sniffing his brandy.

'Don't,' said the Mayor, scratching behind his knee where the hem of his breeches caught a varicose vein. 'The Sergeant couldn't remember it happening in his lifetime. It'll go down in history.'

'What about the chap who dropped it?' asked the Chairman.

'He'll just commit suicide,' said the Governor.

'It was like a Bateman cartoon,' sniggered the Chairman.

'It's not bloody funny,' said the Mayor. 'I'll never hear the end of it. The staff is very touchy about that sort of thing. The ceremonial is their lifeblood. You ought to hear the fuss when I suggest abolishing the slow handclap. Every time it starts I feel like a centre forward who's just missed another open goal.'

'You support Spurs, you should know,' said the Governor, putting a patent shod foot on the mantlepiece.

They brooded and sipped, immersed in their private thoughts.

'Wheeler's going to make a full bid for Premium tomorrow.'

'I thought you said they'd nailed him,' said the Chairman to the Mayor.

'It's coming along. Bibber, the hack they've got working on it, can't substantiate anything yet.'

'Never troubles them usually. He'd better get a move on.'

'It was an omen, wasn't it?' said the Chairman.

'What was an omen?' asked the Mayor.

'Wheeler having the loving-cup poured all over him.'

• • •

Liz and Harry stood poker-faced under the canopy on the pavement outside the door of the Mansion House until Eddie drew up in the Humber. They seemed unmoved by the mellowness of the summer night, the beauty of the fast fading light, the warm zephyrs that frisked about the silk scarves and stoles of their fellow revellers. Eddie got out and stood to attention by the nearside door as they both got in, staring discreetly into the middle distance to conceal his disquiet that she had offered a lift to the Head of Public Affairs in the non-existent company car. It was soon obvious that they had more serious matters on their minds. They sat in their respective corners staring out of the window, immersed in private gloom like strangers in a tumbril.

'That's that then,' Harry said finally, and sighed.

'I'm sure it won't be so bad in the morning.'

'It'll be worse. I'll have to face Wheeler.'

'He can't do anything. It was an accident,' she said, scrabbling for words of consolation and finding only 'q's and 'x's on the rack.

'So was the *Titanic*.'

'I'm sorry, Harry. It was my fault.'

'How could you do that? Just as I was handing it to him? You know what it does to me.' There was no anger in his reproach, only resignation.

'I'm sorry, I really am. I saw you standing there on the other side of the room and you caught my eye and I couldn't help it.'

'Well it's done now. That's my career up the spout. It's round to the labour exchange for old Harrers in the morning.'

'Surely . . .'

'It'll be all round the City tomorrow. The man who dropped the loving-cup. I'm ruined.' He leaned forwards and buried his face in his hands. In the rear-view mirror Eddie saw Liz put a tentative arm round Harry's shoulder and his grip tightened on the wheel. His only consolation was that she looked up to see if he was looking.

'That settles it, anyway,' mumbled Harry. 'I'll bury my shame in the country. But who's going to pay for etiquette lessons from me of all people? I'll have to change my name.' He sat up, braced himself and took Liz's free hand. Eddie noticed that she looked at him in the rear-view mirror again.

196

'Why couldn't it have gone over me? Why did it have to go over him? He looked like Banquo at the feast.'

'Don't worry. It'll blow over,' she said with the conviction of a government spokesman breaking the news of another Chernobyl.

'I can bear the humiliation. I can bear being fired. You know what I can't bear? The thought of the mornings. Until the end of my days I'm going to wake up and greet the new day with a song in my heart and then I'm going to remember tonight and turn over and bite the pillow.'

At a red traffic light Eddie turned round. 'Where to, madam?' he asked, stiff and formal. Liz looked at Harry.

'Any bridge will do please, driver,' he groaned, 'the lower the parapet the better.'

'Shall we drive you home?' said Liz.

'I can't go home. I need you. If you can stand spending the night with a pariah-to-be.'

Eddie made a reflex swerve to avoid a parked car, his full attention devoted to the rear-view mirror.

'I'd better get an early night,' she said, extricating her hand and placing it with the other, demurely, on her lap.

'Please?'

'I've got a meeting tomorrow.'

'So have I,' said Harry, glumly, 'with the Percival Wheeler,' the prospect extinguishing what little ardour he had managed to kindle in his tortured soul. 'London Bridge station, please driver. I'll get the last train. Or the boat train. Whichever comes first.' He lapsed into mute contemplation of his entry into the folklore of the City while Eddie hummed quietly under his breath.

In the slip road in front of the station Eddie jumped smartly out and opened the rear door to cut as short as possible whatever parting consolation Liz chose to bestow. It consisted of a peck on the cheek and a lingering handshake and a hesitant wave to the disconsolate executive as he disappeared through the gloomy portals. It was not until they were driving back across London Bridge that she indulged the convulsions that forced her to stuff a handkerchief in her mouth and clutch the braided straphanger to stop herself holding her stomach and rolling round on the back seat.

'Eddie, you should have seen it. It was priceless. I wouldn't have missed it for anything,' she gasped and lapsed into uncontrollable laughter again, which Eddie joined in. At the end of the bridge he took advantage of a pause for breath to ask where she wanted to go.

'Stop right here,' she said, wiping tears from the corners of her eyes. He pulled over and parked at a bus stop and she got out. She walked back over the wide pavement to the parapet of the bridge, holding her arms tight round her, shoulders shaking. She stood looking upriver past the railway bridge towards St Paul's. He got out of the car and joined her at the parapet, a discreet couple of yards away. The sky was summer indigo, scattered with stars, lightened by the full moon rising over Tower Bridge behind them. He admitted that it was a beautiful night but not in his opinion far enough up the scale to warrant his boss's behaviour. Her eyes were closed and tears were pouring down her face. He tugged at the three little triangles of white handkerchief in his breast pocket and ripped off the cardboard backing.

'Here. What's the matter?' he said, holding out the cotton zig-zag. She took it and raked the tears off her cheeks with the points.

'A month ago I would never have done that,' she sniffed. 'The man's ruined and humiliated and all I could do was throw him on to the pavement and laugh my head off. What's become of me, Eddie?'

He put a tentative arm round her and patted her bare shoulder timidly, as he would a strange dog, wary of being bitten. 'You're just a bit alienated that's all,' he said softly. She sniffed.

'As long as you're useful, come on in. As soon as you're useless, out on the scrapheap. Husbands, wives, lovers, parents, children, flatmates, friends. Throw them out as soon as they stop being useful. Disposable. Consumable.'

'Capitalism alienates us from our true nature as social beings. It makes us into individual competitors for the means of life,' he said, giving her a hug. 'What you need is a nice cup of tea.'

He steered her back to the car and opened the rear door. She went behind him, opened the front door, got in and fastened her seat belt.

'Take that silly cap off,' she said when he got in beside her. He tossed it on to the back seat with the panache of a hat into the ring.

'Eddie?'

'Liz?'

'Will you do me another favour?'

'What's that?'

'Put a sock in the wit and wisdom of Comrade Marx.'

He drove up Gracechurch Street and Bishopsgate and parked in Liverpool Street. They were half-way to the new station buffet when they discovered they had plenty of plastic but no money. They got back into the car and drove to Wilf's Caff by Spitalfields Market where his credit was good. But Wilf was closed until midnight. He suggested going back to the office and was surprised by the vehemence of her refusal. She was equally reluctant to be driven back to her service flat in Chelsea.

'It looks like it'll have to be my place then,' he joked.

'All right,' she said. 'The Bevan Estate, isn't it?'

Declining an invitation is well covered by the etiquette books. Declining an acceptance is not. Even Eddie's quick wits could not come up with a decent excuse. No boss, not even Livery, with whom he had shared many after-hours escapades, had ever crossed his threshold.

She left him and skipped back to the car. She wanted to be lively and impetuous and fun-loving, like she used to be before she had managerial responsibilities. She ran her hands through her pinned and lacquered hair and it fell down on to her shoulders. She got into the car and put on Capital Radio very loud, tapping her foot in time. He was glad he did not have to make conversation. He could plan what he was going to say when he got her home. Cool, matter of fact, we're all good friends. They drove past her basement flat. All the estate agent's signs had been taken down except one which said under offer. She gave it a cursory glance and looked the other way. He drove over the sleeping policemen into the estate and parked between a taxi and an Oldsmobile in a parking lot beside a massive tower block. She got out first so he could lock the door from inside. She looked round her and up to the tops of the towers as if she had just stepped off a tourist coach in some exotic city. He opened the door into the building. It was decorated with posters proclaiming 'No To Private Landlords'. There was a lift waiting. Although he travelled in it at least twice a day he noticed as if for the first time how noisy it was and smelly with disinfectant and scarred where graffiti had been scoured off the graffiti-proof aluminium walls.

They stood facing the door with their hands by their sides.

'We're right on the top,' he said, as they began their interminable journey. 'I bet you've never been in a council block.'

'I grew up in one,' she said. 'My dad was a bus driver.'

They stepped out into a square lobby, the front door of a flat in each of the corners. Moonlight streamed in through a glass door that opened on to a wide balcony. She pushed it open. In the middle of the balcony was the column of a refuse chute. She walked past it to the parapet and looked out. 'This is incredible,' she whispered, gazing down at the panorama laid out below. The full moon hung over Lombard Street. The City was invested in moonshine. The streets were paved, the building were plated, the river flowed with gold. From Bishopsgate to Holborn, from the Barbican to the Bevan Estate, the Square Mile glistered. 'What a fantastic place to live,' she whispered.

'It's OK,' said Eddie.

She opened and closed her fists on the metal rail of the parapet, clutching the empty air. She could see from Tower Bridge to St Paul's. Only the Natwest Tower was as high as they were, casting a shadow over the roofs in the moonlight like the gnomon on a sundial.

'Eddie?'

'Mmmm?'

'Why do you do what you do?'

'Why do I do what I do?'

'Why do you do what you do?'

'Why do I do what I do to who?'

'This sounds like a Mister Bass Man number. You know what I mean.'

'Tell me what you mean.'

'You're intelligent and capable and attractive.' She bit off the last word.

'What's wrong with being a messenger?'

'Nothing. I didn't mean that . . .' She did mean that. 'You could do other things, that's all.'

'I'm my own man.'

'I'm sorry. It came out all wrong.'

'I suppose if I was ambitious and hard-working like you I could end up in a penthouse flat overlooking the City and drive around in a limo and have lovely women back on moonlit nights.'

'I said I was sorry. I mean it.'

'What about you?'

'What about me?'

'Why do you do what you do?'

She shrugged her shoulders and hugged herself.

'What do you mean?'

'You said you were working class. You had all that education and all those advantages. Why didn't you do something useful with it all?'

'Isn't doing my job useful?'

It was his turn to shrug his shoulders. She smiled at him. He put his arm round her shoulders, less tentatively this time than on London Bridge, and she did not shrug him off. Her gold lamé scarf felt crusty and metallic. Moonlight, the spectacular view and the balmy summer air played their traditional part.

'Tell me. What did you do that made Simple spill the loving-cup?'

She pursed her lips and peeked her tongue out upside down.

'Is that all?' he said.

She put her hands at the back of his neck and kissed him impetuously, so that he staggered back against the refuse chute, but not so impetuously that she closed her eyes. She was looking at the moon and the gilded City. He kept his eye on the front doors that led off the lobby.

'I never thought I'd do this,' he whispered in her ear.

'What?'

'Fall for the boss.'

She pushed him away. He had broken the spell, reminded her of what she wanted to forget for an hour or two: that she was the General Manager of Dividend Investments.

'I shouldn't be here,' she said.

201

'You're not the first boss to fraternize with the staff.'

'This isn't exactly fraternal, Eddie.'

'It's all right for men to get off with their secretaries. Why shouldn't women bosses do the same?'

'That's three times you've called me the boss. Am I some sort of trophy?'

He waited for her to walk back to the lift in a huff, hoped that she would. His heart was thumping in his chest. He still could not decide what to do, what to say if she came into the flat. She turned round to him and smiled.

'How about that tea?' she said.

'No. I'll drive you back.'

'I'm thirsty, Eddie,' she insisted, 'and I am the boss.'

They went back into the lobby to a front door decorated with a large brass knocker. Above the number was the name 'Thamesview' done in pokerwork on a slice of log. He stabbed the bellpush, unlocked the door and let her go in first. The brightly-lit narrow hall was painted bright red. Down one side were coat hooks. Down the other were works of art from the Hyde Park railing collection: Stevenson's rocket made of alarm clock parts, an etching on simulated copper of the Parthenon, an elephant head in bright green batik. Liz had little time to browse among them. A door opened and a young woman appeared wiping her hands on a tea towel.

'This is Miss Goodman, darling, from the office,' stuttered Eddie. 'This is my wife Sharon.'

They stood facing each other, equally abashed. Sharon stared at the career woman in short black evening dress and carefully tousled hair. Liz stared at the flustered housewife in a red track suit top and pink polyester trousers and blue slippers with white pompoms.

'I took her to see her new flat. I told you about it, didn't I? She's come back for a cuppa. Seeing as we're neighbours.' It was worse than he anticipated. Neither of them said anything. 'Shall we go in the lounge?' he said.

'I'm sorry, it's in ever such a mess,' said Sharon, scooping up a pile of socks she had been pairing off.

'Would you like to put the kettle on please, darling?'

'Would you like tea or coffee . . .'

'Tea would be fine.'

This innocuous dialogue was dubbed on to furious facial expressions and violent hand gestures behind Liz's back. Sharon stormed out to the kitchen and Eddie gritted his teeth into a smile.

Meanwhile Liz looked round the room. It was meticulously decorated and furnished. Whoever was responsible had taken very seriously the interior designer's dictum that in any decor all the primary colours should be represented, or the eye will wander restless and dissatisfied. There was no danger of that. Red, orange, yellow, green, blue, indigo and violet, and several intervening hues, competed eagerly to please. The stripes on the wallpaper alone accounted for most of them. If the home is mirror of the soul, Eddie's and Sharon's were throbbingly vibrant and alive. 'What a lovely room,' she said, mesmerized.

Eddie switched off the television and folded up the ironing board. 'Sharon's very talented that way,' he said.

On the fireplace above the electric coal fire was an aluminium bust of Lenin wearing a May Day wreath of withered spring flowers. Around it was an assortment of photographs. The largest, black and white, was of a boy in short trousers selling newspapers with a placard round his neck advertising the *Daily Worker*. He was handing a paper to a man in a long coat and a cloth cap.

'Are those your children?' she asked, pointing to two school colour photographs in bamboo frames.

'That's Gary. He'll be in bed. And that's Michelle. She's away on a school trip. That's why her mother's a bit edgy.'

'Nice children.'

His gritted teeth turned into a genuine smile.

'They're great kids. We have a lot of fun.'

Sharon came in with a tray of flowery cups and saucers and put it on a low coffee table. She had changed into a dark blue fluffy sweater and a light blue tight skirt. She had kept on the furry slippers. She had combed her short black hair at the front and dabbed on some green eyeshadow. Liz sat in the middle of the orange leather sofa while the other two occupied the rest of the three-piece suite. They did not have to ask who was going to be mother. The harassed look of suspecting she should be somewhere else, of knowing she had forgotten to do half a dozen things that

203

day, of remembering what she forgot to do yesterday, of anticipating all the things that were still to do before tomorrow, the desperate calm in the midst of haste and bustle and ingrained edginess, were all indisputable evidence of Sharon's status.

'You have a lovely home,' said Liz, toying with a spoon adorned with the municipal crest of Margate. 'Fantastic view.'

'I'd rather have a garden,' blurted Sharon. 'For the kids.'

'They do all right. We've got the caravan on the coast,' said Eddie, encapsulating an argument that had been running for fifteen years. They stirred and sipped to fill the silence.

'I'm sorry for bursting in like this,' said Liz, trying again.

'She has her hands full during the day,' said Eddie, 'don't you, Sharon?'

'I keep busy,' said Sharon.

'Do you have a job?'

'Just from home.'

'Show her, darling,' urged Eddie. 'She's really talented.'

'She doesn't want to see that . . .' They embarked on an oh-yes-she-does-oh-no-she-doesn't routine until Sharon was finally persuaded to lead the way out to the kitchen. In the middle of the kitchen table was a large wedding cake. Imposed on the traditional wedding cake form, three tiers on silver pillars, was a football motif. The base represented Wembley Stadium complete with stands made of icing, the middle tier a less imposing ground and the top a penalty area with goalposts. Little plastic footballers kicked and dribbled and dived round horseshoes and rosebuds on the snow-white icing edged with pink and blue.

'Did you do that?'

'Everything,' said Eddie proudly.

'He plays for Millwall and she works in the office,' said Sharon.

'It's amazing.'

'It's not a bad little business.' She opened a box and took out of a nest of tissue paper a bride and bridegroom, arm in arm, five inches high. She shrugged and for the first time her face cracked into a smile, letting her guest into a girlish secret, and carefully placed the couple on the penalty spot with their backs to the open goal.

● ● ●

Percy wriggled his toes and sipped his tea out of the Charles and Di mug and tried to ignore Sukie springing up and down on her hind legs, begging for a taste of his chocolate-covered shortbread. He enjoyed teasing the little rat, making it beg for morsels which he popped into his own mouth. He closed the file marked Panama Investment Company and put it on the arm of his chair. He leaned his head back and closed his eyes.

'Finished, baby?' asked Nora, picking up the mug and plate.

'Yup. We're in the clear,' he said, balling sheets of flimsy paper in the palm of his hand.

'Beg pardon?'

He opened his eyes and looked sharply at her. He picked up the Harrods bag full of files that lay beside his chair.

'I mean your George. He's in the clear,' he said, putting the PANIC file in the bag with the rest. She still looked puzzled. 'That was the file he was reading when he had his heart attack,' he added.

'Can I ask you something, baby? Was it anything to do with the PANIC file? Was that why you thought he was up to something . . . you know?'

'Yes. One of the reasons.'

She sat down on the pouffe by his side and put her hand on his arm.

'I wish you'd have said.'

'Said what?'

'About the file.'

'What file?'

'That file.'

'This file?' he asked, taking the PANIC file out of the bag.

'He wasn't reading it. The night he had his turn.'

Percy was sitting up now, his eyes drilling into hers.

'What file was he reading?'

'He wasn't reading any file.'

'Go on Nora.'

Slowly, half-laughing, half-sobbing, Nora recounted for the first time the true story of George's last moments. As she confessed she felt a weight lifting from her soul. She did not notice that the light of truth had an apparently opposite effect on Percy.

205

He slumped back in the chair under the burden, the corners of his thin lips twitching, his eyebrows drooping lower and lower.

'You mean it was all made up? All that about him bursting out of his office waving the file around? You mean he was having it away with you in the ante-room?'

'We did it for the best. For the company. We didn't want any scandal.'

'Who's idea was it?'

'Eddie's.'

'The messenger?'

'He said he'd look after everything. That I wasn't to tell anyone.'

Silence fell on the room, broken only by the gentle sussurations of the propeller under the simulated coals and the grinding of Percy's teeth.

'Why did he choose that file?' he gurgled from deep in his throat.

'No reason. He picked out any old file.'

'Any old file,' said Percy, holding the file in two hands as if he was about to swat her.

'Percy? Are you all right, baby?' There was fear in her voice. He was breathing quickly and his face had gone pale. She shook his arm. That fate was so easily tempted to make the excuse for one lover's death come true on another, was too cruel. But he was not finished yet. He leaped to his feet.

'Where's the phone?'

'Percy.'

'I have to make a private telephone call.'

'Upstairs in the bedroom.'

'I'll deal with you when I come down.'

She went out to the kitchen and turned the turkeyburgers down. She could tell from the number of pings and rattles in the junction box that it was an overseas call. She toyed with the idea of tiptoeing upstairs to listen at the bedroom door or picking up the downstairs extension but he was bound to notice. He was in a bad enough mood already. She felt deliciously nervous. She picked up her handbag from the breakfast bar. If he was going to deal with her when he came down she had better put on some more perfume.

●●●

Like many men who have little to hide, Percy, who was hung like a cherub as well as shaped like one, kept his towel round his middle. Sporting little round black sunglasses he lay flat on his back under the warming rays of the sunlamps in the basement gymnasium of Dividend House like a misshape rejected from a tray of gingerbread men. The room was Palladian, with ochre walls and an ornate white marble fireplace and a plaster frieze. The exercise equipment and massage table and sunbeds looked as if they had been parked there while more suitable accommodation was being prepared. The elegance of the surroundings could not disguise the changing-room smell of sweat and embrocation. Spight, the Finance Director, closed the door carefully behind him.

'I've just been talking to the banks. Bad news. There's some-one else in the market for Premium.'

'Who?' grunted Percy.

'They don't know. They're waiting for them to declare them-selves.' Spight's flat and measured tones could have been deliver-ing the shipping forecast. 'We could be in for a battle.'

Percy slapped his stomach with his hands. 'A fight,' he chortled. He raised his head. Spight was not looking at him. It was hard to tell from his lugubrious expression whether this was out of discretion or distaste. Percy reached out and patted the sunbed beside him. 'Come on Spight. Cheer up. You need to relax. Take your clothes off. Lie down and tell me all about it.'

Spight fingered his measle-spotted tie.

'I think I ought to be getting back, Percy.'

'Rubbish. The trouble with you, Spight, is that you're too tight-arsed. Have fun. There's nothing more enjoyable than a good takeover battle. Take your clothes off.'

'I really think . . .'

'Take your clothes off. All of them.' There was a harder edge to his voice. Spight began to undress, hanging his clothes carefully on the nearest Nautilus. He took them all off as he had been ordered.

207

He had not risen so high in the company that he was unable to indulge his penchant for subservience. If Percy's proportions were Rococo, Spight's were Classical, like the Minotaur or a satyr on a vase, his large head matching the pizzle that dangled from his scrawny body. He took off his gold-rimmed spectacles and shielding his eyes with his hands lay down on the sunbed.

'That's better. Ten minutes and you'll be a new man.'

They toasted in silence for a minute or so, Percy glistening like a jellyfish marooned above the tidemark, Spight sere as a white piece of driftwood.

'Tell me about Premium.'

'There's been a lot of concerted buying over the past few days. From overseas. The banks are worried. A foreign institution might be prepared to pay over the odds to get a foot in the London market. The price is near our ceiling already.'

'There is no ceiling.'

'But we agreed the most we wanted to pay.'

'That was for the banks. If you give them a blank cheque they don't make the effort.'

'There's still a maximum price we can reasonably pay.'

'And that's the price it takes to win. I want Premium. Do you understand me? I don't care who's bidding against us, I'll meet his price.'

Percy did not seem unhappy at the prospect. It seemed to make him decidedly cheerful. They lay quietly for a few more minutes until a timer buzzed and the lamp on Percy's sunbed went out. He sat up on the bed with his feet dangling over the side and his hands on his knees, sucking in his belly and admiring himself.

'Can I get up too?' pleaded Spight.

'You're done. Listen. While you're here look at this.' Percy handed him a folder while he sat up and scrabbled for his spectacles. 'I want to squeeze some more fat out of DI before we merge it with Premium. Goodman's got rid of the dealer. Who else can we chop?'

Spight looked down at the folder open at the DI staff list. Each name had a salary next to it. One name had been highlighted in yellow. Spight took the hint.

'Fly seems to be overpaid for a messenger.'

'Now that's a good idea, Spight. Tell Goodman to get rid of him. Right now.'

'On what grounds?'

'That's up to her. She's the Manager.' He smirked and slapped his stomach while Spight put his clothes on.

● ● ●

Eddie was uneasy. He had a feeling that things were unravelling in a way he could not predict. Liz's infatuation for him was distorting a proper rapport with the boss. Personal feelings had no place in business relationships based on self-interest and mistrust. It was different for secretaries. An affair with the boss was just an extension of their surrogate wife status. For men it was different. Wasn't it?

'Pulled a class bird there, Eddie old son,' he said to himself, but it was little consolation. Against his upbringing, his temperament and the natural order of things, he had exposed himself. It did not stop there. He had indulged in personal dislike for Harry Simple in place of the calculated antagonism due to Head Office. And there were other things which worried him. What was Wheeler up to? Why was Norman Foxwell fired? Why was Nora secretly taking files out? These mysteries pricked his cockiness. He pondered them while he opened up the office for the day. There was nothing in the telexes or the mail or Liz's diary or the papers in her desk to shed light on them. The only interesting item of news was that the Stock Exchange had suspended the trading of Premium Insurance shares. There was speculation on the Reuter screen that an announcement would be made later in the morning about a takeover bid.

At half past eight he took a call from Mr Spight for Miss Goodman. He said she was at a breakfast meeting.

'Who's that speaking?' asked Spight.

'Mr Fly.'

'Get her to call me back as soon as she comes in. Goodbye Mr Fly. Goodbye.'

Eddie hung up. 'What's that all about, I wonder,' he said, scribbling on a message pad.

Liz came in a few minutes before nine. Eddie was still carrying in his mind's eye the image of how she looked when he took her to his home after the Mansion House dinner – short black evening dress, tumbling blonde hair, tears and smiles and nervousness. It was how he imagined her when he orchestrated in his imagination their next meeting, in the ante-room perhaps or her little flat in Chelsea. He would also have liked to carry the imprint of her soft lips on his, the feel of her soft shoulders, her soft breath in his ear, but these were more elusive, expunged by the bruise between his shoulders where he had fallen back against the refuse chute. He was sitting at the reception desk sorting the mail into piles, trying to decide if she would prefer to be seduced by Frank Sinatra or Phil Collins when her alter ego came in through the glass front door. In a grey pleated skirt, blue blazer, polished black shoes, a horsey Hermès scarf and with her hair meticulously done up, she looked like an air hostess.

'Good morning, Mr Fly,' she said. Mr Fly. He grinned. But this was not playful formality, the banter of intimacy. Avoiding his eye she picked up the *Financial Times* from his desk and went into the management suite.

'Good morning, Miss Goodman.'

She must really be feeling hot for him if she had to act so aloof. He decided to play her game and stay out of her way for the rest of the day. He would give the reports to Nora to give to her. He went about the business of the morning with bouncing step, humming to himself, distributing the mail with even more chirpiness than usual.

At ten o'clock he called on Norman Foxwell, who was initiating Louise into the secrets of the dealing system. He had let himself be persuaded by Liz to work out a week of his notice to ease the transition. It was doubly considerate of him to give the staff time to organize a party and pass round a clinking brown envelope with a big card inside. The card was a cartoon of a riotous office party which augured well for the leaving celebrations as well as the recipient's future life of leisure.

'Like your tie, Norman,' said Eddie. It was fluorescent pink with blue spots.

'Got it this morning at the station,' said Norman, primping the fluorescent pink silk out over his woolly cardigan.

'Using it to scare the pigeons were they?'

'Leave off, Eddie,' said Louise, 'he looks nice.'

'You can always tell when a bloke's getting short. He runs into Tie Rack for a flash pork pie. Ever noticed that . . .'

But Eddie was not paying attention to himself. Even Norman's tie was eclipsed by a flashing news message on the Reuter screen. He pointed to it.

'Dividend Group makes bid for Premium Insurance,' they said in chorus.

'I'm glad they haven't got my policy,' said Norman. But Eddie did not hear. He was already on his way back to the post-room to phone Premium's head messenger.

Ten minutes later he put the phone down and rubbed his face in his hands. He drummed his fingers on the desk. He fiddled with a bottle of Tippex, uncapping it and capping it again. The light-hearted gaiety of the morning evaporated like solvent leaving only a puddle of unease that spread and hardened into a white crust of anxiety. His friend at Premium Insurance had given him some very serious news. There comes a time in every person's career when they have to face up to responsibility, not only for their own lives but for their colleagues. He stood up and went into the back office, deep in thought, no longer a spring in his step. He paced through the aisles between the partitions, not bothering to carry files or envelopes or reports, weighed down by a heavier burden. He looked at each of them as they worked or pretended to work. Like an old-fashioned boss from the days before professional managers and appraisal systems and computerized personnel records, he knew their names, their family circumstances, their idiosyncrasies, their strengths and foibles, what they could do best, what made them work hard, what made them shirk. Despondency turned to determination. Something had to be done. For all of them. Starting at the top. He turned and made straight for the management suite.

As he went in Liz put the phone down, the green one, her private line. She looked at him like a stranger, and unwelcome.

'Did you buy those Premium shares?' he asked without preamble.

'Since when do you come in unannounced?'

'We haven't got time for that. Did you buy those Premium shares?'

'No. Now leave my office . . .'

'Wheeler is. He just announced a bid. You'd have had some explaining to do if they found out.'

'What are you talking about?'

'Insider dealing. Premium are saying there was buying in the market before the deal was announced. They're demanding an inquiry to try and stop our takeover bid. Because you're a senior manager in the group they'd say you'd bought shares because you knew all about it.'

'Wheeler's buying Premium?'

'See for yourself.'

Liz swivelled round to the screen behind her and read the news.

'That's good for the Group,' she said, trying to conceal her annoyance that she had to learn corporate news from the messenger.

'It's wonderful. Except for us.'

'Thank you, Eddie. You can go now. I shall want to see you later.'

'There's more to it than that. Premium has got a large investment department. Wheeler's going to close down . . .'

The green telephone rang. She snatched it up and turned on a cassette recorder connected to the handset. 'Yeah,' she said in a strangled, gravelly voice with a Midlands accent. 'You've got the right one. Thanks a million for calling back.' She put a hand over the mouthpiece and pulled a pad towards her.

'Have you caught cold?' he asked.

'I don't want to be recognized,' she said in a normal voice, and then slipped into Black Country. 'I'd loik a two tier cake and flowers and a car. What sort of car will it be? Oh grayte. I'll write to confirm. No, that's all I need to know for the minute ta.' She put the phone down.

'You're getting married.' He held the back of the visitor's chair as if to stop it slipping away from him like the rest of his surroundings. 'Congratulations.' His voice had become strangled and gravelly too.

'What were you saying about Premium Insurance?' she asked, thinking about something else, looking down at the pad on which she had been writing.

'I don't understand. Last night . . .'

'Nothing happened last night, Eddie. Nothing.'

'Is it Mr Simple?'

'Who?'

'Who you're marrying.'

'I'm not marrying anyone, Eddie. That was your wife I was talking to.'

Eddie made doubly sure of the chair by sitting down on it.

'I don't understand.'

She stood up from her chair and looked down at him. Bright-eyed, thin-lipped, jutting-jawed, hollow-cheeked, here was an Amazon off to battle. He had seen women look like that before, Russian patriotic posters, Tory conferences, the first day of the sales, Boxing Day foxhunts, Bingo halls on bonanza night, and it was a daunting sight.

'Give me your keys,' she said.

'You what?'

'Give me the keys to the office. All of them.'

Puzzled, he dug them out of his pocket and handed them over. In return she gave him a white envelope.

'You are dismissed. I will escort you from the premises immediately. You may not go back to the post-room. Your personal belongings will be sent on.'

As techniques for firing people go, it had the merit of being short and to the point. No beating about the bush here. No mealy-mouthed guff about it not being personal and what a good chap he was. He had been given not so much the sack as the sandbag and he reeled under the blow.

'What for?'

'Gross misconduct. Embezzlement. Misuse of company assets. Take your pick.'

'Liz, what's going on?'

She flexed her shoulderpads. 'You are going out.'

He folded and unfolded his arms, puffed his cheeks out, blew, sucked, wiped his forehead, generally ran through the repertoire of stress gestures.

'You'd better have proof.'

'How about a tape-recorded telephone conversation with a woman called Sharon at Luxury Limousines, Your Fly Awaits You? I ordered flowers and a cake and the Humber limousine belonging to this office for my wedding in September.' She opened the top drawer of her desk and took out a brown envelope. She tipped the contents into the palm of her hand and showed them to him. 'Confetti. From under the carpet in the back seat of the company car. And by the time we get to the industrial tribunal, if you want to take us there, I shall have gone through the books with Larry to check our purchases of stationery and supplies against inventory. Not forgetting our business relationship with Messrs Peabody the wine merchants.'

'Liz, don't do this to me.'

'You used your position for personal gain. You used me like you use everyone else. Norman, Carol . . .'

'How have I used Carol?'

'Eddie Fly the people's friend. You're out for what you can get. And you know why? You like pushing people around, telling them what they can do and can't do under the pretence that it's for their own good. You think you belong on this side of the desk, Eddie Fly. But you don't.'

He put the white envelope in his pocket. He felt light, light-headed, light-hearted, like a helium-filled balloon slipped from its string. His farewell speech was an eloquent, moving indictment of her misjudgement, her misplaced affection for people like Harry Simple, her misunderstanding of the nature of organizations, her misconception of his motives, her misconstruction of his actions, her misinterpretation of his words, her misapprehension of her own role, her miscarriage of justice, her miscalculation, her mistake. Unfortunately it only came to mind when he was in the lift on the way down. For the time being 'Who put you up to it?' was the best he could drag up from his stunned brain.

● ● ●

Liz put the phone down. She had reported to Spight. She had carried out her orders. She expected to feel soiled, like she had when she threw Harry out of the car at London Bridge station. She did, but the novelty had worn off and she did not let it upset her. Besides she was in the right. Eddie had abused his position. She did not know the real reason why she had been told to get rid of Fly. She suspected there was something more to it than cost reduction. But it was not her job to worry about it. She also welcomed back like an old and disreputable friend the feeling she had had when she fired Norman. Power over other people's lives was a heady sensation, untainted this time by any rejoicing over the sentence. She also felt relief that she would not have to confront every day her stupidity in getting over-familiar with a member of staff. It had been a useful lesson. There were other feelings belonging to a pre-managerial past that lurked in the background but she pushed them firmly away. 'Managers have to manage,' she said to herself over and over again, like a mantra, hypnotizing herself.

She called Nora in and dictated a brief memo to staff to the effect that E. Fly had been dismissed for misconduct. His future presence in the building should be reported immediately to Security. Nora's eyes opened wide. Then narrowed. Then resumed their usual diameter. But they looked at her with new respect. 'He had it coming, Miss Goodman,' she said with quiet satisfaction.

'I want Freda Grafton to clear out his personal belongings. And send her in to me first, will you?' said Liz with natural authority.

The news shot through the back office like a meteor, a sudden blaze of rumour and shock, and just as quickly burnt itself out. A very few, like Norman and Carol, tried to keep indignation alive, but it was soon snuffed out. All that was left were a few sparks of speculation about who would do his job until they hired a replacement.

They would have noticed a close physical resemblance between the Freda Grafton they knew and the woman on the visitor's chair in front of Miss Goodman's desk. A twin sister perhaps. The electrified hair had been earthed and was now combed into softer waves, the inner fury was extinguished along with the cigarettes, the mouth and nostrils no longer breathed smoke but the scent of violets from a tiny can she surreptitiously squirted down her throat on her way through reception.

'I want to talk about Carol Feely,' said Liz.

'Oh very good, Miss Goodman. I was hoping we could at some

stage.' Freda's voice was soft and modulated, her manner self-effacing, words that would have brought hoots of disbelief in the back office were they used to describe the Freda they knew.

'I hired her myself.'

'It certainly wasn't my choice, Miss Goodman,' she simpered.

'I understand she's doing a good job.'

The expression of stupefaction and affront that flitted momentarily across the woman's face belonged more to back office Freda than her look-alike. She gripped the arms of her chair.

'Miss Goodman, I run a very tight ship. I expect a lot from my people. Hard work and a positive attitude.'

'So you should.'

'I'm not sure Carol is right for filing.'

'You know, Freda, that's just what I've been thinking.'

Freda relaxed and folded her hands in her lap. She must have misunderstood. It was going to be easier to get rid of Carol than she hoped.

'It's all down to attitude,' she confided. 'The young people of today think they can do as they please . . . it's all handed to them on a plate . . . they've no respect for authority . . . no manners . . . they don't know what work is . . . it's the schools to blame . . . you tell them something and they laugh at you . . . I've brought mine up different I can tell you . . . in my day you knew you had to work for a living . . . come to work when they like, take days off when they like.'

'Absolutely,' said Liz, 'and then you get someone like Carol. Do you know she'd never had a job when I found her?'

'That explains a lot.'

'We can't keep her where she is.'

'Certainly not.'

'You've done a great job with her, Freda. But you'll have to let her go.'

'As you wish.'

'I hope that's all right.'

'Management has the last word, Miss Goodman.'

'Jolly good. I'm making her temporary messenger.'

As last words go they were beauties. Freda was beyond them. She did not gape, she did not blink, she did not move. This was the moment for her to make her position known, to assert herself, to draw herself up and deliver herself of her true feelings, to bluster and fume and get her own way by force of character and power of words and might of reason, to set fire to a cigarette, to her convictions, to the woman of straw on the other side of the desk.

'Very good, Miss Goodman.'

What else could you say to management?

● ● ●

'Arter-noon, Sah,' said the Sergeant on the front desk as Eddie walked past. Eddie stopped and tried to look him in the eye but failed, so far was the polished peak of his cap pulled down over his nose.

'Sergeant . . .'

'Sah?'

But he could not bring himself to say goodbye.

'Nothing.'

'You all right, Eddie?' said the Sergeant, pushing his cap back. 'You look a bit out of sorts.'

'Right as rain, Frank. Be seeing you.'

He paused for a beat to let the automatic doors sigh open. Then stood on the top step as they chomped shut behind him. The rain that he was right as was drizzling from a grey June sky. It brought Wimbledon to mind, and Lords and Ascot. He would have plenty of time for all that now, sprawled in front of the telly with a can of lager in his hand. He shuddered and stepped on to the cobbles. His umbrella and his coat were still in the office. It was against his dignity to go back for them. He crossed Capital Square and went out into the main road. He could not bear to go home yet. In idle moments he had planned what he would do if he were ever made redundant, in the same way that he mused over whether he would be buried or cremated or what sort of wreaths he would get along with the enormous flowery DAD that looked as if a vital letter had fallen off. He would go round to Mrs MacKerel. He would phone up all his contacts. As soon as he got something lined up he would take a few weeks off and see more of the kids. He would paint the caravan and build the shell grotto in front that Sharon had set her heart on, complete with fountain. The transition would be planned, orderly and calm. But when it actually happened, so swiftly and so brutally, he did not have the heart for any of these things. The thought of telling Sharon, or Mrs Mac, or his poker school, was unbearable. That Eddie the Fixer had been fired for using the office car at weekends? He knew how silly and self-justifying it would sound if he tried to explain the true circumstances, that he was fired because the boss had got too fresh with him. It would ring hollow through every post-room and chauffeur's cubby-hole in the City.

Still he refused to believe that she had done it so abruptly of her own accord. 'Who put her up to it?' he asked out loud. The answer came reverberating back as if it had been lying in wait for the question. Harry Simple. He remembered giving him his card outside Covent Garden. Ever since he had made a fool of himself at lunch Harry had been waiting to get his own back. It was at times like this that Eddie wished he was religious. Then he could have prayed for something terrible to happen to his enemy, like they did in the Bible.

He was disturbed to realize that he did not know where to go. He could have gone to any one of score of cafés and pubs and private gathering places, secret little basement dens near the clearing-house or Lloyds or the Stock Exchange, for a coffee or a drink or a gossip or a game of pontoon. But he did not belong any more. For years he had scurried through the streets on errands, official and private. He knew every short-cut, not only down secret little alleys but through buildings and basements and car parks. A nod to a couple of security sergeants on the way and he could get from the Guildhall to the Stock Exchange without ever walking on a pavement. Now he had no official-looking document case, no badge, no ID, no status, no purpose, no reason, no mission. He did not belong. He was reduced to the lowliest in society, a member of the public.

He started to walk. He did not know where he was going, it no longer mattered. He wandered aimlessly down narrow lanes between massive modern buildings, glittering brass, shiny aluminium, gleaming marble, until he came out on a busy main road, six lanes wide, that marked the boundary between the City of

London and the neighbouring borough. The two sides of the road looked so different that he would not have been surprised to find a border post, a check-point, guard towers, a barbed-wire fence and tank traps down the double yellow line in the middle. The buildings on the other side were only three or four storeys high, of human proportions, mostly London brick, soot-stained, in need of pointing, crumbling, peeling, windows boarded up or covered with mesh and grilles, doors blank wood or metal. Weeds grew from gutters and niches in the walls, high up, too high to pluck a buttonhole from. There were some signs of life, a light left on upstairs or the blather of a radio, as if the last residents were too stubborn or ill to leave with the rest.

He dodged through the traffic and wandered down a narrow street of old red-brick terraces, shop fronts and windows boarded up and covered with graffiti in flowing Bengali script, scuffing through the litter on the broken pavement. At the end was a large white marble church, a Greek temple topped with an English spire. The churchyard was deserted and unkempt, scattered with sodden paper and cardboard boxes. It was raining hard now and he looked round for shelter. The church porch was all that was available. He trudged down a muddy path between the gravestones and up the marble steps. Under the portico he smoothed rain off his hair and wiped his face with his hands. He was surprised to find that the door was unlocked. Suddenly weary and chill, he went into a small lobby sealed off from the body of the church with a wrought iron grille. It was empty. His nose wrinkled at the musty smell of polish and cold stone. He had only been in half a dozen churches in his life, for weddings and funerals. This one was simple inside, with plain green windows and a simple altar and a crucifix. It did not offend him as much as the others. There were no military paraphernalia, tatty flags and poppy wreaths and other gewgaws of the warrior class. There were no gimcrack statues and flickering candles and the opium stink of incense. He sat down on a wooden bench and rubbed his face in his hands.

'There's more to this than meets the eye, Eddie,' he said to himself. His voice echoed inside the church and he looked up nervously, even though he was sure there was no-one to hear.

His mind wandered over the events of the past few weeks. As far as he could tell things had started to go wrong when George Livery dropped dead. The business with the PANIC file, the appointment of Liz, Nora's strange behaviour, including secretly removing files, the firing of Norman, the fall from grace of Harry Simple, the takeover bid for Premium, his own sudden liquidation. And there was more to come. If Wheeler was successful, Dividend Investments would be folded into Premium's investment department. They would all be on the street. He struggled to find a link, a rational, scientific, materialist explanation for all this, but he could see only chaos. Perhaps there was no connection. Perhaps there was no deeper reality beneath the surface. Perhaps they were all adrift in a sea of randomness.

He put his elbows on his knees and his head in his hands. He had always struggled to keep his dignity by controlling his own life. And now he had lost his job and his independence and his identity and he did not know why. Who cared if there was any sense to it? All he knew was that he was a victim. He felt for the first time in his life that he was being played with by forces out of his control. They tore off his wings and they would tear off his legs and then they would tread on him, for sport.

'Pull yourself together, Fly. It's only a bloody job.'

He struggled to find the nugget of faith that could keep him going, a straw to grasp. What would his father have said? He knew what it was like to be hounded and pilloried. Like an echo the old words he had heard so often came back to him. 'Dialectic, son. Every situation had conflicting elements that resolve themselves to make other situations.' Fat lot of good that was when you were in the middle of them. He stood up. Sitting still had made him stiff and cold. Without a backwards glance he went outside. A little man in a corduroy cap and a shabby brown overcoat was waiting for him. 'Spare the price of a cup of tea, guv?' he whined. He had a stiff neck and the left side of his thin face sagged as if he had been sleeping on it too long. Eddie dug into his pocket but he only had pound coins. On impulse he handed one over.

'You're a gentleman, guv. You look as if you could use a cuppa yourself,' said the lopsided man, looking critically at Eddie's muddy shoes and wet suit and bedraggled hair. This was not the most tactful remark to make to someone who had joined the unemployed less than two hours before. In reply Eddie turned up the collar of his jacket, stuck his hands in his pockets and with shoulders hunched set off into the rain.

'No offence, guv,' called the lopsided man. 'You'll catch a chill walking around like that.' Eddie walked faster and heard footsteps coming up behind.

'It'll turn out all right in the end, you see. You've got to look after yourself though.'

'Do me a favour,' said Eddie.

'We've got to stick together. Don't forget that.'

'Bugger off.'

'The children of this world are more astute at dealing with their own kind than are the children of the light.'

'Very interesting. Go and get your tea.'

'Jesus said it. It's in the Bible.'

They were almost running now, the lopsided man two steps behind, like a persistent bumblebee after a picnicker. Eddie stopped and glared at him.

'Look mate. It was for a cup of tea. I didn't pay for a sermon.'

'It's about this bloke and his guvnor gave him the sack. He was useless at his job. He thought he'd never get another one. You know what he did?'

They were at the main road. Eddie stopped to cross. His feet were soaked and he could feel water trickling down the back of his neck.

'While he served out his notice he gave fifty per cent discounts to all his boss's customers and creditors so they would look after him when he left. You know what his boss did?'

'Took him to court.'

'Praised him. Gave him his old job back. What do you think of that?'

'Do you know where there's a phone near here?'

'I mean render unto Caesar. Use money tainted as it is. And then there was the old lady who lost a quid and spent all day looking for it. It's all down to money in the end.'

'I've got to find a phone.'

221

'Follow me, guv. You can get a cup of tea too.'

Eddie followed the lopsided man back down the narrow street towards the church. After a few yards they followed a sign saying 'The Shelter Day Centre' down a narrow passage of blackened bricks to a glass door guarded by a big, muscular, round-faced man. He yanked the door open before they could push it, holding it wide, tilting his head back and raising his eyebrows and opening his eyes so the whites showed all round the pupils. He pointed to a table with a signing-in book under a large notice-board advertising Alchoholics Anonymous, opening times of the local social security office, the Samaritans, free disposable needles, the times of the doctor's surgery, advice on what to do if arrested and other useful items of information. Among them a joker had pinned a brochure about waterskiing in Dockland and a mini-prospectus for the latest privatization.

The lopsided man signed in and to Eddie's relief disappeared through a red door. Eddie turned to the doorkeeper.

'I don't need to sign in. I just want to make a phone call.'

'Your first time is it, friend?' he said in a Liverpool accent, looking him up and down like the lopsided man had done, full of understanding and compassion.

'I'm not staying. I just want to use the phone. OK?'

'You've got to sign in all the same. And why not have a cup of tea while you're here? There's always a nurse on duty if you need her. You're among friends here.'

'Look mate. I'm not a . . .' he bit off his words. 'Never mind. I'll go and find a call-box. Where's the phone?'

'At the far end. Take your time. Have a cup of tea. If you can't afford it you can sign for it. Pay next time.' He winked.

Eddie went through the red door into a large canteen, brightly painted and brightly lit, with blue formica-topped tables and a serving counter down one wall. The favoured seats were round the sides beside the radiators. Most of the customers, middle-aged men, were asleep, slumped on the tables with their heads on their arms. There was a smell of damp and frying bacon and old clothes. At the far end was a door marked Social-Worker-Toilets-Nurse. Eddie walked quickly through the tables, ignoring the lopsided man who was waving to him from a table in the middle. The door opened into a small cream-painted lobby with several doors. The telephone was in an acoustic booth just inside. Eddie took out his diary and picked up the handset and realized he only had pound coins. He went back to the servery where a young woman in jeans and a black sweater and a wooden crucifix round her neck was serving the lopsided man with tea.

'There. I knew you needed one. You look as if you could do with a bacon sandwich too. It's going to be a chilly night tonight.'

Before he could stop her the young woman had poured him a tea too.

'I don't want that,' he snapped.

'Sorry. Coffee?' She had an Irish accent.

'I just want change for the phone,' he said, trying to keep the edge of desperation out of his voice.

'I've poured it now. Go on. You can pay me next time.'

'I DON'T WANT TEA. I DON'T WANT COFFEE. I WANT CHANGE FOR THE PHONE,' shouted Eddie at the top of his voice. He looked round. Everyone was looking at him. Men, woken from their doze, gazed at him with bleary eyes. The lopsided man clutched his arm. The young woman leaned over the counter and put her hand on his shoulder.

'Shh. That's all right, dear. You don't have to have it. Your clothes are all wet. Would you like us to dry them? I can lend you a dressing-gown while they're airing. Here. Take that jacket off.'

'You'll catch your death,' said the lopsided man. Eddie wrenched himself away. He had to get out of here. Before he was sucked down. He turned round and found the doorkeeper blocking his way.

'What's the trouble, Bridget?' he asked.

'This poor fellow's soaked to the skin,' said Bridget.

'He needs a hot drink too,' said the lopsided man. The doorkeeper put his right arm around Eddie's shoulder and held his upper arm in a meaty grip. With the left he clasped his elbow. Eddie did not struggle. He recognized an expert bouncer when he met one.

'What's the trouble, friend?' asked the doorkeeper.

'Look. I have to make a phone call before five o'clock. It's very urgent. Please let me go and I'll find a call-box outside.'

'Why don't you just take off those wet clothes. You don't want to get pneumonia.'

'It's OK. Listen. I've got a home and a wife and a family and a j . . .' He could not get the word out.

'We're all friends here, you know,' said the doorkeeper, hugging him tighter.

'Right. If I let you dry my clothes will you let me use the phone?'

'Of course we will. Come with me.'

The doorkeeper took him through the door marked Social-Worker-Toilets-Nurse and unlocked a room lined with shelves and racks of clothes. He selected a blue towelling bathrobe.

'Don't worry. Everything's been laundered.' He watched while Eddie took out his wallet and diary and pound coins, stripped down to his vest and pants and put on the robe.

'Do you want some clean underwear? It's all new. Only a quid.'

Eddie shook his head violently and clutched the robe round him.

The doorkeeper looked disappointed. 'I'll stick these in the drier then,' he said, gathering up the clothes. 'You can put your shoes back on.'

Eddie went back into the canteen to get change from Bridget, squelching in his damp, sockless shoes. He closed his eyes while she scrabbled in the till. How had he let this happen to him? This morning he had set off to work as usual with his umbrella and his briefcase. Now look at him. He took the change and went back to the phone and with trembling fingers dialled the first number.

He called his friends at City Limited and Office Supplies and Peabody Fine Wines and all the other suppliers to Dividend Investments. He ordered enough forms and stationery and typing paper and telex rolls and pads and pens and pencils and erasers and Tippex and soap and toilet paper to last them a couple of years. He ordered a replacement photocopier, half a dozen new typist's chairs, blotter pads for every desk, a dictating machine for Liz and the playback unit for Nora. He asked for trials of an electronic franking machine and a telephone answering system and a pager.

He ordered wines and spirits and cigars. He arranged that the orders should be back-dated and that he would call in person to sign them the next day.

He put the handset down after the last call and pulled the bathrobe tighter round him. So much for the children of the world. He felt tired and cold and dizzy. Before going in search of the doorkeeper and his clothes he would have a cup of tea after all. He went back into the canteen. The lopsided man was fast asleep with his head on his arms. Many of the men were gathering their belongings, getting ready to trudge to wherever they were going to doss for the night. He bought a tea off Bridget and sat down at an empty table. After a minute or two he was joined by a man of about sixty. His face was aflame with acne. He was wearing a threadbare black Crombie and a black jacket and striped morning trousers. He had a pile of *Evening Standards* under his arm. He put his tea on the table and dropped the papers on the floor, face down, so the headlines could not be read for free.

'Those today's?' asked Eddie.

'Well, they ain't tomorrow's,' said the vendor, gulping his tea.

Eddie handed him a coin. The man drained his cup, picked up the papers and left to ply his trade.

Eddie flipped through the paper. He panicked when he found that in this room what he read seemed frantic and shrill and meaningless, garbled tittle-tattle from a distant world. He forced himself to concentrate, page by page, from the front. So it was ten minutes before he got to the City page. What he read there did not need any effort of concentration. 'Premium Insurance – Mystery Bidder Revealed,' said the headline. The foreign company which had been buying Premium shares was the Panama Investment Company.

'Where are my clothes?' he asked.

● ● ●

Nora dipped her middle finger in the pot of zinc and castor oil cream and came up with a blob, pointed and curling at the top, like soft ice cream from a machine. It smelt sweet and smooth and metallic. She dabbed the cream in and then ran her finger up and

225

down until it was all slippery. He gurgled and she patted the double dimple in the small of his back. She wiped her finger on the terry bath towel on which he lay and reached for the Johnson's baby powder. She turned the top and sprinkled the powder over his pink bottom, massaging it in with her left hand. She put the canister of powder down and carried on stroking. She began to breathe a lullaby, toora-loora-loora, and felt the plump body spread over her thighs grow limp. Still stroking and crooning, toora-loora-lye, she slowly extricated herself so that he was lying face down on the satin quilt, breathing slowly and deeply. Stooping, she folded the terry-towel over him and stroked the fringe of baby soft hair around his bald head. Satisfied that he was asleep, she tiptoed out of the bedroom and went downstairs to make herself a cup of tea.

She carried the tea into the lounge and turned the television on for the news. She usually flicked over to the other channel when the financial news came on. But tonight it led with the story of the takeover bid for Premium Insurance by the Dividend Group. Premium were making a fight of it. There was speculation about who was behind the mysterious Panamanian buyer. There was her baby on the television getting out of the car and walking up some steps into an office building. He looked so imposing and masterful. No wonder he was so tired. He had come in dressed in his suit, tossed his jacket on the sofa and gone straight upstairs. When the item was finished she went out to the kitchen to put the oven chips in. She was half-way up the stairs when she remembered the jacket on the sofa. It ought to be on a hanger, especially as he had to go back to the office that night. She picked it up and noticed the slim black calfskin bound diary sticking out of the inside pocket.

When she went back to the bedroom he was awake, lying on his back on the towel, admiring his reflection in the ceiling mirror. He held out his arms and she undid the buttons of her nightdress and the front of her nursing bra. She sat on the quilt with her back against the padded bedhead and held him while he nuzzled his nose and sucked, making little grunts and gurgles, careful not to hurt her with his teeth.

'There's my baby,' she whispered and patted his shoulder, 'there's my greedy greedy baby.' She sipped her tea, although why this performance made her thirsty she could not say; it was slobbering Percy who ought to be thirsty. After a few minutes he sighed and rolled over and put his hands behind his head.

'I've got to go as soon as I've had my tea, pet,' he said. 'Back to the war room.'

'War room?'

'We've got an office fitted out with all the gear. Spight's there with the bankers. They're analysing what's happened in the market today. Hey. What's the matter with you?' Tears were streaming down her cheeks and she rocked gently backwards and forwards. She put her cup down and put her hands over her eyes. He touched her shoulder but she jerked away.

'Oh Percy, I do love you,' she sobbed. 'That's why I hate it when you lie to me.' She took her hands away from her face, blurred by tears and emotion and make-up like a Hockney polaroid. 'You don't have to lie. I know you have another life. I understand. I've lived with it all these years.' She waved a gangling arm at the corporate photographs over her dressing table, balding men in suits behind desks and telephones and folded hands. 'But they only lied to me when they were ti-i-i-ired of me.' She sobbed again and pulled her large knees up and rested her forehead on them.

'Come on, Pet. You're my favourite, honest.'

'Boo-hoo-hooo-hoo.'

'Look, let's talk about it when this Premium business is over, shall we? We'll go away for a couple of days, just you and me. Right now I have to get back to the office.'

Far from stemming the tide his words opened the floodgates. She wailed and thumped the satin quilt. He got out of bed clutching the terry-towel round his waist.

'Please, please, you don't have to say that.'

'It's the truth, pet.'

'It's not. Be honest with me. You're going to see Sally.'

Had she been less overcome by her own misery she would have been intrigued by Percy's reaction to her accusation. This was not the defensive, embarrassed, defiant philanderer exposed. This was a man in the sudden grip of fear. With a spasm that would have impressed even Signor Galvani, his eyes popped and his shoulders jerked back and his hands shot up as if an electric cattle prodder had got him in the back. He dropped the towel. His penis, no great oak to begin with, had shrunk to a little acorn, and the rest seemed to have been sucked right back up.

'Where did you get that . . .?'

'I won't lie to you. In your diary. You left it downstairs.'

Percy had not got where he was by avoiding crises but by finding solutions. By the look in his face and the way he held his hands, as if warming them at an open fire, it appeared that in this case strangulation was the solution of choice.

'I'm sorry, Percy. I shouldn't let it upset me. I don't want much. I don't want to be seen with you in public or intrude on your life. (Sniff.) I love our evenings here. Looking after you. (Sniff.) It's nice to feel wanted. (Sniff.) It's hard to be reminded that there's always someone else. (Sniff.)'

He gripped her on the shoulders, near the neck. She was no longer so confident that she could throw him across the room if she wanted. His soft white fingers felt endowed with new strength. He seemed to swell in front of her, his chest rose, his head went back and he looked down on her as if from a great height. As a precaution she folded her hands chastely across her breasts ready to break his hold and smack him in the windpipe if he got too rough.

'You had no business going through my diary. I'll forget that. And you forget Sally . . .' he began to squeeze and shake her.

'How can I forget her, Percy? How can I forget her?'

He relaxed the pressure. 'Her?' he asked. 'Who?'

Nora had a chilling *déjà vu*. Her mother had suffered from Alzheimer's. Conversations with her consisted solely of beginnings. Perhaps it was just stress and overwork with Percy. She put her hands on his wrists.

'Sally. You remember her, don't you baby?'

Percy suddenly discovered an alternative solution to physical violence. He relaxed his grip.

'Sally? Of course. Sally. I was going to tell you about her, pet, honest.'

He sat down beside her on the bed and put his arm round her shoulder.

'She's an old girlfriend. From before I met you. I promised to meet her for a drink.'

Nora sniffed and patted his knee and stood up, buttoning her nightdress.

'I should have known it would never work. A man like you. It was a silly dream. Perhaps one day I'll meet . . .' she started to sob again. Percy picked up the terry-towel and put it round his waist.

'I'll have a quick bath. Then I'd better go.'

'What about your tea? It's beefburgers.'

'I'd better go. I'm late.'

When he came down after his bath Nora had changed into a long housecoat buttoned to the neck. She had cleaned off all her make-up and combed her hair straight back. She helped him on with his velvet-collared coat and closed the door behind him, not waiting to watch him walk down the path.

• • •

*MIDSUMMER*

It was Midsummer Day. The gorgeous sun rose into a clear blue sky. Clear and blue, that is, above the blanket of thick grey cloud which protected the good citizens of London from the harmful effects of the solstice – sunburn, heatstroke and the dreadful melanoma of cheerfulness. Eddie shared the mood of nature. There was no spring in his step, no summer in his heart as he plodded along Lombard Street to his meeting with the journalist Bibber. He had spent a sleepless night thrashing his limbs in his bed and his suspicions in his fevered brain. At five o'clock, as the unseen sun rose into the heavens to begin its longest journey, his mind was made up. But not made easier. Did blind Samson have second thoughts as he was led to the pillars? Delilah deserved what was coming to her but surely he felt a twinge of remorse, a twinge of nostalgia for what he used to feel for her. And did he have no feeling at all for the innocent among his victims? Like Eddie he may have given himself the traditional advice doled out by the robust to the depressed. 'Snap out of it,' he said and forced himself to stop beside a window-box sponsored by the Sun Bank of Florida. He hooked his umbrella on his elbow and plucked a red carnation for his buttonhole. 'Rise up, you have nothing to lose,' he proclaimed as he threaded the stalk into the lapel of his best charcoal-grey three-piece suit. And immediately, like a small miracle, his heart felt lighter and he started to hum to himself in a rusty baritone. 'Ti-tum-ti-tum ti-tum-ti-tum . . .'

He met Bibber in the Stag. It was a minute after opening time and the barman was locking back the doors. The hack was already sitting in a corner veiled in smoke and staring into his pint, looking as if he had been there all night. He gave Eddie the customary journalist's greeting.

'What'll you have?'

'A large Grouse. Water no ice.'

Bibber hauled himself wearily to his feet, sucked in a lungful of smoke for the journey and padded over to the bar. He came back with two glasses of Famous Grouse and a jug of water. Before Eddie could protest that one was enough his host swigged down one of the scotches and chased it with a gulp of his pint.

'Before we start, Mr Fly,' he coughed, 'I should tell you I've been making some inquiries. I found that you are not the General Manager of Dividend Investments.'

'A triumph of investigative journalism if I may say so.'

'You disappointed me, Mr Fly.' It was apparent from his general demeanour that Bibber's life was a tissue of disappointments.

'I never said I was.'

'I discovered you're the messenger.'

'Wrong again, Mr Bibber. You ought to check your sources. I was fired yesterday.'

The hack eyed Eddie's scotch as if he regretted his investment. Eddie swirled it in the glass, hard enough to bring it to the rim, like the dregs of medicine. He should get up and leave now. He was a sacked messenger. Not worth a quote. He could take his hurt and shame and hide it somewhere else and try to put the last ten years of his life out of his mind. Bibber expected nothing. He sat kippering himself in smoke and disappointment and the hack's indifference to those who have no information. The scotch hit Eddie's bloodstream at the same time as his resentment. He would tell Bibber to spite him.

'The Dividend Group has made a takeover bid for Premium

Insurance. A large parcel of shares has been bought by PANIC, the Panama Investment Company. PANIC is holding out and driving the share price up. But PANIC is a customer of Dividend Investments. Someone in the Dividend Group leaked the news of the takeover bid to PANIC.'

He watched Bibber for his reward, the flush of interest and respect. But the cork-tip face and the nicotine eyeballs remained impassive.

'How do you know?'

'We used to deal a lot with PANIC. Then the General Manager died and it stopped. The new General Manager, Miss Goodman, got wind of it. She has been secretly investigating the files. She fired Norman Foxwell, the Chief Dealer, because he knew too much. Her boyfriend, Harry Simple, works at Head Office. I think he's behind it.'

'Where's your proof?'

Eddie finished the rest of his drink. Nurtured in the night his words were solid facts. In the light of the public bar they were bubbles puffed from his lips and popping into specks of slime. Bibber had not even opened his notebook.

'In the files.'

'Show me.'

'They're in the office.'

'Can you get them?'

'A girl called Carol Feely can get them for me. But it's dangerous. And she might not get the right things. We ought to go in and look for ourselves. Then we can go through Miss Goodman's diary and her desk.'

'It's not enough to show that your office did business with PANIC. We have to show a connection.'

'I know. I can get us in if you know what to look for.'

Bibber reached inside his pocket for a buff-coloured envelope and took out a glossy black and white photograph. It showed a dark little man with a luxurious head of hair, a kiss curl over his forehead and a neat little moustache getting into a taxi. 'Have you ever seen this man before?' he asked. Eddie shook his head. Bibber stubbed out his cigarette in the overflowing ash tray and stood up. Instead of feeling relieved Eddie was angry that he had made a fool of himself, angry that he had wasted Bibber's time.

'I've got to make a call,' wheezed the hack. 'Same again?'

While he was away Eddie played flicking a beer mat up from the edge of the table and catching it. Twice he missed, his fingers snapping in the air. It was just after eleven o'clock and the bar was beginning to fill up, mostly well-dressed young men from dealing rooms, some middle-aged men from back offices, all on their own, drumming their fingers on the bar, downing doubles and triples, first of the day, looking at their watches and hurrying out again. All he had to do was stand up and walk out with them. Before he could make up his mind Bibber came back with the drinks. He looked puzzled.

'I talked it over with my editor,' he said. 'For some reason he told me to go ahead. But we have to take the Fraud Squad with us.'

'Why?'

'Makes it legal. And it gets us a better story.'

'I don't understand.'

'Even if we don't find anything we can say the police are investigating them.' He lifted his glass and clinked it against Eddie's. Eddie picked up his Grouse and swallowed it in one go, like medicine. Perhaps it would stop him feeling sick.

●　●　●

Liz stood in the middle of reception like an ancient despot receiving tribute from the ends of the empire. Around her on the floor and on the desk were stacks of cardboard boxes. A procession of bearers came from the lift with still more, under their arms or on trolleys.

'What the hell's all this?' she spluttered. Carol shrugged and signed a delivery note for two hundred reams of typing paper. Liz snatched it out of her hand. 'There must be a mistake. You've brought it to the wrong place. Take it back.'

'Can't do that Miss. It's ordered,' said the delivery man, pushing his green forage cap to the back of his head.

'Who by?' flamed Liz, turning to Carol.

'E. Goodman it says here,' said the delivery man, pulling his cap down over his nose.

'Mind your backs,' called a smart young man in a blue suit, dragging a massive photocopier on a trolley through the door, helped by two men in brown coats pushing from behind. Liz threw herself in front of the juggernaut.

'What's this?'

'The latest,' said the young man. 'Does your automatic double-side with sheet-feeder and full colour, your electronic exposure, your fifteen reduction and enlarging modes, your hundred copies a minute . . .'

'It's not mine. I don't want it.'

'Somebody in here does. Miss Goodman for one. She signed the order. If you wouldn't mind stepping aside Miss, we're blocking the gangway . . .'

A queue was building up in the lobby. In the middle of it was Harry Simple looking sporting in light tweed and a racing trilby and a yellow rose in his buttonhole. He stood on tiptoe and waved boyishly at her, unsure of the welcome he would get, hoping for a smile and fearing rebuff. He was clearly not expecting her expression of astonishment and fear. He had not noticed that he had been upstaged by the entry behind him, with a triumphant ping of the lift, of three men in gas-masks and boiler suits with canisters on their backs. Liz's first thought was hold-up. Her second was fire. Her third, consequent upon the first two and sure to embarrass her later, was not where the alarm was but where had she left her handbag? Harry squeezed in past the copier as it cleared the doorway.

'Gosh. You having a party? I have to talk to you. Urgently.'

'Who are those men?'

They answered for themselves. 'Pest Control and Fumigation Services, madam,' said their leader. He wheezed as he spoke and there was a nicotine yellow tinge about his face and hair, as if he had too often neglected the mask that dangled round his neck. The man behind, a lean and fit young man with a smart shirt and tie beneath his boiler suit, corroborated the story. 'Fleas,' he said, nodding vigorously.

The third man was taking no chances. He lurked behind the other two with his gas-mask already over his face and a cloth cap pulled over his forehead.

'You can't come in here now. It's full of people. The staff are working.'

'It'll soon be five o'clock, madam. We'll start just as soon as they've left. We like to catch them while it's still warm, see. It's more effective.' He flexed his fingers in a sort of hopping motion in front of her eyes and she shuddered.

'Sign here, please,' said a middle-aged man in black jacket and grey trousers and wing collar, thrusting a print-out bearing a litany of saint's names under the logo of Peabody Fine Wines.

'I didn't . . .' Liz began, then noticed her signature was already on the sheet. 'I'll sort this out later,' she said and signed.

'Liz. I've got to talk to you,' said Harry. She looked round for the fumigators but they had disappeared. 'It's urgent.'

She instructed Carol to collect all the delivery notes and bring them to her office. Harry led the way through the cartons to the management suite. He closed the padded door behind them.

'Eddie,' she growled, collapsing into the farting swivel chair. Harry looked round but they were alone. 'What do you want?' she snapped. His romantic good looks were made even more fascinating by the pale, fevered look of a man in the grip of great emotion.

'Wheeler let me go,' he said, slumping into the visitor's chair. 'Actually not so much let me go as threw me out of the window.'

'I'm sorry,' she said, with the depth of feeling of a telecom voice simulator. 'It was hardly a surprise.'

'Doesn't make it any easier.'

'Why have you come here?' she asked, shuffling through the papers on her desk.

'I wanted you to know.'

'Thanks.'

She picked up the position report and studied it.

'Is that all you're going to say?'

'What do you want me to say?'

He leaned forwards, swivelling his hat in his hands. 'I thought you'd be interested. I thought you'd give me some help. I mean I haven't got anyone else.'

'It's what you wanted isn't it? To get out of the City? Go and run your finishing school.'

'I can't buy the place until the divorce comes through. Daff would get the money I made on Premium.'

'Give War-wick Kingmaker a call. He'll find you a job.'

'I'm not going through that again. He makes you write to all your chums asking if they know of any jobs going. I'd rather stick it on the side of a bus.'

'Redundancy is no stigma these days.'

'No stigma? You don't know my friends. It'll be all round the members' pavilion by the end of the first over. Poor old Harrers. His head's in the basket again. Anyone got a pole to stick it on?'

'You've got to use your contacts, Harry.'

'Contacts are for tickets to Wimbledon and a box at Twickers and the odd share tip from the inside, not touching them for a billet.'

'War-wick would get you something within twelve months.'

'Twelve months? What am I going to do for twelve months?'

'I know it's hard. You'll find something.'

'Listen, Lizzie. I had an idea.'

'Gosh.'

'I'm going to sign over our money to you. You can buy the place. Then we can run it together. Before the divorce.'

'I don't know if you've noticed but I have a full-time job of my own. And I'm going to make a success of it. I'm not leaving it now Harry. Besides. It's not our money. It's your money.'

He sat up and braced his shoulders and looked at her with his lovely grey-green eyes. She felt a tightening behind the breastbone.

'I love you. I want to be with you. I want to build a new life with you. That's what I called my nominee account. New Life. It's for us. A true partnership. I want you to be my partner.'

Her reply came in a rush, breathy and full of emotion. She felt exhilarated and fearful. She knew that in this room, of all places, she ought to be measured and rational, to let good sense and judgement restrain her feelings for him. But she could not help speaking from the heart.

'Oh Harry,' she sighed, 'you're finished. You're finished with Dividend. You're finished in the City. You're finished with me.'

'Liz . . .'

'You're a wonderful person. You've got so much to offer. You've got lots of talent. Lots of experience. You're handsome

239

and attractive. There are so many women who would be glad to have you share their lives with them.'

'But not you.'

'Not me.'

'I won't take that. I love you.'

'It's not personal, Harry.'

He looked like a beaten spaniel, shoulders sagging, arms dangling between his knees, staring down at his shiny brown brogues and twiddling his hat.

'I'm sacked, am I?'

'Yes.'

'I'm no use to you any more. That's it, isn't it?'

She declined to comment.

'If you get rid of people because they're no use to you any more you soon won't have anyone left, you know that, don't you?'

'Perhaps.'

'Is it hopeless?'

'Nothing's ever hopeless. Sometimes you have to find a different hope from the one you had before.'

Harry pondered his words. When he pondered he usually gave the impression that he was giving his brain time to catch up. But now it seemed a genuine pondering, a weighing of the pros and cons of what he was about to say.

'Enjoy it while it lasts, old girl. You've got another couple of months at most. Wheeler's closing this place down. He decided weeks ago.'

The flatness in his voice took her by surprise. The charm and elegance and suavity had gone. The composure had wilted with the yellow rose in his buttonhole. It was not just the slackness round the mouth, the slouch that had replaced the courtier's stoop that reminded her of the down-and-outs who haunted the streets when she came to work in the morning. It was the look he had in his eyes that it was no use pretending any more.

'He told me to go out and hire a no-hoper, a second-rater, someone from the slow lane. I found you. My advice is to take your reference and your redundancy and come away with me.' He had good grounds for bitterness and resentment. But there was no rancour in his voice. It was a statement of fact.

'You're lying.'

'Ask him.'

'I'm asking you.'

'And I've told you. This is your last chance.'

She opened the top drawer of her desk and took out a new packet of Camels and her lighter. All her concentration was dedicated to stopping her fingers trembling.

'I'm sorry. It doesn't change anything. Now if you'll excuse me. I have a job to do.'

He stood up and turned to go. She looked up at his broad back and closed one eye against the smoke that curled from her nostrils. 'One last thing,' she said. 'Your New Life. If anyone ever found out that a Dividend Group director had bought Premium shares through a nominee account a few days before a takeover bid, that director would be in serious trouble.'

It was the best she could think of on the spur of the moment.

● ● ●

'..If..anyone..ever..found..out..that..a..Dividend..Group.........
director..had..bought..Premium..shares..through..a..nominee...
account..a..few..days..before..a..takeover..bid..that..director....
would..be..in..serious..trouble..'

Bibber licked the end of his pencil and waited for more. He was a changed man. The aura of disillusion that used to cling to him had wafted away. His skin had colour and tone, his eyes sparkled and a smile played around the corners of his bluish mouth. 'It's like the old days, Eddie,' he had whispered while they set up in the dining-room, 'when I started in the business. The stake-out, the waiting, the disguise. The cameras loaded and primed. The excitement. The adrenalin. It was like going over the top. Someone gives the signal and pow' – when he said pow he punched the air—'pow. The terror on their faces, flashes going everywhere, microphones in the face . . . I thought all that was behind me.'

'Didn't you ever feel bad about what you were doing?'

'The public has a right to know, laddie.'

'It sounds dead sleazy to me.'

'You have to forget your conscience sometimes. It's tough I know.'

'What paper were you on?'

'*The Times*. I followed the Royals for twenty years.'

He put away his pad. The policeman slipped his miniature tape-recorder into his pocket and jumped down from the dining-room table. His Gucci-style loafers had left marks on the teak. Eddie automatically scrubbed at them with the sleeve of his boiler suit. Lucy would go spare. He should have remembered to put the mats on. The policeman had not bothered to replace the ceiling tiles either. The entrails of the building were laid bare, raw concrete and silver pipes and snaking cables. But there was no time to put it straight. The policeman was already out of the door into the lobby, Bibber at his heels. Eddie pulled the gas-mask down over his face and followed them.

They met Harry as he came out of Liz's office. He looked through them. But he could not walk through them. The policeman barred his way.

'Might I have a word before you go, sir?'

'No, I'm in a hurry.'

'It would be better for all of us if you did, sir.'

'I'm nothing to do with this place. She can take care of her own vermin.'

'Please, sir,' said the policeman, pointing inside the office.

Confronted with such confident authority Harry retreated before the three fumigators. Eddie, bringing up the rear, closed the door. Everything seemed muzzy and dreamlike from inside his mask and he could hear himself breathing.

'What's going on?' asked Liz. 'This office is clean. There's no infestation here.'

In reply the policeman unbuttoned the top of his boiler suit and pulled out what looked like a season ticket holder. He flipped it open.

'Inspector Frost, Fraud Squad, Snow Hill. I should like a word with you about shares in Premium Insurance and a nominee account called New Life? If I may? Sir?'

For a moment Harry was stunned. He gaped. He gawked. He gawped. Then he recovered his composure. Frost was lean and fit and well-dressed, like an accountant. Nevertheless Harry tried the local-squire-to-the-village-bobby approach.

'Now look here, officer, something tells me you've got the wrong end of the stick . . .'

He rabbited on as if he were accused of parking his car on the village green. Frost remained unmoved. When Harry finished he asked him to accompany him down to the station to help with a few enquiries as if he were inviting him to come and look at his collection of postage stamps.

'I really don't know what you're talking about,' blustered Harry, changing tack, looking desperately back at Liz, who avoided his eye.

'We're talking about your using privileged information about Premium Insurance obtained from Mr Wheeler in the course of your employment.'

'That's not true. He never tells me anything.'

'You expect us to believe that?'

'Ask him. Go on. Get him in this room and ask him yourself. He's probably at the bank. A hundred yards from here. I'm not leaving with you unless you have a warrant for my arrest.'

'Do you have a warrant for anything?' chipped in Liz.

'A warrant to search these premises, yes.'

'Only to search? Then if you wish to interview Mr Simple about his private affairs you may do so outside.'

'Liz,' pleaded Harry, 'I'm not leaving here until this is cleared up.'

'So you deny having an account called New Life,' said Frost.

'You're twisting my words,' said Harry. 'I bought Premium shares. But I deny having obtained the information from Wheeler.'

'Who did you get it from then, sir?'

'Her,' he said pointing his outstretched arm.

'Miss Goodman?' asked Frost.

Liz's peal of nervous laughter reverberated inside Eddie's mask. 'That's nonsense,' she said. 'Where would I get the information?'

'You said you got it from your messenger,' pleaded Harry.

'Eddie Fly?' chortled Liz. 'The messenger? I wouldn't believe him if he told me the time of day. I've dismissed him for misconduct and dishonesty.'

Eddie's face felt very hot. Moisture, probably perspiration, trickled down his cheeks and his eyes smarted.

'The messenger, eh, sir? I think you'll have to do better than that,' said Frost.

'Now if you wish to interview Mr Simple further may I suggest you do it outside the premises. His private share dealings have nothing to do with Dividend Investments.'

'I think it goes deeper than that, Miss Goodman. I wonder what you know about the Panama Investment Company. PANIC. They have been investing very heavily in Premium shares and they are a customer of yours.'

'There you are, you see,' blurted Harry, 'it's her. She got information from PANIC and passed it on to me.' He was treated to another derisory chuckle, this time from Bibber.

'So an offshore investment company got wind of the takeover, passed it to a business contact who passed it to a director of the company doing the takeover? It's novel, anyway, isn't it Inspector?' he wheezed.

But Frost had finished with Harry for the time being. He pushed him to the side of his plate for later.

'About the relationship with PANIC, Miss Goodman?'

'We have no dealings with them. Certainly not while I have been Manager here.'

'This is not our information, miss. May I see the file on them?'

'All our files are confidential.'

'Then I'll have to find it for myself.'

'Wait. I have to tell Mr Wheeler about this. I've only just joined the company you see, officer.' She smiled and attempted an eyelash flutter which, under the stress of the moment, turned into a heavy blink. Eddie could not help admiring her presence of mind. Although she had to clench her fingers to stop them trembling she looked bewildered and innocent.

'Dashed good idea,' said Harry. 'Get him over here. He'll clear things up.'

'I can't stop you,' said Frost. For the first time he hesitated. Sneaking round premises was one thing. Bearding company chairmen was another. 'Perhaps we can arrange an interview at some other time . . .'

'We'll get him right now,' said Liz, reaching for the telephone. She pointed to the sofas. 'Make yourselves comfortable, gentlemen.'

While they were milling round for seats Eddie quietly slipped out of the door. In reception he ripped off his mask and hurried through the stacks of boxes to the post-room.

'Eddie,' squealed Carol, and threw her arms round his neck. 'You came back for the party. You can have a joint one. You and Norman. They'll be ever so glad to see you. Everything's been a right mess since you left. And they all blame me.'

'Later, darling,' he said, pushing her away. 'Blimey. What happened to you?'

'Don't worry. I'm going to change for the party.'

He held her at arm's length. She was wearing a crisp white cotton shirt fastened at the neck with a little blue bow and a neat blue skirt and sensible flat shoes. The jacket that matched the skirt was hanging over the back of her chair. She had little gold studs in her ears and no more than a touch of make-up.

'I get a clothes allowance for being messenger. I'm permanent staff now. Miss Goodman's going to send me to college on day release. Office practice. Miss Goodman says if I do a good job and keep my nose clean . . .'

Eddie glanced round the post-room. It wasn't his any more. He tried to clear the lump in his throat.

'What's got into you, Carol?'

'The working class works, remember. I took your advice. Play their game. Lie low. Wait for the historical moment.'

'You won't have long to wait, darling,' he said, going behind the desk. He yanked his desk drawers open. They were full of shoes and tissues and make-up and chunky paperbacks with gormless women in Victorian dress on the front.

'Where are all my things?' he asked in desperation.

'She went through them, didn't she?'

'Who?'

'Miss Goodman. She ransacked the place.'

Eddie slumped down in the chair and put his head in his hands.

'Of course. I should have known.'

'What are you looking for?'

'The evidence. Never mind. It's too late.'

She came round behind him and put her hand on his shoulder.

'It wouldn't be Norman's black book would it? The survey of all Dividend Investments' past business relationships? The one you hid behind the bottom drawer?' He nodded and sighed. 'That's down in the cellar,' she said, 'along with all the other stuff I guessed you wouldn't want her to find.'

He jumped to his feet and hugged her.

On their way back from the basement the lift stopped and opened at the ground floor. People were pouring out of the lifts and through the doors and into the square with the desperate urgency, the controlled panic, the now-or-never haste peculiar to fire alarms and Friday nights, as if the weekend would escape if it were not caught by the heels. Eddie saw a familiar figure fighting his way towards them through the exodus.

'Fly!' roared Percy, barging through the crowd. It sounded more like a general instruction than a summons. Behind him, a weaker salmon, struggled Spight. Eddie pushed the doors-open button. Anyone who had ever doubted Percival Wheeler's fighting mettle should have seen him now. Heavyweight boxers, prop forwards, Sumo wrestlers, icy hockey players and any other brand of professional gladiator would have quailed before him. He took in Carol with a passing glance, as one would a crocodile handbag or a halogen spotlight or any other decorative accessory, and glared at Eddie. 'I thought you were fired.'

Eddie held up the gas-mask dangling round his neck.

'I was. I've got another job.'

'Do you know anything about this?'

'What, Mr Wheeler?' he said, tucking the black book firmly under his armpit.

Percy thumped the wall with his fist. At the fifth floor he charged out of the lift ready for action. In reception he gazed round at the higgledy-piggledy cardboard boxes. The door of the back office was open and exuded the soothing strains of Frank Sinatra. Wheeler was not soothed. 'What's going on?' he roared.

Eddie shrugged his shoulders. 'Must be the cleaners,' he said.

'The people you want are all in Miss Goodman's office.'

Percy ignored him and headed for the main office. His path was blocked by a rastafarian in the career uniform of a cleaning operative of Dividend Sanitizing Services.

'Out of the way,' bawled Percy, jostling past him and knocking dusters and aerosols flying.

'Hey man, relax. How about a little courtesy?'

'Do you know who I am?' As Wheeler bore only a superficial resemblance to the benevolent industrialist beaming like a traditional uncle out of the portrait in the management suite the operative did not notice the likeness.

'Can't help, man. You got anything in your pockets that could jog your memory, driving licence, rent book, something like that?'

'Get that uniform off and get out of my building,' his employer snarled, and continued his trajectory. He was almost through the door when Louise, in a shiny yellow strapless cocktail dress, a plump canary, came from behind a partition carrying an ice bucket. Her free hand flew to her mouth and moved down to her naked breastbone and then she saw Eddie and assumed the best.

'Oh Mr Wheeler. It's nice of you to come . . .'

Percy pushed past her into the main part of the office. Partitions had been pushed back to clear a space in the middle. Jammed in between the desks were the staff, the few men in shirtsleeves, the women in skimpy summer dresses and glamorously made up to prove that they were not drudges all the time but as fascinating as the women who decorated the magazines and paperbacks that stuffed their handbags and their desks. In the middle of them was Norman, in an orange shirt and his brave pink tie.

'Goodman,' snarled Percy, 'where's Goodman?' He stormed back through reception into the management suite and, without formality, into the General Manager's office.

'What's going on in here, Miss Goodman? It looks like a New Orleans knocking shop in there and you're having a tea party.'

Connoisseurs of Percy's moods would have been more in awe of his menacing calm than the fury he had previously exhibited. Only Harry recognized the symptoms and cowered in his armchair. Nora was being mother, handing round the milk and sugar. Liz was behind her desk, calmly ticking her way through the position report. Bibber and Frost were side by side on the sofa, still in boiler suits and dangling masks.

'Indian or Earl Grey?' asked Nora.

'Earl Grey for me,' said Spight, misjudging the mood of the gathering.

'This is Inspector Frost of the Fraud Squad,' said Liz, standing up. 'He has some questions about our relationship with the Panama Investment Company.'

'One sugar,' said Spight, still a jump behind. He had clearly not been briefed as to the purpose of the meeting. He was left in no doubt when Frost explained.

'Oh Harry,' said Percy, 'you let me down. My word is my bond. A clean nose and a straight bat. I thought I could trust you.'

'Then why didn't you ever tell me anything?'

'I was taken in, officer,' said Percy, turning to Frost. 'He was my right-hand man. He signed our code of conduct as well.' He shook his head and tutted, a sadder and wiser man. 'Does he have shares in PANIC? Or was it just for a pay-off?'

'Wait,' cried Harry. Eddie had often read about strangled voices but this was the first time he had ever heard the genuine article. 'I had nothing to do with PANIC. I'd never heard of them. They're a customer of Dividend Investments. Why don't you look in the file?'

Their conversation was punctuated by the clatter of falling china. All except Nora looked down at the pool of milk spreading over the beige carpet. She was looking at Percy. Percy looked at her. 'I suggest you get a cloth, Nora, there's a good girl' he said, the milk of kindness suddenly in his voice.

'But . . .'

Percy was in no mood for buts. Head-butts perhaps, but not conversational buts.

'Get a cloth, Nora. We'll clear this up once and for all. We'll get the PANIC file. Show us where it is, Miss Goodman.'

Liz led the procession. Harry marched between Frost and Percy. Bibber came next, scribbling, then Spight like an acolyte, with his cup of Earl Grey. Eddie brought up the rear behind Nora. They marched into the back office. Cigarette smoke swirled around the air-conditioning vents. Half-empty paper cups littered the desks and empty ones littered the floor. A light glowed on the portable CD player. Jackets and cardigans festooned the backs of chairs. But it was deserted. They went straight to the Filomatic. Liz opened the flap and was confronted with a fully-stocked bar with bottles, glasses, ice and savoury snacks. She quickly stabbed a button and the shelves revolved until they came to P-S. She riffled through the files, pulled one out and gave it to Percy. Like a lector before the first reading he ceremoniously opened it and handed it to Frost. The policeman flipped through it expertly, the others waiting with bated breath and baited curiosity. Only Eddie heard a faint scuttling beyond the partitions behind them, like mice behind the skirting board. Frost seemed disappointed.

'There were a few transactions some years ago but nothing recently,' he said.

Percy smiled and opened his hands wide. 'You need look no further, officer,' he said and pointed at Harry. 'There's your man.'

'You've got no proof,' whimpered Harry.

Bibber reached inside his boiler suit and into his pocket. He took out a photograph. He held it so they could all see the dark little man with a luxurious head of hair, a kiss curl over his forehead and a neat little moustache. 'Do you know who this is?' he asked.

'That's Sally!' exclaimed Liz, turning to Harry. 'You introduced me to him at the Colonial Bankers. You said he was an old friend of yours. You said he was Panamanian.'

'Are you sure?' asked Bibber.

'Positive.'

'Salvatore Rossi,' said Bibber, handing over the photograph to Frost. 'Director of the Panama Investment Company.'

Harry looked at Liz like a faithful old sheepdog about to get a bullet in the forehead. He opened his mouth, closed it and acceded to his fate. He nodded to Frost.

'Let's go,' said the policeman and, taking his elbow, steered him to the door, followed by a sprightly Bibber. As they passed, heads appeared one by one over the top of the partitions and round the side, witnesses to the Procession of Shame: City Cheat Led

Away in Handcuffs. They looked on in silence. Only Nora was visibly moved. One hand at her throat, she silently sobbed.

'The canker of corruption must be cut out wherever it shows itself,' intoned Percy. 'The good name of the City must be upheld. Justice must seen to be done . . .'

'Oh, Percy,' cried Nora, unable to restrain herself any longer. 'Oh, Percy.' And she threw her arms round his neck and wept on his shoulder. 'I'm sorry, baby. I'm sorry. I should never have doubted you.'

'There, there,' said Percy, simultaneously patting her back and trying to push her away, forcing a smile at the others.

'I thought Sally was a woman. I should have trusted you.'

Percy was having difficulty with his smile. Instead of pushing her away he wrapped his arm round her neck and pulled her face tight into his chest. The strength of his affection seemed to be causing her breathing difficulties.

'All right everybody,' he called, 'go home now. The show's over.'

'No, wait,' said Liz. 'I have something to ask you first. Something we have to clear up right now.'

'If it's about Salvatore Rossi it's *sub judice*,' growled Percy, still keeping a tight hold on Nora.

Liz took a deep breath, her hands clenched in front of her, as if she was about to burst into an aria.

'I want to know if you have decided to close down Dividend Investments in the next few months. We all want to know.'

A Mexican wave of surprise washed over the silent partygoers looking down over the top of the partitions.

'I had decided that, yes. But after this evening I have changed my mind,' said Percy. Surprise was followed by relief and one or two clapped their hands. 'I'm closing it down on Monday morning.' The crowd rhubarbed and scuffled and Louise fell off the upturned waste-bin she had been standing on. Liz looked as if she was being whistled off the stage. Percy discarded Nora and held up his hand for silence.

'I have had doubts about the quality of management and the standard of performance of this institution for some time now. I put in Miss Goodman to improve it. I thought she was a capable

250

manager. She has failed. Performance has remained unsatisfactory. Even if she and the rest of you are not directly implicated in the scandal of Mr Simple, you are implicated by association. As soon as I have completed the takeover of Premium Insurance all your business will be handed over to them. Come on Miss Truelove. I have no more to say.'

With eyebrows lowered he set off for the door followed smugly by a sniffling Nora. Their way was barred by Eddie. He stood holding the black binder in both hands.

'I've got something to say though, Mr Wheeler,' he said. His knees were trembling and he heard his voice sound thin and squeaky, as if he had been sniffing helium.

'Out of my way.'

'Not until you tell us when you set up PANIC.'

Percy looked like the chairman of the board at a shareholder's meeting when a maverick shareholder has the cheek to slip in an unplanted question.

'Nonsense. Out of my way.'

Eddie had to dodge back to avoid Percy's imperious arm.

'It all came clear when Nora here talked about Sally. Salvatore works for you, doesn't he? He runs PANIC on your behalf. It's all in here,' he said, holding out the black book. 'It analyses all our business relationships. PANIC was one of our biggest customers when you set up DI. We had money out to them all the time and under market rates. Lending PANIC money at cheap rates was a good way of creaming off cash belonging to the Dividend Group, wasn't it? How many other of our overseas customers do you own?'

'You're mad. I won't stand and listen to this.' He tried to push past, but Eddie shoved him in his swelling chest. He was surprised how soft he felt. Percy staggered back and Nora caught him.

'The ten per cent of the Dividend Group wasn't enough for you, was it? When you had Dividend bid for Premium Insurance you were bidding against your own private company. The more the price of Premium shares went up, the more you had to gain.'

'Prove it.'

'That's why you got into such a state when Mr Livery died. You thought he'd rumbled you. You panicked. You had Norman

251

fired because you thought his study would show Liz the preferential treatment PANIC was getting. You had Nora get the files out for you so that you could doctor them. And you had me sacked.'

'I said prove it.'

'I don't have to. Nobody does. All they have to do is investigate it and you're done for.'

'Who'll listen to you? You're a messenger.'

'They'll listen to me,' said Liz, bravely.

For the first time in that longest day Eddie felt that what he was doing was right. It made him feel good. For as long as he could remember he had struggled to keep his independence and his dignity by conniving and compromise. But now the historical moment had arrived and he had come out in the open. His knees still trembled and his voice seemed reedy but he was given new courage by his audience. He basked in the warmth of solidarity. They were tired of being manipulated, tired of being cheated, tired of being made fools of by people like Wheeler. He was doing it for them, the ordinary people, as well as himself, and it filled him with strength. Above all Liz was beside him, backing him up. He had not been wrong. She was a different sort of boss, she wanted the world to change, and she had come down on his side.

His revelations did not deflate Percy. On the contrary. To the disinterested observer it appeared that they inflated his confidence and swelled his ego and enhanced his charisma even more. His stomach rose into his chest, his head went back so that he looked down his nose, he seemed to swell before their eyes like a bullfrog. He was about to do what he did best. A deal.

'Poppycock. These are absurd speculations. Offensive and out of order. I would take extreme exception if you were not making fools of yourselves. If they are ever spoken outside these walls I will sue for slander. They could do this company a great deal of harm if they fell on the wrong ears. As PANIC is an overseas company it could never be proved either way. You can only damage yourselves.'

He looked each one of his audience in the eye and finally came to rest on Liz.

'You have also misunderstood my intentions about Dividend

252

Investments. I said I was closing it down. That is true. What I did not tell you was that you are all being offered a transfer to Premium's investment department and that I am offering Miss Goodman here the position of General Manager on a three-year contract.'

Eddie stared open-mouthed at this effrontery. It was as good as a confession. Liz looked at him in disbelief and then at Wheeler. She stood up straight, her arms by her side. Her chest swelled and her head went back so that it looked as if she were looking down on Wheeler from a great height. Eddie waited for her to deliver her condemnation. Instead she held out her hand and Wheeler shook it.

The atmosphere of the back office suddenly changed. The technical aspects of the issue went over the heads of the audience behind the partitions. They belonged to the majority of people, including jurors in insider dealing trials, for whom the workings of the Financial Services Act remain a mystery. But they grasped the essential, which was that their jobs were safe and life would go on as before and it was all thanks to Eddie. They broke into applause and nodded to each other like an amateur crowd scene. Liz made a few hesitant steps towards the hero of the moment before she was beaten to it by Carol, who slipped from her perch and flung her arms proprietorially about his neck. By uncanny coincidence the setting sun shook off the clouds that had cloaked it all day and shone through the west-facing window of the office in all its midsummer glory. Optimism and joy lit up the company. They kissed or shook hands or clapped each other on the back, whichever was most appropriate or pleasant. Norman flicked on the CD player. Louise activated the Filomatic to bring back the cocktail bar. Percy presided over the growing hubbub with the sunny smile he usually fixed on for staff Christmas parties.

'What about me?' asked Nora, slipping her arm through his, 'now that we've forgotten that silly misunderstanding about Sally. We wouldn't want anything to jog my memory would we?' She wrinkled her large nose and pouted her lips. His smile remained resolute.

'I need a new personal secretary,' he said. 'Would you like the job?' His voice sounded strained.

'Oh, Mr Wheeler,' she sighed.

Meanwhile Eddie stood by the telex machines staring numbly at the revellers and trying to extricate himself from Carol's embrace as she pulled him among the dancers. Liz pushed her way through the joyful throng towards him. He had not seen her as vibrant and happy since the day she first came to the office.

'I owe you everything, Eddie,' she said, smiling but slightly embarrassed. 'I'm sorry I was so abrupt yesterday . . .'

'Shh. It's all right. I'm glad it's worked out for you. Are you happy?' She nodded.

'I've made it at last. Thanks to you. I've learned a lot. I know I can be very successful.'

'What about Mr Simple?'

'Poor lamb. I'm so sorry about him. But he won't get more than six months.'

'You're going along with Wheeler, then?'

'What else can we do? If he goes down we all go down. You can't change the way the system works, Eddie.'

'It's changed you though.'

She shrugged her shoulders and forced a smile. 'Come on. Let's square things with Mr Wheeler before he goes.' She took him by the hand and they threaded their way through the party to their Chairman who was being shepherded to the door by his new secretary. He glowered at Eddie.

'Mr Wheeler, I think we should do something for Mr Fly here. As you know he was summarily dismissed,' said Liz.

'What do you suggest?'

'One month's pay for every year of service?'

'All right,' he grunted.

Eddie looked at Liz, Percy's new manager. He looked at Nora, Percy's new secretary. What could one man do on his own?

'Thanks, Mr Wheeler,' he said at last.

'Thank *you*, Eddie,' said Liz.

Had he rehearsed this little scene in his mind he would have furnished himself with a jumble of powerful and conflicting emotions. So the real thing took him by surprise. It took the others by surprise too. They were not used to staff laughing in their faces.

'Come on Carol,' he chuckled, putting his arm round her.

'Where are we going?'

'The Samuel Pepys. The jokes are on me.'

254

# EPILOGUE

• • •

# *After the Midsummer Banquet*

'So we got our man,' said the Mayor, looking pleased with himself.

'Not our man,' said the Chairman, scratching the side of his thin nose. 'A man.'

'Old Duffer Simple's boy,' said the Governor, despondently.

'Never mind. We'll see him right when he gets out.'

'He did us a good turn. The heat's off us for a bit. Look.' He held up the *Business Times* and flicked a headline with the back of his hand. 'City Keeps Its Nose Clean,' it proclaimed.

'A happy ending,' claimed the Mayor, and they dipped their faces into brandy goblets big as nosebags.

# A SELECTED LIST OF HUMOUR TITLES
## AVAILABLE FROM CORGI

THE PRICES SHOWN BELOW WERE CORRECT AT THE TIME OF GOING TO PRESS. HOWEVER TRANSWORLD PUBLISHERS RESERVE THE RIGHT TO SHOW NEW RETAIL PRICES ON COVERS WHICH MAY DIFFER FROM THOSE PREVIOUSLY ADVERTISED IN THE TEXT OR ELSEWHERE.

*All Corgi/Bantam Books are available at your bookshop or newsagent, or can be ordered from the following address:*

Corgi/Bantam Books,
Cash Sales Department,
P.O. Box 11, Falmouth, Cornwall TR10 9EN

Please send a cheque or postal order (no currency) and allow 80p for postage and packing for the first book plus 20p for each additional book ordered up to a maximum charge of £2.00 in UK.

B.F.P.O. customers please allow 80p for the first book, and 20p for each additional book.

Overseas customers, including Eire, please allow £1.50 for postage and packing for the first book, £1.00 for the second book, and 30p for each subsequent title ordered.

NAME (Block Letters) ................................................................................................................

ADDRESS ................................................................................................................

................................................................................................................